Sword of Light

Troy S. Reaves

DEDICATION

To my editor, my inspiration, my wife and my Muse. This book would not be possible without Nemesis and the Goddess in my life.

Prologue

It was happening again. The stronghold trembled with a crack of thunder that rocked the stone beneath ~~the structure~~. The smell of burning flesh and brimstone invaded the boy's nostrils even before he could open his eyes. It was happening again, and Gregor was certain he would not survive this time. The evil invader had come ~~once more and~~ knew where to find him. The young weapons page forced his eyes open, knowing he had to prepare for what ~~lay~~ waited beyond the open doorway. The coal that smoldered in the forge glowed, ~~but~~ yet no heat emanated from the fuel there. He steeled himself for what would happen next. As if Gregor's thoughts had brought Master Riley into being, the knight of Bella Grey slammed into the doorway between the armory and the room where Gregor slept. The knight's body was wedged firmly into the door frame blocking any path of escape as his head twisted impossibly, now looking over his own back, and ~~faced~~ facing fully ~~toward~~ the boy sitting frozen with terror on his worn cot. "Death is in the keep of the Knights of Bella Gray, Gregor! Gather weapons from the armory and arm yourself!" Even before he had finished speaking, the plate armor the knight wore had begun to drag his body to the ground.

His dead eyes staring into the smith's workroom, Master Riley's body folded slowly forward into the armory as if attempting to point Gregor toward the right path. Gregor climbed over the dead knight, praying that there were survivors among the stronghold's residents as he gathered the iron swords from the nearby weapons rack. In his rapidly beating heart, Gregor knew there would be no one living in the keep, and yet he was unable to stop the futile exercise.

The dead were everywhere as Gregor moved through the halls. The boy almost welcomed the crimson mists that covered most of the corpses, shedding a tear for each face he could still recognize. (The Knights of Bella Grey had always counted on him to serve them well in his duties and he used that inspiration to keep himself moving toward the death he had avoided so many times) Gregor wondered if it was a sin to hope for release from his weak body and spirit as he moved to face the creature that longed to devour him.

A guttural howl, just barely recognizable as human, reached Gregor's ears. The sound had come from the main hall and Gregor forced himself to run toward it, knowing all too well the source. He cast away all the weapons he carried but one, carrying the sword clumsily as he ran. Lord Clamine was dying, and though Gregor did not know how to stop the one that had slain so many, he knew he had to try.

Gregor felt the heat emanating from beyond the doors of the main hall. It was the only heat he had felt in the keep but he took no comfort from it; there was only an intensity that became pain as he opened the giant door just enough to pass through it. The demon, forced into a crouch because of its great height, had bent forward over its victim and dominated the room. Lord Clamine hung from the wall beneath the creature, with his own sword's blackened hilt protruding from his chest. The creature before the boy was no stranger to him, yet still the fear welled up in him as it always had. Gregor felt there was something different this time, as if some line had been crossed and that this time there would be no retreat, no escape, for him. Gregor decided to take control of his destiny; his terror had gone on long enough.

He brought the sword he was carrying to the ready with a resolute movement and felt a surge of strength he did not recognize as his own. "Take me, coward! Do you not tire of torturing this old warrior over and over again? Take me and release him! Let Lord Clamine die!" Gregor looked into the eyes of the Master of the keep as he spoke, drawing inspiration from Lord Clamine's actions. There was very little strength left in the elder knight, and he was using all that remained for one purpose now, raising his voice in prayer to the God of Light. There was still hope in the voice that uttered that prayer.

The boy felt the heat from the demon invade his mind. *Release my favored pet? I cannot do that, boy, despite your entreaty. Both of you will serve me, each in your time, and this knight's time is now.* The demon twisted Lord Clamine's holy blade into the knight's chest once more, a darkness overtaking the blessed light that normally suffused it.

Gregor began to rise to his feet, intent on charging the demon and saving Lord Clamine or dying in the effort, but the past could not be changed, and a gentle white light enveloped Lord Clamine and Gregor, bringing a sense of peace and safety as it had each time before. *Rest my son. This Knight of Bella Grey has pledged his life to me, and I would never deny my most humble servant's final request on your* behalf. *You will be spared and in time you will wield the power to bring justice for what took place here. You will become my sword and you will avenge those who were slain here today. Pledge servitude to your God. I have set your path before you, but you must choose to follow it.* This thought calmed the turmoil of emotion within Gregor as he brought his forehead to rest on the cool stone floor. He felt his destiny had found him.

The gentle power that flowed into the boy as he received the answer to his entreaty was the same as it had been in the past when he had issued the challenge. *Your Master is at my side as was promised when he entered into my service so many years ago, and you will destroy this creature when you have the faith to do so. The Gods and Goddesses can only guide and bestow divine blessings to the faithful. You must find your own strength and your own faith. In time you will, my son.* The roaring stopped. The heat cooled. Gregor thought that he must finally be dead, reasoning only death could bring such complete quiet. He brought his head from the stones just in time to see the demon suddenly vanish with a howl. The weapons page was glad the demon had vanished, though he was at a loss to reason how. Only Lord Clamine remained, with the blade of the knight's broken sword still pinning his unmoving body to the wall. Gregor noted that the sword's hilt was gone.

Gregor felt the presence of the knight's spirit as gentle, familiar words sounded in the boy's mind. *Rise young one and bury my body. My soul passes to the next realm. No longer do I fear. Death has come, and with it, peace. Now I pass the burden to you. The God of Light has dismissed the Tharnorsa into the Abyss, but the demon has taken the hilt of my sword. The blade remains within my torn flesh. Remove the blade and keep it with you always. Remember me and I will watch over you. There will come a time when you will face this demon that has brought his powers against us. It is your duty to bring the hilt and blade together before you will face him once again. Tonight you bury the dead and pray that their souls are guided swiftly home. The priests in the village will aid you. Take the blade from my body and go quickly.*

1

Once upon a Knight

A shudder passed through Gregor as he sat up in bed in his parents' meager home. The sweat poured from him as he shook the night from his eyes. The dream was coming more frequently of late, though the memory had never left him. It had been six years since the destruction of the keep he had called home, six years since he had helped the priests lay to rest the last of the Knights of Bella Grey. The blade he kept strapped along his back reassured him even as it reminded him of the tragedy. His stance was proud with the steel between his shoulder blades. The knights would have been impressed at the man he would become in the passage of time.

There had been little peace in the youth when the memories were still fresh in his mind. Truth of the matter was Gregor had spoken little since the destruction of the knights. The priests who had tended the dead were concerned. His frequent trips alone into the wood and his refusal to speak about what had happened were a constant worry for the local clergy as well as his family. His father reassured his mother that their son would speak when he was ready, and they had to allow him time to make his own peace. Gregor was still deciphering the events of that fateful night, and he had told no one everything that had happened. He had no desire to be sought because the unknown God had communicated with him.

Gregor thought most of the villagers would simply think he had been driven insane by the shock. He could find no good that could come from revealing the demon's direct threats to his mind, either. If Gregor should couple that with the direct contact from an unknown God, then he was certain the priests would take drastic action to save his immortal soul. They would certainly lock him away for "proper cleansing." Gregor knew well enough that the rites of purification administered by the local priests often ended in death, though family members were assured that the unclean soul had been purified. Gregor may have been young, but the horror he had witnessed had made him cautious and somewhat wise beyond his years. The weapons page was certain that he would require training of some kind to move out into the world, but there were no warriors with whom to apprentice within the village, and passing mercenary companies had little patience with one so young. The determined look in the boy's eyes had caused one or two sergeants to consider his request. One so earnest might prove to be a solid investment with proper training, and something in the boy spoke of powers as yet unseen. However, they always turned him away in the end, and, if they had been asked for a reason, not one would have been able to say exactly why.

***

It was the planting season in the village of Bella Grey, named for the near constant mists that shrouded the farmlands in the area. Gregor had set out into the woods near his home at dawn. Each morning before his father called him to the fields, the boy had taken to hacking at the ancient trees in the forest with two short swords taken long ago from the dead knights' keep. The old trees neither noticed nor objected as the fledgling warrior released his fury, however there was one within the forest who kept a vigil with the boy. The hidden guardian of the forest felt no need to reveal himself at first, as the weeks had grown into months and Gregor's strength increased. No grace or dexterity came to the ineffectual swinging of the swords in the boy's hands. His thrusts and slashes were tainted by too much anger to provide any real benefit. Gregor would have proven to be no threat to the one who watched over him high in the tree branches, but the ranger admired the young man's devotion to this haphazard training. His decision to drop in on the wildly swinging youth one overcast morning could have been a poor one if the young warrior had been more skilled. The ranger quite literally dropped between the boy and the tree where Gregor was currently practicing his strikes. The young man was taken by surprise, and both his sword blows struck violently at either side of the tree. The force behind the swings would have imbedded them into the trunk quite neatly if Gregor had maintained his grip on the hilts. The ranger could not help but laugh as the boy's arms flew out to his sides and the short swords bounced harmlessly into the struggling brush and grasses near the tree.

"So, the farm boy was not looking, but only striking. This would seem a poor way to sharpen one's abilities." The leather-clad man could not help laughing at his own joke as he leaned against the abused tree. "Perhaps you might want to open your eyes during your exercises, unless of course it is your intention to fight the invisible by sense of smell." This seemed to tickle the ranger even more and he doubled over with laughter. Gregor could not help but wonder how long it had been since the dirty, long-haired man in front of him had actually spoken to another person. The sticks and leaves tangled in the wild man's hair as he bent over laughing gave Gregor a good measure of the man's personal hygiene. The smells wafting off him surely offended even the forest creatures, although Gregor could see how such a scent might be a successful deterrent to being attacked, or for that matter even approached. The wild look in the stranger's dark green eyes suited the rest of him. At his side the ranger wore only a small hunter's knife in an unremarkable, aged leather scabbard.

The ranger regained some amount of control and addressed Gregor once more. "Good to meet you, young man. My apologies for my abrupt appearance, but I could think of no better way to make you aware. There are many dangers in the wood and one should not focus to the point of distraction on any task. I am Galant Silverwing, protector of these woods as was decreed by the elders of this forest, and devoted Master Hunter of all that would disturb the natural balance. May I know to whom I speak?"

The wild look in the hunter's eyes seemed to disappear, giving way to a focused intelligence that took the young man's measure. Gregor saw no threat in the man's stance or words, and brought his own dark blue eyes to meet the stranger's before he spoke. Even while Gregor stood at his full height, the ranger before him was a good bit taller than himself. "I am Gregor, servant to the Knights of Bella Grey, or I was before the destruction of the Order." A light breeze blew Gregor's shoulder length hair, the color of winter wheat, across his face and the boy lifted a callused hand to brush away the errant strands.

"So, you have come into the wood to mar trees and frighten small animals?" The woodsman asked with a slight grin.

"No, Master Silverwing, I strengthen my skills as I can with no one to guide me." Gregor frowned in response to the ranger's grin.

"I have watched your daily training in the wood for some time and have to wonder why one so focused cannot find a proper weapons handler to guide him. Despite your best efforts, you have no natural skill. You should present yourself to the militia within the city of Travelflor. It would be just a few days' walk, and with my word to the captain of the soldiers there you would be granted an audience at least. I can draft a parchment for you to carry to the soldiers if you wish."

Gregor had no desire to leave his home to join the militia of Travelflor. "I have a calling beyond service as a soldier. Did you know the Knights of Bella Grey? I was with Lord Clamine when he was taken from this world."

"Lord Clamine was a good man and a devoted warrior. I hope he did not suffer when he died. How is it the knights were destroyed and you are still alive?" The ranger cocked a curious eyebrow at Gregor, awaiting his answer.

The young man felt compelled to relate the details of what had brought the destruction of the Knights of Bella Grey, holding nothing back. Master Silverwing listened intently to all Gregor said before he spoke again.

"So it appears the God of Light that Lord Clamine pledged his life to has chosen you. It is no light burden you carry, Gregor, and I hope you are up to the task." Silverwing's gaze softened as he considered the young man before him once more. "Despite your best efforts, your hands are betraying you with every swing. I would prefer that you not practice on live targets in my forest. I suppose it has become my responsibility to share my training area with you until you can assist me in my patrols. We will have to speak with your parents. That shouldn't present a problem, should it?"

Gregor stood in stunned silence. He couldn't believe his luck in finding a possible mentor. The time the man had spent in the forest alone had obviously affected the ranger, but Gregor was in no position to turn away any offer of aid. "I am sure they will be glad to have you receiving some guidance in your training. The animals and trees will no doubt be happy to see you relocate as well. We will check in with your parents right away, and after that go to my encampment deeper in the forest." Gregor only nodded in response. Silverwing smiled, noting the boy's silence. "You don't say much, do you? That is an honorable trait for any student to possess."

The ranger paused momentarily and looked thoughtfully beyond Gregor's shoulder. His eyes seemed to lose focus for a moment. The ranger frowned a bit as a great shadow darkened his features, as if a cloud had blocked the sun. His words came forcefully, with all humor gone. "You should know one final thing if we are to continue. Trust all that I say and follow my instructions without question or hesitation. *Drop to your knees and place your head at my feet, or we part company!*" There was such power in the hunter's voice that Gregor bowed before his new instructor. When the boy's head touched the cool earth near Galant's boots, he was surprised to find that the man had launched himself into the air using Gregor's back to gain more height. There was a great roaring growl, followed by the thunderous noise of some great beast charging from somewhere behind the boy. The unknown creature's howling was answered by a sharp whistling noise resembling a disturbed hive of angry hornets. The noises stopped as quickly as they had begun, and the boy dared to raise his head. The ranger came fully into view and appeared to be standing on a great mound of matted gray and brown fur. There were multiple arrow shafts, grouped tightly, sticking out of the remains of a snout. The dead bear's eyes had been pierced with an arrow in each, and several more arrows served to secure the creature's muzzle. The shots into the muzzle appeared to have come from some height. Gregor reasoned that even if the bear had been charging, there was no way the ranger could have shot into the animal while standing on the ground. The angle was all wrong for a direct shot. The hunter had somehow shot two perfect blinding shots into the eyes of a charging bear while jumping into the air and piercing its muzzle with three more shots....from the air? It was then that the boy noticed something mingled thickly in the blood that had already begun to congeal around the dead bear's muzzle. It was thick yellow saliva, the color of a dying sunflower.

Master Silverwing stopped staring down at the dead bear and took notice of Gregor. Tears ran down his flushed countenance as he began to speak in a low tone more befitting a funeral than the slaying of an animal. "This pile of fur was once Papa bear. He was the alpha male when I came to this forest. He was a strong protector, and his cubs are all strong as, well, bears, I suppose. Papa bear was more than a bear to me. He was a friend, and now that he had grown too old to remain unchallenged, I was trying to help him find a safe place to scavenge until he passed. It looks like he tried to make a home in some caves where I knew some diseased rats were living. Old bastard must have eaten one and got the sickness." He shook his head. "Damn, foaming sickness has come to the forest! I thought I had contained it since the rats couldn't survive it very long. I marked the cave to keep other animals out, but Papa bear either didn't care to heed my scent or could no longer smell, although I doubt there was any problem with his nose. He always was willful." Galant absently wiped away the tears cleansing his cheeks. "We will burn the body. I can't chance scavengers coming upon him and spreading the sickness." Silverwing looked to the sky where already the sun had begun burning away the morning gloom. "The balance in nature will remain constant even when all appears in chaos. You would do well to learn that if you learn nothing else from me. The natural order needs little aid from the likes of us. Rangers exist to protect the lands from the *unnatural* forces." The ranger turned back to Gregor. "Looks like you have come to train with me when I may need the aid of a strong hand. We will need to watch for changes among the animals of the forest until the sickness has passed, and burn the remains of any we find infected." The ranger cleared the surrounding area near the bear's corpse and set it alight with remarkable efficiency. Silverwing paused only briefly once the fire burned to say a whispered prayer for the dead.

***

Galant's concerns about the foaming sickness were unmerited. The ranger had said that the natural balance would be maintained, and the forest had looked after itself where the disease was concerned. The small rodents who had carried the infection died within a few days. Gregor and the ranger became close companions, tracking through the forest day after day. The rigors of the trail strengthened the young man and it was not long before his constitution matched that of his new Master. The woodsman insisted that Gregor learn to escape danger before he would train him in the martial art forms. The student complimented the teacher with the patience and perseverance he demonstrated every day.

***

Gregor caught his wind as Silverwing stopped abruptly in front of him as the pair completed their morning patrol of the forest. "When you face an overwhelming opponent, it can be far more advantageous to stay away from the threat you have spotted. I teach you avoidance, and the art of measuring a threat, so that you can know when to engage and when to flee." Gregor nodded with understanding as the ranger continued. "See there?" Silverwing pointed toward a small copse of trees where there was a glint of metal as the sun filtered into the clearing ahead. Gregor crouched as Silverwing's hand waved him down, though he could hear no movement from the clearing. Silverwing's voice dropped to a whisper. "The one we see is no indication that there are no more present. Poachers are cowards and travel in packs like wild dogs. I leave these to you, Gregor. What is your plan?"

Gregor took a moment to take stock of the ranger's words and his own weapons. The short swords at his sides gave him little comfort as he considered facing organized bandits. "Plan? The best plan would be to quietly circle around the clearing and see what it is I face." Sweat dripped down his cheek and Gregor could only hope his mentor did not hear the trembling in his voice.

"A valid thought and a serviceable plan, I suppose. Go on then and I will watch for anyone sneaking around the campsite. It is quiet so be aware of where you place your feet. These scoundrels will surely hear you if you break a stick as you move." Silverwing drew his bow into his hand and pointed toward the outer edge of the trees.

Gregor grasped his short swords and moved as quietly as possible, keeping the metal gleam Silverwing had noted between himself and the trees as best he could. He was beginning to feel a bit confident in his careful movements as he rounded the far side of the grove, daring to move in closer. Only the sound of a slight breeze disturbed the leaves of the trees, but it was enough. Gregor sighted the shield hanging from the tree in the center of the clearing that had reflected the morning sun's light. Someone was hunting, but it appeared that they were not hunting animals. Gregor rose to shout a warning to Silverwing, nearly having an arrow pierce his throat for the effort. "Down, Gregor! Now!" Silverwing's yell sent birds into the air from all the nearby trees as yet another arrow flew at the boy, sinking into the tree which Gregor had shifted behind for cover. Another arrow narrowly missed imbedding itself in Gregor's shoulder, its fletching whispering in Gregor's ear as the boy dove into the trees behind him. Silverwing's pupil lay in the underbrush, drawing each breath as if it were to be his last. He could still hear nothing, yet another well-placed arrow struck near his head.

As quickly as it had begun, the lesson was over. Silverwing moved blithely into the clearing, calling for Gregor with the unmistakable sound of laughter in his voice as he chastised his student. "Well, so much for the 'Let us see how many there are and take them' approach! Come on then, Gregor, and bring my arrows with you! Reflect on what you have learned while you dust off your clothes!"

The initial swell of anger that surged through Gregor gave way to his own laughter soon enough. Silverwing was a cunning mentor, that much was certain, and even when suffering the man's twisted sense of humor the boy could not deny the effectiveness of his training. "You are an evil Master, Silverwing! One day I will get the better of you!"

Silverwing waved a greeting as Gregor entered the clearing where the shield hung, the boy noting the worn symbol of the Knights of Bella Grey at its center. "Good luck in that pursuit, Gregor. Many have issued such a challenge and no single enemy can claim that victory." Silverwing held out his hand and replaced the arrows in his quiver as Gregor passed them to him. "One day, with time and training, you will be able to stand at my side as an equal. It will be interesting to see who can outdo whom when that time comes." Silverwing's smile shifted into the studied look of a mentor once more before he continued. "So, tell me what you have learned."

Gregor adopted his mentor's serious look before forming his reply. "What is behind you can kill you just as easily as that which is in front of you."

"And?"

This time Gregor could not restrain his own smile. "Never underestimate your opponent, never think the enemy is going to engage you honorably, and never trust a ranger! You could have killed me!"

"Any reasonable archer could have killed you several times, I assure you. You move like a cow bearing a calf in her belly. I guess stealthy movements will never be your strength. Good thing you can drop quickly." Silverwing grinned as a fiery flush colored the boy's cheeks.

"Damn you, Master Silverwing! I grow tired of dodging through trees, nipping at your heels. When are you going to train me to fight?" Gregor regretted the anger in his tone, but Silverwing chose to ignore it.

Silverwing cocked an eyebrow at his pupil. "Good! We begin your bow training tomorrow. Remember, Gregor, that each lesson builds on the last and you will do well."

***

Galant Silverwing rarely spoke of anything outside the woods and his training was rigorous enough that Gregor had little time to be concerned about his mentor's past. Most of the pair's time was spent running through the thick woods with Gregor dodging low branches and slipping on protruding roots. When the ranger was off on errands beyond Gregor's ability, the young boy that was quickly developing into a man of some strength spent his time in the woods, taking what peace he could from the thick scents of the wild flowers and the cleansing mist that formed a nearly constant blanket over the forest floor.

***

When Master Silverwing began teaching Gregor the art of weapon handling, he insisted that they focus on the bow before the sword. His reasoning was this; Gregor was marked by a lack of dexterity, and Silverwing felt the bow would improve his hand-eye coordination while also adding an amount of control to the boy's choppy movements.

Gregor listened intently as Silverwing expounded the virtues of the bow on the fine clear morning the day after he had been taught the value of flight. It had been a full season since the pair had met. As the crops in the fields grew heavy with their bounty, so the young man had grown.

Gregor was more than ready to take a weapon, any weapon, into his hands, knowing that each day brought him closer to matching swords with his mentor. "We learn the bow before the blade because if your enemy becomes aware of us, then a wounding or crippling shot from a distance better serves us. It is rarely necessary to kill the woodland creatures, except for food, and small game can be trapped with snares when the need arises. Even the interlopers from the cities that come to hunt for *sport*," the ranger spat out the last word with vitriolic scorn, "make better messengers to other would-be sportsmen with an arrow in their thigh. I personally enjoy shooting them in the leg and whooping like a madman."

Silverwing let out a gibbering howl and flapped his arms wildly to demonstrate the proper execution of this technique, making Gregor take a few rapid steps back. "If I am particularly annoyed, or if they are repeat offenders, then an arrow or two in the buttocks usually prevents another incursion. There are some pleasures to be taken in the performance of one's duties." He smiled, full of mischief, no doubt thinking of Gregor's trials the day before. "It is my personal feeling that all should find some amount of happiness in whatever they choose to do, except for those who perpetuate evil. Evil should be summarily destroyed once it is discovered."

The last words seemed to Gregor to be out of place. These statements would have been more appropriate coming from one of the Knights of Bella Grey than the rough-cut Galant. This wasn't the first time the woodsman had let slip glimpses into his beliefs. Gregor had wondered about Master Silverwing's past from their very first encounter. There was the curious nature of his name as well as the odd thought the man sometimes voiced. Silverwing made some sense when taken with the longbow being the hunter's weapon of choice. Still, there was an unspoken amount of weight that the name carried. Gregor considered it a title rather than a given name, which only served to confuse the issue more.

***

Gregor's targeting with the bow could only be termed random at best, even while he attempted to fire on the still targets Silverwing had fashioned of cloth sacks. Galant often had to subdue laughter, although just as often the ranger could not restrain it. Silverwing had some time ago assembled a pulley system, to teach tracking and leading moving enemies, and the ranger's dismay only deepened with each day the boy left the targets untouched. After being driven from nearby trees by the random shots Gregor unleashed, birds watching this curious development in their forest got in the habit of perching directly on the slow-moving targets. This seemed to give them the best advantage, because no creature was safe in front of or behind the path of the target itself.

"The best I can say of your skills with that bow, Gregor, is that there might be some level of intimidation involved in the delivery of your misfires. Anyone who would see the amount of intensity you have in your eyes before you release the shaft would be certain to attribute a great deal of skill to you. It would stand to reason that your enemy might think you are missing on purpose as a warning." Silverwing wiped away tears of laughter before delivering the words Gregor had longed to hear since his training had begun. "My young one, I feel that you have no more to gain continuing your training with the bow. Despite the strength of your arms, your trembling hands will never master the steady hold required to sight with the bow properly. We will begin your blade training immediately, before any innocent forest dwellers can be harmed by your pitiful aim. I can only hope the long hours committed to the bow have bestowed some amount of dexterity and, more importantly, balance, as we take up the blades. I fear, if this is not the case, you will be relegated to using a heavy mace or club that might benefit from your strength."

Gregor still bore the twin short swords from his previous home with the Knights of Bella Grey, and his infrequent practice sessions when Silverwing had left him in the forest while on unknown errands were still marked by a lack of dexterity, but the power behind his thrusts and slashes was increasing. The bow training had served to increase his ability to weigh his strikes as he wielded the two short blades, and Gregor felt certain his mentor would be surprised at his skills.

When he announced that the blade training would begin, Galant had taken the young man to the village smith to fit him for proper chain mail. Galant had explained that it would do no good to train without the interference of armor. Considering the ranger wore only leather armor, Gregor had found this strange, but he could find no reason to question Silverwing at the time. More curious was the warm reception the ranger received from the blacksmith, who was notoriously ill-mannered to everyone. Gregor was amazed once more by how little he actually knew the man who had mentored him the past season, and, as the harvest neared, Gregor could not help but wonder where the road with this mysterious ranger might lead.

Then there was the matter of the long swords that the smithy had kept maintained for Master Galant. "I was wondering when you would pop in to check on your weapons, Lord Silverwing. I take it the bow I acquired has been serving you well, as you aren't dead from being alone in those woods." The smith had said with a rough chuckle.

"The longbow has proven more than adequate. Few poachers leave the wood without feeling its sting." *Silverwing assured him*

The smith moved into the rear of his shop to retrieve a long package wrapped in silk cloth. The man laid the package on the counter in front of Gregor and Silverwing with the kind of reverence one would normally reserve for a holy artifact. "They are a beautiful pair of swords, Lord Silverwing, and I admit I would be happy to inherit them if you should pass on into the realm of the God of Light." As the blacksmith spoke and slowly began opening the package, it was all the young man could do not to spout out the numerous questions that flooded his mind. One thing he knew without asking; Galant Silverwing had been a knight of some merit in years past. This knowledge answered none of the riddles concerning the ranger and only created more unanswered questions. Gregor was stunned to silence with admiration as Master Galant drew the weapons from their simple leather sheaths, with the blacksmith grinning broadly at the wonder reflected in the boy's eyes. Gregor's time with the Knights of Bella Grey had given him great appreciation of properly crafted and well-balanced weapons, and the two blades that lay before him were exquisite, crafted of an alloy he could not recognize, and ornately carved with gilded hilts. Each of the hilts of the twin blades was decorated with golden dragons intertwining their serpentine forms down the full length of the handle, their long necks curving outward to form the branches of the guard. The dragons' bodies were woven around nearly identical intricately cut crystals in the center of the grips. Golden claws appeared to suspend each crystal at the top and bottom within the handle. The crystals showered every surface near them with a spray of multicolored light, reflecting the fiery glow from the forge. Gregor could only imagine how beautiful they would appear in full sunlight. He thought he would faint if Sir Galant passed these blades to him even for training. He could imagine the feints and delivering strikes he could deliver with these weapons. His blows ~~felled~~ giants and deadly creatures of the night, the blades glimmering with power and purity. No evil beast or man could stand before him with his enchanted blades and practiced movements. Master Silverwing pulled him from his reverie as quickly as Gregor had become lost in it.

The ranger smiled at the smith, removing the huntsman's knife, and the belt where he had carried it, from his waist. "Won't have much use for this knife any longer, I suppose. Pass it on to one of the local huntsmen when they come to have their weapons tended. It has served its purpose well over the years and I would hate to see it go unused."

Silverwing secured the belt and scabbards that were meant to carry his weapons as he placed his order with the blacksmith, restoring his swords to their proper place. "Master Ian, I need a chain mail shirt and two properly balanced long swords crafted for this young man. Please take his measure and I will have him pass by again for proper fitting in a couple of weeks. Would you be able to forge these in a month's time?" Silverwing smiled briefly, awaiting the smith's answer.

"If it was anyone else asking me, they would be told it would be done when it was done. It will be ready for you in three weeks, Sir Galant, and the boy will bear weapons and armor worthy of his mentor."

"You will need a bit of coin for the sweat of your labors, Master Ian." Silverwing drew several coins from a small leather pouch at his side, only to receive a hard look from the smith before he could place them on the counter.

"Do not insult me with the offer of payment. Your service to these lands is payment enough." The smith's crossed arms and furrowed brow showed he would hear no more such nonsense from Silverwing on the matter, and the ranger respectfully dropped the coins back into his purse.

The smith bowed to the ranger. The bow was returned in kind with the respect usually reserved for the meeting of kings. These men were both men of honor of a kind few common people could understand. Gregor felt humbled to be in their presence.

***

"Well, I guess you want to know about the blades and how I came to have them?" Gregor felt that he might just have heard the biggest understatement ever from Master Galant. The ranger may just as well have said he was only a fair shot with the bow. "The story is a long one, but we have time until proper blade training can begin. Sit on the stone and practice listening. It is one of the most useful skills I can teach you." Sir Galant began to relate the story of the creation of the Golden Dragon, Keepers of the White Light.

The Order of the Knights of the Golden Dragon had taken their name from the God of Light they served and the beast whose hide was formed into the armor they originally wore. Gregor learned from Silverwing's story that the original warriors were drawn from an elite guard unit in service to a Lord of the House of Materon. "The dragon-scaled armor worn by the first knights remains in service, worn by elite guards of the House of Materon to this day. No one dares to challenge the guards that wear the armor, and the lands overseen by the House of Materon enjoy peace and prosperity even at the worst of times. Perhaps you will see the great keep where we originated one day in your travels."

The knights had always numbered ten men and women chosen from the strongest and most devout warriors the lands had to offer. The first ten warriors shared a vision from the God of Light, and were drawn to the Temple of Light by their dreams. The head priest who oversaw the temple at the House of Materon educated the holy warriors as healers and bestowed the power to channel divine blessings from the God of Light. Holy weapons were granted to each of the first warriors, and they were charged with protecting all the lands from the evil of men and beasts. Priests gifted with special sight were dispersed to the various Temples of the Light. When any knights left the Order, these priests trained the replacements before they took their place among the Knights.

Tradition dictated that the blessed weapons were passed from the fallen or retiring members to the new warriors, and in this manner the Order remained strong for 400 years. "The breaking of the sword carried by Lord Clamine has never happened. Only a terrible curse of unknowable strength could have torn the sword into two parts. The other weapons were retired with their owners when the Order of the Golden Dragon was broken years ago. It has been thirty years since the last of the knights, besides Lord Clamine and myself, were committed to their final rest and their weapons sealed within the tombs. Lord Clamine went to the God of Light without his weapon, the blade of which you bear. The sword still has some role to play in destroying the evil responsible for this tragedy."

Gregor was moved to ask Master Silverwing how he had been separated from Lord Clamine. "You were the last of the Order. What could have made you leave the Knights of Bella Grey?"

"I was following the path set before me as Lord Clamine was following his own. Neither of us knew where our paths would carry us, but we both trusted our faith to sustain us. Lord Clamine established the Knights of Bella Grey to train warriors from across the lands the Knights of the Golden Dragon once protected. Many of these holy warriors still train orders of knights of their own and protect the lands as we once did. I chose to study with the priests of nature, the druids as they are called, to gain greater insight into the workings of the world as a whole. My heart is heavy with sorrow wondering if I might have made some difference, but the God of Light had other reasons to keep me in this forest. We cannot possibly understand why all things happen as they do. Many knights were killed in service to the God of Light; they gave their lives for their brothers and sisters within the Order, and we made terrible sacrifices to save the common people in the time the Golden Dragon existed. I have little doubt that you, Gregor, will come in time to question your own faith as I have, but know this; it is when you would most easily turn from your faith and the God of Light that you must find your own strength and carry on. The God of Light never loses faith in you. I have watched you, fueled by anger and hatred for the loss of Lord Clamine. I share your sorrow, but we cannot live in the past and progress toward the destiny set before us."

Gregor reflected on these words for the first of many times. It was much to bear for one so young. Gregor had somehow been drawn into the service of a God he did not know, to serve a purpose he could not begin to guess. He could not believe the potential Silverwing seemed to see within him was there at all. He vowed to honor the loss of Lord Clamine and raised his head to the God of Light who had touched him so long ago. Gregor *would* find the power and faith he needed. He could find no peace until he did.

2

What Goes Up

The time of harvest had come, and Gregor spent a few weeks helping his father take in the produce of their farmlands. The young warrior felt the call of the earth as he and his father drew the bounty of the rich soil, and wondered if he was really meant to pursue great deeds as a sword bearer. The vegetables and grains he had harvested every season from these fields gave him comfort in their ability to be known, to be understood and appreciated. His rough hands were better suited to a hoe and fishing pole than the hilt of a sword, as Lord Silverwing would remind him all too soon.

"Oh, how I grieve for your lack of dexterity. Is there no amount of balance forced into you that your limbs cannot undo? God of Light, please bless and keep this boy untainted by war so that he might not injure those nearby that would aid him! Once more, Gregor, and for all that is pure, concentrate!" Master Silverwing was a weapon master the likes of which Gregor had never seen, even among the best of the sparring warriors that had numbered among the Knights of Bella Grey. It seemed Gregor's strength training with the practice swords was of little use in preparing to actually wield true weapons. The swords prepared by the village's blacksmith were art in steel, but no special prowess was bestowed with the care in their creation. The first weeks of hacking at stuffed practice dummies had tuned his muscles to some extent. Nightfall after each sparring match with Master Silverwing brought aches where Gregor had not known muscle existed. Still, the dance of his mentor's blades was an inspiration. The slow movement as he would parry aside Gregor's awkward thrusts only enhanced the beauty of the two blades. Those swords were weapons made for the valiant, and Master Silverwing seemed impervious to attack with the weapons in hand. Gregor often found himself distracted with dreams of wielding such fine blades with the grace of a true warrior.

"Master Silverwing, I am never going to be able to bear the blades as you do. My strength is the strong assault, the swift cleave that takes the enemy by surprise with the muscle of the attack. You are a dancer and I am a clod. You strike from a natural place of balance honed by years of practice, and I strike with the swing of a smithy." Gregor was sad to admit it, but certainly his mentor must see this obvious fact.

"There is truth in your words, Master Gregor, but the failure in your ability is a lack of insight into the trainer. You do not have the hands for two blades. Sheath one of your weapons and follow me." Silverwing turned to travel deeper into the tall trees. The ranger paused at the base of one of the oldest oaks in the wood and gazed skyward toward the blended yellows and reds coloring the leaves above him. "Beautiful, isn't it? No man could match the burst of color that nature produces without any effort. This one should serve our purpose." Silverwing began climbing into the giant tree that would have taken ten men touching wide spread hands to measure its girth at its lower trunk, his grace all the more apparent as he ascended into the upper branches. "Come up, Gregor! The view from here is beautiful! Leave one of the swords at the tree's base."

Gregor could not imagine what the ranger had in mind, but he allowed his curiosity to propel him into the tree's branches to join him near the upper portion of the tree. It had been a long time since Gregor had climbed up into the higher reaches of any of the great oaks, and he had to admire the profusion of leaves that formed the canopy. Silverwing stood on a thick branch near where it emerged at the center of the tree, extending outward to form a portion of the crown. Its branches divided at Gregor's back a few steps behind the shaking warrior. Despite the thickness of the branch Gregor's legs were splayed across, the young student felt certain it was best not to look down, and he had no intention of standing up. "What is so fascinating way up here?" Gregor focused on his mentor as he posed the question, not wanting to dwell on the distance to the ground from his high perch.

"Everything! The smells, the sights, the colors as the sun's rays come through the leaves of the season! Look around you!" As if to illustrate his point, the hunter spun around in a tight circle on the narrow branch. Gregor felt dizzy just watching.

"I will take your word for it, Master Silverwing." Gregor had not released his grip on the branch where the ranger stood, and felt no hurry to do so.

The ranger obviously had other plans for his student and turned toward Gregor, pulling him up by his chainmail chest piece.

Gregor marveled at the man's strength as his feet dangled just above the branch where Silverwing stood. "It is time for a lesson in balance, Gregor." The ranger smiled as he gently lowered Gregor's feet to the branch. "The thing to remember is that if you trust your balance, you can focus on the defense and offense you use against your opponent. Just have faith in what I have taught you, Gregor, and you should be fine."

Gregor extended his arms briefly and tried to breathe, still focusing on his mentor. "What? You want me to spar with you? Up here?"

"Exactly, this time using one blade instead of two. I am sure you would fall out of this tree if you tried to fight me with two blades. In fact, I should probably only use one blade, too. Even the odds a bit." Silverwing leaned into the air and dropped one of his swords toward the earth. A solid thunk indicated the blade had landed well into one of the tree's roots.

"You can't be serious! What if I fall?" Gregor's voice, which had only recently lowered in tone to that of a man, chose this moment to resume the fluctuations of the boy he once was.

Silverwing looked at the young warrior as if he were amazed at the question. "Well, no doubt it will hurt quite a lot. Still, falling from a tree is not nearly as bad as being stabbed to death by a sword. Come on, then, arm yourself or see how well you fall. Try to miss the root if you slip." The ranger slapped the flat of his blade at each side of the tree branch where they stood, bringing his sword up to the ready.

Gregor felt he had little choice in the matter and brought his own sword up to the ready as well. The melee had begun. The young warrior decided to open with a direct thrust. Silverwing answered the attack by gently deflecting Gregor's blade and replying with a feint to the young warrior's throat, causing Gregor to lower his sword and step back. "Well done, Gregor! There is no room for powerful swings here. Losing your balance when crossing swords leaves you defenseless. Notice your feet have not betrayed you in your retreat."

Gregor smiled. "Master Silverwing, how many knights have you trained in this manner?" The warrior's blade feinted in an attempt to take his Master in the shoulder.

His mentor swept the incoming blade into the air past his shoulder, taking a step closer to Gregor before speaking. "You are the first I have trained in such a manner, and no doubt will be the last. This is terribly dangerous, wouldn't you agree?" Silverwing brought his sword up defensively, awaiting Gregor's next move.

Gregor decided to assume a more aggressive posture, matching Silverwing's step forward with one of his own. The two swordsmen stood dangerously close to one another, their blades touching to form an X between them. "What now, Master? I will take you if you back away and you will take me if I step back. Let's call it a draw and end this madness."

Gregor realized his error when Silverwing grinned at him. "You assume one of us would be willing to give way. You may find the drop to the left the more favorable." As he finished speaking, the hunter shoved Gregor backward, causing the young warrior to lose his footing. As Gregor spun his arms trying to regain his balance, his mentor slapped his unstable student's right shoulder with the flat of his blade. Gregor had no time to look before his feet were leaving the safety of the narrow branch. 'Jump and bend your knees! Trust your feet and you will be fine!"

Gregor's first action, based purely on faith, was to follow the shouted directions of his mentor. He was shocked to find that he did not plummet to the earth and break his neck as he had expected. After a remarkably short fall, Gregor's feet struck a branch slightly broader than the one he had fallen from, with a handy limb extending just at the right height to give him something to grab. "I bet you are a heck of a dancer, too!" Silverwing shouted as he leapt down to the branch where Gregor had landed. "Shall we continue?"

Gregor grinned at his mentor, despite the hammering in his chest. "Do I have a choice?"

"You always have a choice, Gregor. The thing that makes it matter is that you make the right one." Silverwing sheathed his sword and extended his hand to help Gregor back to his feet. "There is an easier way down if you trust yourself enough to follow my step." The hunter stepped off the branch and jumped down through the branches until he rested on the ground.

Gregor held on to the branch that had saved him from a more rapid descent as he waved to his mentor, shouting his reply, "I think I will take the slower path, Master Silverwing."

Master Silverwing had sheathed his blades, waiting while Gregor climbed to the ground. His mentor's words were unexpected as Gregor moved to join him. "I have other duties outside this forest that have been too long neglected. You have learned much with me, but I feel only time and the road can teach you more of the skills you need. You are an adequate swordsman and even your bow skills have improved, though I would not think you are ready to survive with your abilities as a hunter alone. I must deliver you to the Temple of Light at Nactium, and there we will part company for a time. The city is down the west road, about five days' travel if you push. Prepare your pack and take as little as you can. I will come to your parents' home to get you tomorrow. Pray for safety and guidance tonight and sup with your mother and father. It will be some time before you see them again."

Gregor made no effort to mask his confusion at the ranger's words. "Why are you taking me to the temple?"

"It is where you will learn the ways of the warriors of the God of Light, Gregor. The God has chosen you for some purpose that I cannot prepare you for, nor even guess what it may be. Only the God knows why you have been called. I have done all for you that I can, and you are a man worthy of the honor of the Golden Dragon. The priests must educate you further to prepare you for the title of knight you are meant to bear."

***

The dawn and Master Silverwing came too soon. The young man had risen early to dress in his armor and secure at his sides the swords Master Ian had crafted. Despite Gregor's lack of prowess wielding two blades, he took some comfort knowing he had them both. Gregor kissed his mother good bye, and hugged his father tightly, promising his parents he would return when he could, despite his mentor's words the day before. The road from the village seemed dark with the unknown, and even though strength emanated from Lord Silverwing beside him, Gregor was afraid. It was an insidious, penetrating fear that leeched into his very bones with each step down the road through the forest.

The pair spoke little as they made their way, with the knight of the forgotten Golden Dragon educating Gregor in the worship of the God of Light. Silverwing explained that the knights were more than just warriors, often assuming the role of healer and sometimes priest to those who were isolated from their faith. There was much the boy, who had so recently reached manhood, did not know of life. Master Silverwing prayed faith could carry him. He would feel much better once Gregor had been educated among the priests in a proper house of worship. So much depended on Gregor, so much Master Galant could not tell him. The burdens of these lands would be too much for shoulders so slight, and there was still time, Lord Silverwing thought. He could not have known how short time really was, or how shadows drew closer to striking every day.

3

Divided Highways

Something in the darkness of the nearly moonless night set Gregor's teeth on edge. Silverwing and Gregor ~~gotten~~ had were a little over halfway to the city of Nactium after three days' hard travel, and there was no reason to think anything would keep them from entering the city in a couple more days at their current pace. Still, this deep night caused a tightening in the chest of the young swordsman that he had not ever experienced. Gregor had learned not to dismiss the warnings his instincts offered, and he brought both his blades from their sheaths even before Silverwing's voice broke the silence of the night.

"Stop," Lord Galant's bow appeared in his practiced hands as if by magic. "Ready your weapons and put your back against mine. Bring them up but not too high. There are two at my back and four more at either side, moving in pairs. If you strike to kill, you will expose yourself. Parry and feint as best you can, and for God's sake stay at my back. I can't help you if you move away from me."

Gregor moved as instructed and two forms clothed in shadow appeared from the trees near the road. He was steady at his mentor's back though he wanted desperately to charge his attackers. A droplet of sweat trickled down his cheek slowly as the figures approached. He could barely discern their forms in the night that held only a sliver of moon. They had obviously planned their ambush carefully. "Watch their feet and remember our training. These are professionals, not mere road thugs. They must have been following us for some time." Gregor was amazed at how calmly his mentor was considering the current state of affairs. The first arrow Master Silverwing loosed was whisper quiet, and the only indication it had struck true was a ragged moan followed by a soft thud to Gregor's rear. There was the sound of rapid movement in the direction Silverwing faced, indicating the ranger's attackers had grown bolder, or more desperate, at the loss of one of their number. A rush of footsteps sounded as Master Silverwing drew his blades, dropping his trusted bow to his side. Gregor took no time to check who his mentor faced, bringing his blades up as he snarled deep in his throat at the approaching pair of brigands.

The hooded figures moved cautiously toward him, taking the measure of their victim. Each bore a vile dagger in their right hands, with a jagged edge made for tearing. There were wicked spiked balls, roughly a quarter stone's weight to Gregor's trained eyes, which were hanging from the left hand of each attacker, attached to one another by thin metal links of chain. Gregor could only guess at the purpose of these strange weapons. His enemies paused as they entered the road, planting their feet and slowly spinning the odd weapons in their left hands as if the killers were a matched pair of jugglers. Gregor brought up his blades defensively as the pair pivoted onto their boot tips to release, and the missiles flew from their hands in unison. Gregor realized the purpose of the missiles too late as the thin iron chains between the spiked orbs encircled his blades and moved down toward the hilts of the swords. He managed to drop the blade of his stronger arm quickly enough to shed one of the vicious missiles, but the other stuck true to its purpose. His weaker hand took the full impact of the spikes and the weight of the metal balls buried the spurs in his hand. He had no time to dwell on the excruciating pain. The work of their initial attack complete, the killers moved to engage him. The first strikes were easily parried as Gregor gave himself over to his training and the protection of his swords. The pair before him moved into and out of his reach with cunning and patience, as if he were a mouse cornered in a barn when the cats had come to play. The blood dripping from his left hand told them all they needed to know of his wound, and they seemed to be enjoying wearing him down.

Gregor felt a grudging respect for the assassins, for surely they must be trained in the arts of death, as they toyed with his defenses. He didn't know how long he could last without being mortally struck, and he knew full well, as the melee progressed, that they could slay him with ease. Master Silverwing was firm at his back, and Gregor resolved to hold as long as his mentor required. The only reassurance the young warrior had was a near constant clang of metal at his rear along with grunts of disgust and pain that were not Master Galant's. The fight seemed to go on for hours, when all at once everything changed. Silverwing shifted to one side and turned, bringing his shoulder to meet Gregor's on his weaker side.

"This youngster is not worthy of your skills, dark ones. Flee into the night or face the fate of your companions." There was a soft thud behind Gregor and Master Silverwing, emphasizing his words as the last of the four assassins he had faced struck the ground. Gregor did not dare to look away from the two men before him, though he could sense by his mentor's tone that Lord Silverwing was smiling. The pair considered the offer momentarily before slashing violently at the ranger and the student, but the killers could not match Lord Silverwing's skilled blades. The ranger's blades extended expertly and in one smooth motion stabbed through the leathers they wore, burying a sword to its hilt into each of the attackers.

"As you wish," Silverwing uttered the words almost conversationally. He pulled the blades free and shoved Gregor back, driving an elbow into his student's chest. The movement, intended to protect the young warrior, cost the ranger some amount of his own protection. The men swung their vile daggers in a final act of defiance. Silverwing's thrusting elbow forced Gregor beyond the reach of the killer directly in front of him, but the other facing Master Silverwing drove his dagger into its intended target, burying the jagged blade in Silverwing's shoulder. The dagger remained where it had pierced Silverwing's leather shoulder guard as the last of the assassins fell dead, joining their fallen companions.

"What are we going to do with the bodies, Master Silverwing?" Gregor felt no remorse for those slain, but he did not feel it was right to leave them in the road. "We have to get aid for your wound as well. Your shoulder; should I remove the blade? It seems the jagged edge might tear it apart and I am no healer."

"Hold, Gregor," Master Silverwing spoke through gritted teeth as once more he retrieved his bow. The ranger sighted carefully before loosing a single arrow into the darkness with a whoosh of breath and a curse. A flapping of leathery wings was the only indication that he had come close to his intended target, and the curse that escaped him told Gregor that his mentor had missed. "There will be the hells themselves to pay for the lack of aim in that shot! We are exposed every moment we remain here. Do not trouble yourself about my wounds. Our God serves us as we serve him, and I can bind myself readily enough. Cut the shoulder guard away from the blade, and I will mend the wound. Apply as little pressure to the dagger as possible."

Gregor removed the shoulder guard as instructed, casting aside the ruined chunks of hardened leather as he cut them away. The wound bled grievously, no longer restricted by the padding beneath the leathers. Master Silverwing removed his leather glove from the hand opposite his wounded shoulder, focusing his strength as he prayed in a whisper for the divine power he required. A gentle blue and silver light enveloped the huntsman's hand as he moved his palm over the wound. "I will need you to remove the blade, Gregor, so I can heal the wound properly." The open flesh began to knit almost immediately as Gregor drew out the jagged dagger, covering the wound in fresh pink skin. As the bleeding stopped, Master Silverwing set about cleaning his leathers with a cloth from his pack. "It is not the worst I have had, but it will take time to heal completely. The priests will be knitting bone in my shoulder and curing the wound for some time. It is time for you and me to part company, Gregor. It is far later that I would have thought, and the price on my head must be great. The services of the Brotherhood of the Black Hand are much too expensive to be wasted hunting travelers on the roads." Master Silverwing examined the dagger closely, pointing out the tell-tale markings on it as he did. "The obsidian handle and the fist carved on the hilt are unique to each blade. The owners form them when they become initiates of the Brotherhood. Each weapon leaves a signature mark as it pierces the flesh. They rarely group into bands of more than two, and I have never heard of this many working as one before. It is too hard to cover their tracks in so large a group. Most of the people within these lands never encounter more than rumors of their existence. These are black times indeed, Gregor, and you must be constantly on your guard. The mark of the Overseer of the Brotherhood himself appears to be on me. The bat I failed to slay that flew from the trees is his servant, and will bring word of the failure. Such interest is curious. Look here, "Master Silverwing knelt beside the body of the one who wounded him. "See the ring, here? This man was no novice. Few bear this bit of jewelry outside the proven members of the evil Brotherhood. Curious that he should lead a band of so many that were untested. I assume we were to be their final trial before the rite of passage into the Black Hand. This one must have fallen out of favor somehow and been seeking to redeem himself. Yes, dark times for us all. The Overseer is the one who slew one of my students long ago and disappeared into the darkness. The bastard was little more than the leader of common brigands at that time. I have spent much coin and many years looking for him. Tales of his ascension into the higher ranks of the Brotherhood of the Black Hand were obviously accurate, and it would appear my inquiries have not gone unnoticed. Gregor, you must take my swords to the Temple of the

God of Light in Nactium. The priests there will recognize them and will complete your training." With this, Silverwing handed Gregor his swords and took Gregor's in return.

Gregor was overwhelmed by the words of his mentor. He was honored and confused by the implications of Silverwing's trust, with the giving of the ranger's sacred swords into his care. "There must be some other way to send word to the priests at Nactium. You honor me with your suggestion that I am fit to bear your weapons, but I feel your faith in my abilities is misplaced. What if you are mistaken about the target of these killers? Would they not have struck you down long ago if that were their intention? Even with the final strikes they made against us, as your blades pierced them, they did not appear to attempt to kill us. Cutting our throats would have served them better."

Silverwing met the young warrior's eyes before taking Gregor's wounded hand in his own. "You assume too much, Gregor. Trust my knowledge and I will trust my faith. There is no time to send word to the priests ahead of you, even if I reach Travelflor by tomorrow. Let me heal your hand. It seems the dread spikes have bitten you deeply. You are lucky that they were meant to slow instead of cripple you." It took only moments for Master Silverwing to restore his flesh.

"How am I to find the city without you? These roads are no paths I know." Gregor felt the fear that was becoming his near constant companion return. He marveled at his bare hand that had only moments before been punctured and bleeding. Gregor flexed it several times, curling his fingers into a tentative fist. A slight tingling sensation slowly worked its way out of his joints. He marveled at the divine healing wielded by his mentor. The stories of great deeds and acts of healing were one thing; it was very different to experience it.

His mentor's answer came gently. "Gregor, our God will guide you through this night to safety, and it will take time for others to be sent. With any luck, they will be tracking me. Stay off the road and keep a straight path. Travel in that direction as straight as you can until the sun rises, then follow the sun across the sky for at least a day before you rest." Silverwing paused to orient Gregor in the proper direction before continuing. "That should take you deep enough into the forest to elude any that might follow. You should come upon huntsmen as your travel these woods, or more likely they will find you. Mention my name and they will keep you safe, but do not tell them where you are going. Those who live off the bounty of the forest can be trusted, but there is no way to know to what lengths the Black Hand might go should they discover who you really are. I will send word to the Temple once I know what must be done. Guard yourself against the wild predators in the wood. They can be vicious, but if you are noisy enough the animals should stay away. I doubt they would find the smell of you appealing in any case." Master Silverwing paused for a moment, drawing two leather pouches from his belt, one appearing to be empty, while the other was heavy with coin. He deftly transferred a few coins and gems to the empty pouch before tossing a few coins to the ground where the corpses lay. Silverwing handed the lighter bag of coins and gems to Gregor. "This, and the gifts of the woodsmen, should take you to Nactium with enough for a proper inn and a donation to the temple once you arrive. The coin I have left here should be ample to make sure our friend disposes of the bodies and follows me." Master Silverwing raised his voice enough to be heard in the trees as he spoke of the "friend." This time the arrow sighted flew true, as an unidentified watcher fell from his perch among the branches. "Don't worry, Gregor, he is not dead, just startled. The blessings of our God have many faces, and I have little doubt this man serves some purpose yet to be seen. He won't be following you in any case." Master Silverwing's smile was infectious, and Gregor found his heart was lighter for seeing it. "We have no time to waste. Take my swords and go into the wood, my brother, and know that the spirit guides you. Do not stop until sunset tomorrow. You should be out of harm's reach for now. Just follow your feet west until you make it to the walls of Nactium." The two parted ways, Silverwing continuing down to the road as Gregor moved off into the forest.

The shadow that had been hiding in the tree dropped to the ground with a volley of curses that would have burned a sailor's ears. "He is a reasonable shot maybe, but I take orders from no one. I will, however, take the coins and cover these as I see fit." Boremac mumbled more curses as he kicked some fallen leaves and debris over the bodies of the assassins. "Amateurs. Better off dead than stupid." He took just a moment to think over his options. Obviously the Hand wanted one of those two dead instead of him. Even with Boremac's skills, he had to admit this bunch would have been difficult to slay alone. As it was, he had been watching the group of assassins' movements for two days without drawing their attention, no mean feat.

"So the sloppy young warrior would have required no effort to take which means they must be after the ranger. So capture the ranger…that will be fun, to be sure, and give me a chance to trade with the Hand for my life. No honor among thieves, but the Hand, they are something else altogether. My handsome life for a scraggy ranger? Works for me." Boremac took to the shadows he had known so well all his life and set out after Silverwing.

4

Strange Relations

"I can do this. I grew up with the woods all around me. I trained with the great Lord Silverwing. How could I possibly go wrong?" Gregor spoke aloud in the dark night for the first time since leaving his mentor. Another howl pierced the darkness, and Gregor's hands went instinctively to his mentor's blades. "Master Silverwing entrusted me with his weapons and I have no right to end up lost and eaten in this forest. Follow my feet. Yes, well, my feet have found every root and rabbit hole this forest has to offer. What next, Master Galant?" Gregor knew all too well what was next, as another wolf answered the first. He couldn't be sure, but the calls seemed to draw closer each time the throaty howls broke the silence. Gregor doubted there were any deer near to distract the pack. He was quite sure he knew who was on the menu tonight. He longed for a fire, but knew better. The killers they had defeated may not have been alone, and the woods could host any number of poachers or rogues. He had no desire to draw any more attention to himself than necessary, and he dared not stop tonight.

The rising sun was little comfort as it broke the horizon, but at least the wolves had not found him. Gregor prayed his luck would hold for another day. The passage through the wood wearied him to the bone, and he could not rest again until nightfall. His aching legs reminded him of this unpleasant fact with each step. "Keep the sun at my back until it carries over me at midday, then follow it. Simple enough. A bit of luck may even bring me a path for a while. It seems strange how the trees take ones voice. Should be glad of it I guess. Surely the woodsmen would think I was quite cracked wandering out here in full chain mail talking to myself."

"I would have to agree with you. Of course, any hunter worth his bow would have heard you clattering through his wood soon enough to avoid you altogether." The hunter in question rounded a tree in front of Gregor, a grin breaking his weathered features. "You have cleared this bit of wood of game. It seems my only recourse will be to get you out of my hunting grounds and hope the deer return in a day or two. Come. I have a cabin near here. Let's see if we can get you somewhere else. I am called Dakin. You must be lost."

"Thank you, Master Dakin; I am in your debt. I am Gregor, student of Master Silverwing, sent on an errand in his service. He has graced me with some skill and a bit of direction, but little else, I fear." Gregor felt himself flush as he bowed before the huntsman. "He said the hunters of the wood were kind and would lend me aid. I am glad to see it is true."

"No need to honor me with titles, sir. Dakin will suffice, and anyone possessing merit enough to train with Master Silverwing has my deepest admiration, and no small amount of pity, besides." Dakin laughed at his own jest. "I understand he is a terror to poachers and brigands alike that happen into the forest under his protection. I can only shudder to think of the trials he must have put you through as his pupil." He punctuated his words with a hearty clap on Gregor's back as he began to go deeper into the wood. "It is good to keep the sun at our backs and the breeze in our faces. Let's be off."

Dakin spoke little as they made their way deeper into the forest, and Gregor was glad. The hunter kept a quick pace, and talking would have wasted Gregor's breath. Dakin shared bits of lore concerning the local flora and fauna, and Gregor found he was as modest as he was knowledgeable. Dakin had spent all his life in these woods, with his parents at first, until they had died, taking up the safe-keeping of the land as his father had done. He seemed somewhat sorrowful that no brave pup from the local villages bordering the forest had been sent to learn the hunter's ways. The keeper of the wood had no son or daughter to train, and feared he might be the last guardian of this forest once he died. Gregor was surprised to learn that Dakin's fate was shared by many of the roving hunters, since there just weren't many fair maids that would choose the forest over the farm. Many of the young men and women that might have taken up the call were fleeing the villages for the promise of wealth in the cities.

"Can't really blame the young ones. The merchants come out all showy and full of tales of this hero or that. This life is a hard one, but no less fulfilling. The woods are getting more dangerous all the time, though, with the incursions of poachers and worse. Goblins been sighted, I hear. Small groups for now, but the mountains and hillocks don't suit them so much since the hired blades and adventurers been going after them. Someone is making ready for war, I imagine, and those warriors that drive the goblins from their caves control who mines the mountains. Yes, times are getting tough for man and beast in the forests."

Gregor couldn't help but wonder at Dakin's words. He had heard some rumors of such things, but had mostly dismissed them as tales of bluff from the far traveling tradesmen. The only goblins mentioned in his village had been the ones that come and take naughty children away when they stray from their beds at night. He resolved to ask for more information once they reached Dakin's home, deciding to keep in step with him for now.

Dakin's home was a sight to behold. The cottage was nearly indistinguishable from its surroundings. The walls were supported at the four corners by trees of considerable diameter, creating a natural camouflage for the roof angling gently upward inside the cover of their boughs. Greenery of various sorts seemed to grow out of the walls themselves, as vines had traced patterns up and over every surface. The doorway itself was the only sign of man-made intervention; intricately carved with runic symbols Gregor could not begin to decipher. He could make out forms of trees, flowers and a few animals, seemingly scattered at random, with strange symbols forming pictures at nearly every exposed surface. The arched entrance was just a hand taller than he was, and bore the same runes etched into it. Only the top of the doorway remained in its original form, stripped of bark and worn smooth.

"Do you like it?" Dakin's pride could be heard in his voice, as Gregor marveled at the entrance. "My great grandfather found the trees and built this family home, oh, a hundred years ago, for my great grandmother. A woman can't much see rearing children in a cave. The forest seems to have taken to our line quite nicely. Haven't had to do much in the way of directing the plants, not that they would have much let us anyway. Those older markings at the base of the archway there are from my great grandfather's own hands. He asked the Goddess of the wood to protect his kin, and devoted his line to protect the wood in return. Each man of the family has made his own mark in his time, reaffirming the commitment and asking for his own blessings." Dakin sighed, tracing his fingers across what Gregor assumed were the hunter's own markings. "Haven't had mine answered yet, and I am not getting any younger. I am sure the Goddess will send a new protector when she sees fit. Come inside and let's get you some food. Looks like you been traveling through the night and this day is nearly gone."

The mention of food made Gregor realize just how hungry he was. The interior of the house was simple compared to its exterior. There was a wood stove and a table with four chairs. Two beds were positioned near one another off to one corner of the single room, and a beautifully carved bassinet had been positioned under the only window, not far from the larger of the two beds. Gregor noted a bit of late sun still shown on the baby bed. Delicate vines creeping in the window had formed a halo around the upper edges of it, and small pink flowers had sprouted everywhere. "Three generations of huntsmen were raised here and slept in that tiny haven. The scent of the flowers never quite goes away. We have always just let the petals drop where they will. Never more than one child, and always an extra chair at the table, just in case there was a visitor." Dakin smiled and motioned toward the table. "Go on and rest a bit. Might want to take the armor off. Gets a bit warm in that chain mail, I would imagine. If you would like, there is a shirt and leggings in the chest near the stove there. You could take a chance to clean your undergarments and dry them by the stove while we eat."

Gregor thanked his host, and removed his chainmail armor. Pegs along one wall meant for hides served to keep the armor, and he found himself very comfortable in the spare clothing the hunter offered. Gregor felt the tension of the past few days drain from him, as the smells of cooking venison and the gentle tug of the perfume from the flowers penetrated him. It was a simple meal of meat and hardtack, with warm broth to wash away the journey through the wood. Gregor was comforted to find a warm meal with such a gentle soul. He and Dakin spoke little, except for praising the food the wood provided. Each man concerned himself with the business of eating. The meal finished soon enough, and Dakin pulled the plug on a large jug in an almost conspiratorial fashion. "I have been saving this for a special occasion. Trader said it is a fine brew. Called it the drink of kings. Haven't tried it yet, but what better time than now to share it? Don't know about 'the drink of kings' part of it, but the scent is promising. Care for a cup with me?"

Gregor hesitated before answering, and decided the truth was the best reply. "I have not imbibed anything stronger than ale, and so would not be one to measure its worth. If it pleases you, I would share a cup with you."

Dakin took two fine glasses from a cabinet filled with various herbs and seasonings. "These poor cups have seen little need of use with me. My father acquired them for my mother when she carried me in her belly. A special gift for the next of our line, I suppose. My mother was a city girl when they met, and wine was a treat for her they could scarcely afford." Dakin filled the glasses with two fingers of the dark golden fluid and bid Gregor to rise from his chair. "A toast to new friends. May we each find our paths clear, and the breezes gentle in our faces as we travel them." Dakin sampled the amber liquid with a smack of his lips. "Well, I will say this for it, kings may frown, but it suits me just fine." Gregor felt his face flush as the liquid passed his lips; the burning sensation it caused ran across his tongue to his belly with no hint of lessening. There was a warm glow, almost a haze that passed across his eyes, as Gregor sat down hard in his chair. He felt an awkward smile break across his face as he nodded his head in agreement. He made note to sip slowly lest he embarrass himself.

The drink gave flight Dakin's words, even as it quieted Gregor. The woodsman had learned much of recent events from the traders and fellow huntsmen he had encountered. Despite the numbing of his own tongue, Gregor was able to learn a great deal from Dakin. The young warrior asked a few slurred questions, cautiously sipping his own drink, when the hunter would pause to take a breath or refresh his own goblet. Goblins did indeed exist, and were making quite a nuisance of themselves for the merchant travelers. The demand for trained blades and marksmen had steadily increased, and prices for goods traded between the cities had grown with them. Local militias had their hands full with the usual brigands, and the raiding parties of the goblins were staying well outside the reach of the regular soldiers. There were rumors of worse things, as well.

Orcs, the boar-faced humanoids that had infrequently raided isolated villages for pillage and slaves, seemed to be growing bolder and more organized. These tribal creatures grew easily a head taller than the average man and had great strength. The orcs had long ago learned rudimentary metalworking, fashioning brutal weapons similar to the great axes and two-handed swords wielded by human warriors. The humanoids' great strength allowed them to wield the weapons with one hand and carry hide shields with the other that were large enough to use as makeshift sleds to carry away their ill-gotten spoils. Villages that before had been able to repel the creatures could no longer stand against them. Villagers had been slaughtered, and piles of ash and cinders were all that remained of their homes and farms.

The demand for iron and steel had made wealthy men of traders and blacksmiths alike, as the call for arms and armor increased. Governors of the various lands were under constant attack by the farmers and tradespeople in the outlying areas for their lack of aid. The city dwellers were safe enough behind their walls of wood and stone, but times were growing treacherous for all, including the leaders of men walled within their homes. The slums of the cities spawned their own evils, and as the populations grew with the displaced villagers, the number of brigands and rogues multiplied to exploit the newcomers. Brigands were banding together for safety, making the roads more dangerous. The larger packs of lawless men were mounting more effective strikes against the merchant caravans that carried wares between the cities and towns, and the wild predators of the wood grew fat on the bodies of those who fell in the resulting frequent raids. No one dared stay long enough to bury his or her dead. The merchants found the only safety in movement and the only profit in survival.

"I tell you, Gregor, be cautious as you go. Silverwing must have you on a mission of some great need to send you out alone. I hope your skill is up to the swords you carry at your sides. Must be a very important trip you are making for Silverwing to equip you with such fine blades." Dakin looked at him intently, concern furrowing his brow. "You feeling okay, Gregor? You aren't looking so good. Looks like the drink has the best of you, as a matter of fact." Gregor was not feeling well at all. Dakin's words fell on deaf ears, as Gregor slipped into the darkness that had been closing in at the edge of his vision for some time.

***

Gregor opened his eyes slowly to find nothing. Nothing so complete that even darkness was absent. He was aware of his own existence in spite of the complete lack of anything else around him. Gregor could only think that the drink, so sweet and burning at once, must have killed him. The God of Light must have been taking his time deciding how to deal with his monumental failure, holding him between the world he had left and the one in which he would spend eternity. Mists began to coalesce in the nothingness and the darkness became palpable. He felt pounding in his head the likes of which he had never known. The burning that had recently warmed his throat and belly suffused every part of his body. Gregor found his boots resting on a shiny, inky surface that held his weight, though it appeared as glassy as the smooth surface of an undisturbed lake. Odd waves moved just below the surface, and flashes of crimson light seemed to brighten random areas with no apparent pattern or purpose. He flexed his legs to jump away from one that burst just under his feet, and found he could not move.

"Do not worry, Gregor. No harm will come to you here. You are my guest, and our meeting has been too long delayed. I consider that an error on my part. It was news to me that Lord Silverwing had taken a student. It seems his own failures have taught him nothing." The figure speaking seemed to form from the mists themselves as he emerged from the darkness. His appearance drew the random flashes into a rough circle that served to light the cloaked figure as he approached. A deep hood hid the face, and Gregor was both drawn to see the figure's face and terrified that the hood might be pulled back to expose it. "You see, it was intended that the last of the Golden Dragons should join his brethren at the foot of your God. What pawns they were in a game they could not possibly understand, yet he managed to undo all my careful plans! Lord Galant Silverwing only managed to delay the inevitable, however, and you may rest assured he will be dealt with when I am ready. The hunter has become the hunted, and the Overseer has never failed to fulfill a contract. You are of little consequence to me, though my associate has taken a keen interest in something you possess." The form moved toward him with a rush, causing the robes he wore to flutter as if some great wind blew from nowhere. A clawed hand, roughly human but covered in shimmering scales that reflected the bloody light from the floor, emerged with the palm up as if seeking an offering or some kind. "You could give me that blade and perhaps you would no longer be of any interest to me at all. You might even be allowed to live. Come, farm boy, and give me the blade. You have only to desire to do so and I will take this weight from you. It is such a terrible curse you bear, and knowing you are powerless must make it all the worse for you."

Gregor answered with a single thought, though his lips refused to give voice to the word in his mind. "No."

The burning in every part of Gregor's body intensified as the tormentor's hand withdrew into the folds of his robe. "You will suffer greatly. The limits of my imagination will be tested with the tortures I will devise for your impudence. I can assure you, there are no limits to the pain I can bestow. Rest well for now, Gregor, knowing I will not come for you until your Master begs for mercy at my feet. Your mentor will be ready to greet you when at last I see fit to release you with death. Rest while you can." The nothingness returned and Gregor trembled.

***

A reassuringly familiar voice brought him from his stupor, and light flooded his eyes. "Gregor, wake up! Oh my Goddess, what have I done? Gregor, please wake up! Master Silverwing is going to kill me if you don't wake up. Oh, thank the Goddess, you are breathing! Easy, boy. Thank all the heavens! You were out cold, and then you were thrashing about. You went dead still, and you stopped breathing and I thought you were dead for sure! Pumped your chest like a bellows, but you never moved. You okay? Speak to me, boy, please speak to me, Gregor!"

"Stop shouting at me." Gregor thought his head would crack with the racket Dakin was making. He felt like a bull had kicked him square in the face and stomped on him for good measure. Every muscle sang its own caterwauling fury, and he couldn't move at all for several moments. The light through the window of Dakin's home told him it was still early morning, but Gregor thought it would take a bit of time before he was ready to get moving again. "It was just a dream. The drink, I guess."

"That must have been a dream straight out of the hells to warm you like that. You were burning up when I touched you. Here, drink this." Dakin held out a wooden cup, but Gregor was hesitant. "No, don't worry. No more of the hair of that dog. That dog bit you good. Just some spring water and bitter herbs. Tastes terrible but it will make you feel better. Let me get you some breakfast if you have the stomach for it. Need to get your strength back after that fever. Never seen anything like that." Dakin mumbled to himself, while assembling the meal. "You have really got to stay away from the spirits. They definitely take you."

Gregor tentatively sipped at the bitter water, and found it at least made his stomach stop burning. "You don't have to worry about that, Dakin. No, you don't have to worry about that at all!" The refreshing spring water brought him back to himself sooner that Gregor would have imagined possible. The sizzling boar meat gave him a hunger in no time, and it wasn't too much longer before he began turning over the events of his dream, if it was a dream. Gregor held on to the remnants that were trying to flee from his mind as much as he could, and what he remembered scared him. He doubted seriously it was a dream at all. Someone was after him and

Master Silverwing. Gregor somehow knew they were after much more, as well.

***

Gregor was enjoying the scent of the greenery since he had left Dakin. Knowledge brought as much comfort to the warrior as experience, and Gregor had learned a great deal of the woods while in Dakin's company. The hunter had taken time to tell him what plants and berries would aid the warrior if he caught fever again, or ran out of provisions before another hunter happened upon him. He smiled to himself, thinking the huntsman was probably enjoying the bounty of the wood again since Gregor had departed. The weather at least was favoring him, and he had good made progress since leaving Dakin.

His host had packed a bag of dried meats and more of the bitter plants for Gregor before allowing him to go, saying it was the least he could do. "Loud as you are in that armor, I doubt you will find much game," Dakin had chided him when the hunter had sent him on his way. "Rest easy in your travels, Gregor. Master Silverwing is well thought of among the guardians of the woods, and as deep as your path seems to be taking you, they will probably be all you encounter until you make a road. The wolves shouldn't trouble you as long as you set a fire at night." Gregor had been glad for all the wisdom Dakin had shared.

***

The howls at night didn't trouble him nearly as much as the remnants of the dream the drink had brought. The visitor had

53

wanted the broken blade Gregor carried with him. Gregor could not fathom why unless the figure was somehow in league with the demon that had destroyed the Knights of Bella Grey. What kind of person would have dealings with a demon? Gregor wished Silverwing were present now. The visitation, which is how he had come to think of it, once more answered none of the questions that plagued him. It only brought more questions. All he could do is make his way to the city of Nactium and find the Temple of Light as instructed.

The travel was made easier as Gregor followed the deer tracks, and he managed to keep a steady pace. There would be no hint of civilization for several days to come. Peace won out over the worries that Gregor had felt weighing him down, and he became more certain with each day that the God of Light was watching over him. He came to the bank of a great river that neatly broke his intended path. The armor Gregor wore made swimming across impossible, even if he had known how to swim. "Well, this is not supposed to be here. I must have gone off course somewhere, otherwise I am sure Master Silverwing would have mentioned this river." Gregor noted that the river seemed to bend in the rough direction he intended to travel, though what lay beyond the curve of the waters was obscured by trees huddling close to the banks. "Nothing to do but look for a bridge or shallows in that direction, I suppose." Gregor set off down the smooth bank along the river, trusting that he had made the right decision. The path fate had chosen for him would prove eventful very soon.

**

There was trouble ahead. Gregor heard it long before he saw anything. He had been traveling along the river for the second day, still having no luck finding a place to cross, but glad to have the smooth path near the water's edge. Somewhere ahead he could hear the angry howling of a large number of wolves. A coarse, vulgar language that sounded completely alien to him answered the pack's throaty growling. Great shouts and cries of pain that were almost human grew in volume as Gregor ran alongside the river. Barking howls and yips filled the air to accompany the strange caterwauling. Gregor drew up abruptly to watch a curious melee that was taking place on an open area of grass near the river's opposite edge. Small, dark green and brown humanoids bearing long sticks tipped with yellowish bone shards were fending off a large pack of wolves. The beasts ran into the loose circle of poorly armed humanoids, attacking with vicious efficiency. Gregor could see no reason to fear either the wolves or the goblins from where he stood on the safety of the opposite bank, and moved closer for a better look. None of the participants took any notice of his arrival, so focused were they on their opponents' destruction. Gregor noticed almost immediately that the goblins seemed to be particularly intent upon protecting one of their number that jumped and screeched from the center of the circle. This individual was distinctive because, unlike the others, it wielded a short crude sword and carried a hide shield. There was a wolf's skull fastened to its head with what appeared to be straps formed of hide, and it was clothed in makeshift hide armor as well. The center of the circle was littered with several bodies, both of slain wolves and goblins.

The wolves also seemed to be guided by leaders of their own kind. Two larger wolves, one with an auburn cast to its fur and the other with a gray coat that blended to white, moved around the ~~circled~~ goblins at opposite sides of the circle formed by the wolves. A growl or bark from one or both of them signaled a few wolves to break away from encircling the humanoids. Their intention was obvious as the wolves broke the ranks of the yelling goblins, with one of the wolves always angling its charge toward the goblin leader. This fact had not gone unnoticed by the shield-bearing leader, either. The largest concentration of the dead wolves lay at his feet. Still, despite his apparent success, the circle was growing tighter as the goblin force weakened with each attack. Gregor found he was hoping the wolves would kill the goblin leader.

It seemed the large gray wolf had grown weary of seeing its brothers and sisters slain. There was no warning as the huge animal charged into the circle, knocking the goblins out of its path as they moved to block it. The goblin leader turned to take it head on, bracing his feet and bringing his shield full to face the beast. A great howl erupted from the large auburn wolf, and at once the wolves encircling the goblins moved as one to take the remaining spear-men. Gregor was entranced as the action unfolded. The auburn colored pack leader moved into the path of the spears before it, biting one in half with its terrible jaws and knocking another aside with its paw, as it surged toward the goblin leader. The large gray wolf quickly closed the distance between itself and the diminutive leader, and the goblin leader's full attention was focused on the great gray beast as it leapt into the air. The goblin was quick and resourceful, taking advantage of his position as he made himself as small as possible under his shield. He brought the short sword's blade through a small hole in the center of his shield and braced for the airborne wolf's impact. He had obviously practiced the maneuver many times before with success, and it served him well now. The gray wolf landed heavily on the shield and fell away. It did not struggle to rise, and Gregor said a small prayer for its sacrifice. The leader rose and shouted, apparently full of his victory, just in time to have his throat torn out. The clenching jaws of the fiery large wolf that had come from his rear had neatly delivered vengeance. The fight was ended with the goblin leader's death, as his followers fled to the woods. Few made it as far as the tree line before the pack had them, and Gregor doubted those that made it to the trees fared much better in the forest.

He turned his attention away from the fleeing goblins and their pursuers to watch the pair of pack leaders. The gray wolf was on its side near the body of the dead goblin leader, and the auburn wolf was now standing near its companion's body. It tentatively touched the fallen animal with its muzzle, as if checking for signs of life. Gregor watched in wonder as the auburn pack leader sat back on its haunches facing away from him and began to transform. The front legs became arms as the fur that covered it thinned and shortened, and hands replaced the front paws. The body lengthened, with fur appearing to draw into the creature's hide, revealing tanned skin along a well-muscled back that was clearly human even at this distance. The fullness of the figure's hips was the only indication it was female, as soft auburn hair lengthened from her scalp, stopping just at her shoulders. Gregor felt embarrassed for his intrusion, but could not bring himself to look away. He watched her run her hands over the large gray wolf slowly, as if seeking the wound. Her body tensed as blood spread across the fur of the wounded animal. The figure's head lowered as she brought her hands together, seemingly where the short sword had penetrated. Moments later the gray wolf stirred, and Gregor noted the rise and fall of its chest where the hands of the female lay. He found he had been holding his breath, and released it in a rush. He drew air into his own starved lungs, and moved closer to the edge of the river. "Hello! You there!" Gregor shouted to the woman, wanting to let her know she was not alone. She glanced at him over her shoulder, and without pausing to acknowledge him, she scooped the wounded animal into her arms and turned toward the forest. Gregor could only marvel at her strength, as a moment later she disappeared into the woods with her arms full of the great gray beast. He was glad to know the animal had been rescued, but he was curious to know by whom. He had never heard of such a creature that could change form this way. Gregor shook his head, once more amazed at how little he knew of the world. It seemed pointless to stand wondering at the strange course of events, so he once more began moving along the river's edge.

***

Tana was worried. Problems were plenty her forest with the incursion of the goblin tribes. The wolves were slowly starving or being killed as the goblins encroached more and more. Their normal game was slaughtered, and the interlopers seemed to be appearing everywhere. Lone wolves, driven out to hunt by hunger, had even begun attacking grazing animals that strayed too far from their herds. Men would come into the forest soon seeking the animals, thinking the packs were to blame. Things were bad enough without this new complication. A soldier, or mercenary more likely, had seen her change. She yanked her pack of clothes from the tree limb where she had left it, and moved near where Fang rested. The leathers were such a trial to deal with, but it looked like she was going to have company soon one way or another, so best to be dressed for it. Tana strapped on the delicate blade she kept for encounters with poachers, and strung her bow and quiver across her back. Her tall form was clothed and ready in moments. "Well, girl, let me see if I can get you on your feet again, and we will go find this new problem together. We can beat him to the bridge easily enough."

***

Gregor found a crossing point the next day where a great tree spanned the river half a day's march from where he had camped the night before. He was glad to have a chance to resume his path properly, even if it meant moving across the river to the forest of the unknown female. His dreams had troubled him, and Gregor wondered at the safety of entering the forest of a woman who clearly held sway over the animals that called it home. Her flight the day before was a sure sign she did not wish to be bothered. It had not taken Gregor long to reason this out, as he gnawed at a breakfast of seasoned boar meat and hard tack. The breakfast also served to remind him he was running out of provisions, and food had been hard to come by as he had traveled the river's edge. The simple farm boy in him longed for a fishing pole and a bit of luck, but his days of plucking hapless fish from the waters near his home were over. Gregor looked into the surrounding trees on the far side of the river, and seeing no more reason to delay, he started across the ancient tree that formed a bridge where it had fallen. Someone had been using it regularly for that purpose, as the branches had been cut away to make a relatively safe path across the breadth of the river, though there was no mark from saw or ax to indicate it had been felled for this purpose. Still, Gregor had learned his lessons well enough in the woods, and he watched where he placed his boots as he slowly made his way. The whisper of an arrow, followed by the appearance of the same near his right boot, made him aware that not only was he not alone, but that he was in a very bad spot. Gregor had no desire to alarm the archer, who could easily have put the arrow in him if that had been their purpose. Any question about whom that archer might be was answered with a low growl just ahead of where Gregor stood. He very slowly tipped his head up to find that the large gray wolf he had seen wounded the day before was in fine health, and currently blocking his path just a few paces away.

"Can you swim? She can. Fang can just about swim like a fish when she has the need. I bet that chain mail would drag you right to the bottom, if the current doesn't take you first. I want you to think hard about that for a moment, and then we are going to talk. Can you hear me okay out there? I don't want to shoot you just because you can't hear me." The voice could not be called musical due to the hard edge of her tone, but Gregor found it strangely evocative in spite of his current predicament. He longed to look up at the face of the woman of the forest, but he decided he had better not.

"Yes, ma'am, I can hear you and I can't swim in this armor or otherwise." Gregor's heart felt like it might fly out of his chest, but at that moment he could not have said if fear or exhilaration was the primary cause.

"Good, I am glad I have your full attention. Rest assured you have mine as well. Now, you are going to look up slowly, and if I even think you are going to draw those blades, or try running back across this tree, then you better learn to swim in that chain mail quick. You understand?"

Gregor felt he was doing well not to fall off the tree at that moment, so she didn't have much to worry about. Still, there could be no harm in reassuring her. "Yes, ma'am, I understand." He brought his hands up slowly to show he was more than willing to comply.

"Bring your chin up. I want to see your face while you tell me exactly why you are in my forest and where you are headed. You will also tell me exactly who you are, and why I should care. Watch him, Fang."

Gregor brought his chin up as instructed, and was struck silent. The woman before him stood a bit taller than he, and was exquisitely formed from her life in the forest. The muscles of both her arms were taunt with the pressure applied to her drawn bow. He had no desire to taste the sting of the arrow she held nocked and ready. Her green eyes glittered with intensity even at this distance, though a nonchalant look colored her features. It appeared she had pretty much planned this meeting as just another part of her daily routine, and was ready to be done with it. If she had any hesitation about firing, Gregor could find no indication of it.

The woman drew the bow away slightly from its sighting position, addressing him before assuming a proper targeting stance once more. "Are you going to start talking, or am I going to shoot you? Let me make it easy for you. What is your name?"

Gregor decided after only a moment's deliberation that the truth would serve him best once again. He raised his voice so that it would carry unhindered to her, finding strength in it he had not noticed until now. "I am Gregor, honored with the title of weapons page to the Knights of Bella Grey until they were destroyed. Lord Galant Silverwing was my mentor and now has sent me to Nactium for education with the priests at the Temple of Light within its walls. The blades I carry are those of my mentor. He was wounded in a melee with bandits and, fearing more would come, he sent me through the wood toward the city of Nactium following a path west."

A smile crooked her mouth as Tana answered the voluminous information she received. "Well, that was a bit more than a mouthful. Do you always share your life story with strangers, or has the potential bite of both my bow and my companion influenced you? No answer required, as the positive influence is obvious. It was more of a rhetorical question than an actual inquiry. Why do you want to go to that city anyway? Your armor and stance show training as a warrior, not a priest. I doubt there is much the temple priests could share with you in the area of martial pursuits."

Gregor took her pause as an invitation to continue his story. He noticed with some amount of relief that her bow was lowered slightly, and no longer at the ready, though the lady before him still kept her arrow nocked. "I believe I am to be educated in many things within the temple. My knowledge of the God of Light is limited, and my healing abilities are lacking. Master Silverwing indicated that the priests of the temple would be able to complete my training and allow me to more fully enter into the service of the God of Light. The sword hands of the Light have been severed. It is my hope to number among those that are to serve as protectors of the common peoples and slayers of the evil forces that have grown so numerous in recent days." Gregor felt himself come to his full height as he spoke. He did not know where the last words had come from, but he felt the truth of them bring him strength. The statement brought him something else he had not expected; something he had not really felt since the terrible dream he had experienced in Dakin's home. Hope, pure hope that could not be shaken by doubt about his own abilities or fear of the unknown trials that he would face. Despite his current predicament, Gregor smiled.

Tana lowered her bow and waved her hand, urging Gregor to come across the tree. It appeared her interview was over, and Gregor would be allowed to continue. Fang seemed a bit more judgmental than her mistress, not quite ready to give up her position until Tana called her. "Come to me, Fang. He means no harm, and there would be sin in drowning him. Let's see if we can get him to his precious city, and out of our forest. My name is Tana, not that you will have much need of it after today. The walls of Nactium are little more than a half-day's walking from here. The wolves are nervous enough without another interloper in our forest, so I will take you to the gates myself. Be sure you keep up. The sooner I am rid of you, the sooner I can get back to tending these woods."

Gregor felt his words and honesty had been well invested in the mistress of the forest as he fell into stride beside her. There was a well-worn path leading from the tree bridge that allowed the two to walk abreast with Fang taking up watch between them. Gregor found his new companions equally quiet, though he was able to learn a bit about Tana with gentle questions. She ignored most of his inquiries, though she confirmed that she was the protector of the wood.

The huntress had lived almost her whole life among the trees she called home, making fast friends with the wolves that lived there. She followed the ways of the Goddess of Nature revered by most rangers and druids within the wilder lands. These chosen people taught the ways of nature to the villagers and farmers outside the cities, and sometimes acted as healers to the more remote settlements outside the reach of the temples.

Tana's view of the cities and the people within was easily understood by her few remarks concerning them. "City dwellers have forgotten the gifts of the wood and the link to nature we all have. The druids are little more than wild priests to the city dwellers. We carry no more importance than the farmers that provide their homes with fresh meat and grain. You seem like a good sort for a man. It is a pity you would choose to poison your innocence seeking counsel within a city that has spawned so much evil in recent years. Be wary of those you choose for companions, and do not let me find you in my forest again. There is nothing for you in the wood, and it would be a shame to see harm come to you."

The words were very clear in their intent, but somehow Gregor suspected this was not to be the end of his and Tana's association. Fang gave a low growl as Tana finished speaking, appearing to be displeased by her companion's words. The large gray wolf had acquired a taste for the remaining dried meats Gregor shared as they traveled. When Tana was about to dismiss him at the road, the wolf nuzzled Gregor and playfully nipped his thigh. He tried not to jump at the pinch of her jaws, and lost his balance, falling toward Tana as Fang neatly stepped to one side. Tana quickly turned to catch him, setting Gregor back on his feet before the warrior's full weight dragged them both sprawling to the ground. "Now, what is this about, Fang?" The huntress cautioned the wolf with a severe look. "He needs to go, and so do we. Are you so easily swayed by treats? There will be no living with you for a while, I see." Tana brought her attention back to Gregor once more, favoring him with a small frown. "You need to make haste if you are going to make the gates before sunset. The guards of Nactium lock the walls tight after nightfall, since the goblins and orcs have become more aggressive. You will shine like a beacon with that armor and the blades you carry, so I would not advise waiting for the brigands that haunt the road to come out for their nightly patrols. A single warrior would serve as a prime target for them, I would imagine." Fang signaled her displeasure at Tana's words with a bark. The gray wolf pushed at Tana's back, forcing the huntress to take a step closer to Gregor. Tana turned to look down at Fang, clearly annoyed by the animal's interference. "Don't worry about him, Fang. I am certain this brave warrior can make his own way to the gates before nightfall."

Gregor felt that Fang had her own opinion of his abilities. The wolf turned back to eye the young warrior, cocking her head to one side, and once more pushed Tana toward Gregor. Whether it was the hope of more food or a genuine concern for Gregor's safety, the warrior could not say, but something in the wolf's stance indicated that the beast was not ready to leave him. Gregor felt compelled to speak. "There is one more favor I would ask of you. Master Silverwing and I parted with such haste that he gave me no indication of how to find the proper temple within the walls of Nactium. Have you been within the walls, and if you have, could you tell me where I might find the Temple of Light? I assume a city so large has many temples dedicated to the Goddesses and Gods of the lands."

Tana seemed openly frustrated by this request, and Gregor regretted it immediately. "Yes, I know the city well enough to take you to the city watch and the jailers. I am also familiar with the judges who have set poachers free, lining their pockets with ill-gotten coins, and the governor who issues bounties for the packs that seek only to hunt in their own forest without molestation. You will find that the streets are well marked, and except for the occasional pickpocket, few will trouble you. The streets are patrolled regularly, and I am certain that with a bit of coin you can receive an escort to the temple you seek."

"So I should be able to hold out my purse and find a guide to the main Temple of Light easily enough in any tavern?" The innocence of the young man's smile affected Tana. Gregor's honest reply to her vitriolic words caught Tana by complete surprise, and as he finished speaking, laughter equally honest broke from her of its own volition.

Tana regained her composure quickly and blushed at her own reaction to his words. "Forgive me, Gregor, but Master Silverwing is not unknown to me, which is why you are not swimming to the city as we speak. I would have thought the ranger would send someone more prepared to the treacherous city you approach. The merchants and rogues alike would be at your heels, smelling an easy mark. Gregor, you do not even have the basic skills to make it to breakfast in the inn at the gate. May the Goddess bless you, and hopefully me, as well. It appears we are to journey together to the city after all. I hope you are happy, Fang." Tana fixed Fang with a baleful look before turning down the broad dirt road. Gregor closed his mouth with a click of his teeth as he hurried to catch up.

***

The group made the city gates by evening, though Gregor was winded from the increased pace. The bandits who must have been shadowing the road gave them no trouble, and there were few travelers so close to nightfall. Gregor had noted the slow moving caravans of merchants that had stopped along the road, making camp together well before reaching Nactium in order to to take advantage of the safety of numbers. Great bonfires had been set, awaiting the igniting touch of flame in anticipation of a long night at the camps. Gregor saw that many rugged looking mercenaries serving as guards had organized patrols, moving around the ring of wagons. The hired swordsmen appeared to be little more than paid thugs themselves, and although they did not challenge him and his companions, he found himself wondering just how safe the huddled merchants and tradesmen really were. Tana had aired similar thoughts after they were out of earshot of the roaming guards. "I doubt the tradesmen would find much comfort in traveling with those mercenaries if a large group of brigands set their minds to organizing an assault. The smarter rogues would wait until the merchants were set upon by a goblin horde, or worse. There is little safety in numbers outside the city gates, and bonfires do not deter the boar men when such a large prize is set before them. No doubt the 'guards' would flee to the woods in hope of saving their own skins, only to return later and see what the orcs had left behind. There is truly no honor among thieves, even well paid ones."

Gregor's curiosity was piqued by the mention of orcs so close to the cities. Dakin's stories had indicated that the humanoids had stayed away from the more populated centers, and he said as much. Tana's reply was punctuated by a snort of derision. "That may be true where Dakin hunts, but then again, he has not seen the goblins in the numbers I have. The orcs I have encountered are far more aggressive than their weaker brethren. Less than a moon ago one of the wolf packs was attacked by a handful of them that were hunting game in the forest. The wolves' howls roused me from sleep, filling the night with their pain and anger. I transformed, making haste to the clearing where they were desperately fighting for survival against an enemy of a strength the poor creatures had never encountered. Most of the pack were dead by the time I arrived, and the scene was one that terrified and enraged me all at once. Dead orcs and wolves littered the copse of trees. Several of the wolves that still breathed were hanging in their boughs. I will never forget the sounds of feeble growling silenced with the cracking of bones and rending of hides.

Tana shook her head sadly at the memory. "The orcs in the clearing fought over bits of meat torn from the dead wolves like mongrel dogs, grunting and striking at one another. I had seen orcs before, but there was one among them the likes of which I had never seen." Gregor witnessed a tremble pass through her as Tana continued. He wanted desperately to reach out to her, but found he had no words to offer in comfort. "The light of the full moon reflected off his back, giving him an odd glow, like sunlight passing through blood. He tore at the meal before him, consuming one of the fallen orcs and tossing away the bits he could not readily break in his jaws. The others in the war party kept a good distance from the creature, though they seemed to be gathering more meat for him. Two other dead orcs had been thrown within reach of the creature's long arms. There was little hope for the wolves that remained, so I returned to the place my bow and other equipment was stored, intent upon ridding the forest of this evil. The orcs had taken to the forest in search of more meat when I returned. I tracked and killed them each in turn as they bumbled through the trees, the stupid bastards, until only their leader remained. The grotesque humanoid still remained where it was when I had last seen it, gnawing and tearing the remains of the dead orcs at its feet. The large beast must have caught my human scent and decided it was more interested in softer flesh. It dropped its meat and pointed its nose into the air, turning to face the stand of trees where I stood with my arrow nocked. The eyes of the creature gave me a moment's pause; they were unlike any eyes I had ever seen.

Tana frowned slightly. "It may have been a trick of the moonlight, but this creature that vaguely resembled the orc kind had eyes that glowed like embers of a dying fire. Two red-hot coals shone out from under its heavy brow, and the tusks protruding from its mouth seemed impossibly long. I had no time to consider what this could mean, as the huge monster began loping rapidly toward me, not so much running on two legs as using its arms and legs to move with greater speed. My first arrow put out the fire of one of its eyes, but it barely even slowed. I sent a second arrow into its other eye, blinding it but slowing it only a moment, as once more it caught my scent. It took several more arrows and finally my blade, buried deep it its chest, to kill the creature. Nothing held its body together once it fell dead. The only sign of it ever having existed was an area of dead grasses in the rough outline of its body where it had fallen. I did not dare touch the ground that night, and when I returned to the area the next day, the grasses had already begun reclaiming the spot."

"Demon spawn." Gregor's features hardened as he recounted his encounter with the demon that had destroyed the Knights of Bella Grey, and almost killed him as well. The demon's eyes were burned into his memory forever, and Tana's description of the creature she had seen brought the image of the demon to the surface once more. "Master Silverwing shared stories of the mating of creatures from the Abyss with humanoids of the lands, but never anything like this." He made note to make inquiries of the priests once they arrived at the temple. Somehow he doubted he was the only one who had been visited by the evil figure that had invaded his dreams in Dakin's home

5

Food for Thought

A great wooden gate stood at the entrance to the port city of Nactium, as foreboding as it was impressive. Two guards stood at either side of the entrance, clad in dented plate mail and bearing wide-bladed halberds in addition to personal hand weapons hanging from their belts. Each tower at the sides of the gates was host to several militiamen who bore crossbows at the ready. They were moving about constantly, searching the deepening twilight for any threat in the surrounding area. Gregor was shocked from his examination by a high-pitched voice emerging from one of the helmeted guards flanking the gateway. "Tana! Welcome back to the city! We see you have brought a new friend with you, too. He looks very clean to be another poacher. Are you giving tours of our great city now, in addition to capturing unwary bandits?" The guardsman in question sounded younger than Gregor, and he wondered why one that could not even grow hair on his face would be trusted to secure the city's walls. Times were difficult indeed when mere boys filled the ranks of the city's protectors.

The boy's incautious prodding was answered by a low growl from Fang, and a ridiculing remark from her mistress. "Watch your mouth, boy. Fang would have at you if not for her respect of me.

That bladed spear you hold would not protect you. I doubt you have the strength to wield it properly in your slender arms." Fang emphasized Tana's words with her own feral bark. The young guard was caught by surprise at Fang's bark and dropped his halberd. He moved to pull his sword awkwardly from the sheath at his belt, but the blade did not wish to be exposed, and the hilt would not budge.

The guard next to the boy issued a barking laugh of his own at the young one's antics before addressing Tana himself, "I recommend you tie up that dog of yours, Mistress Tana. The guard cannot afford another wounded soldier in the infirmary. I would like to see this one cut his teeth in battle before there is a need to stitch him up. What is your purpose in darkening the great doors of Nactium?"

"I am bringing a pilgrim to the Temple of Light. This warrior was lost after fleeing into the forest, pursued by the bandits you guardsmen are supposed to keep at bay. The streets of fair Nactium are not safe after dark, as you well know, so I will be bringing him to the temple myself." She turned to look at Fang intently. "No need for you to worry the poor defenseless guards, Fang. Go on into our forest and rest. I will find you soon."

The guard's sharp answer to her words came quickly enough. "That dog is lucky no hunter has found her yet. She has a lovely hide, and with a bit of work would make a fine rug." The other guards laughed with him at his jest.

"Most hunters would find her more than their match. Those that might be foolish enough to track her would find my arrows are hard to swallow. Now if you will excuse me, we are due at the temple. I believe this pilgrim's God would be displeased to know he was delayed by halfwits." Tana moved through the open gateway, Gregor trailing behind her before they had a chance to reply.

***

They walked through the city at a slower pace, allowing Tana to point out the various places that Gregor might find useful, as well as the places he should definitely avoid. Even at night, there was a clear division between the sections of Nactium. Gregor felt he would be able to find his way with little effort after Tana had left him with the priests. The low buildings where craftsmen practiced their trades were marked with carved pictures and names on the signs hanging from the eaves. The loaf of bread clearly denoted a baker, and the anvil and hammer was the location of a smithy. Tana noted which tradesmen she sometimes dealt with for supplies, and suggested that Gregor should seek them to supply his needs as well. She promised to take him around once the trades had opened for business the next day, and make sure their association was known so he would not be cheated. Tana, for her part, had grown to like the naive wanderer that had come to her forest, and whether she liked it or not, she felt some responsibility for him.

The simple warrior had been overwhelmed by the grandeur of the Temple of Light itself, which was more a complex of various devotions to the facets of the God he was chosen to serve than a simple place of worship. The sheer number of priests and acolytes that maintained the main house of prayer was beyond anything Gregor had ever witnessed, and the libraries of books made him eager to find a tutor in the many languages of the varied tomes. He was welcomed with open arms by the Brothers and Fathers of the God of Light, and felt immediately at peace among them. Safety emanated from the very stone of which the walls were formed, and every tapestry and statue scattered throughout the many buildings spoke to him. When Gregor and Tana had first arrived, she too had been moved to pay respects at the foot of the magnificent altar devoted to the God. They had bowed their heads and knelt as one before the candlelit dais. Gregor felt the touch of the great power he had had experienced when he had been saved from the Tharnorsa that had destroyed the Knights of Bella Grey. Tana would speak later of the soft light that suffused his bowed form while she had listened to Gregor's simple words of honor.

The Father who had come to greet him offered rooms for the pair after Gregor had explained why he had come and who had sent him. The priest did not appear surprised at the hour of his arrival, explaining that they had expected him, though his companion was not foretold. "The God of Light keeps his own counsel, and we simply do his bidding," Father Oregeth said with a smile. "We have ample housing for the two of you, and Tana may stay with the sisters of the temple if this would please her." He turned to Tana with a nod. "They would probably enjoy the opportunity to speak with a servant of the Goddess of Nature. She has no proper sanctuary within the city, though we do our best to serve the needs of all the higher powers within these walls. Sadly, there are few written records concerning the Goddess of the wilds, despite every person's reliance on Her special gifts. We gather what information we can from the worshipers bringing food and supplies for our stores here."

Tana declined the offer respectfully, with some amount of regret. "These are dangerous times, Father Oregeth, and there are matters that require my attention before I return for Gregor tomorrow. It would be best if he were able to get a good night's rest before beginning his studies, I am sure you will agree." Tana nodded to Gregor and Father Oregeth. "I will return for him at midday tomorrow, if that will give you enough time to arrange his introduction to his tutors."

Father Oregeth moved his hands in a sign of blessing toward Tana, touching her lightly on her forehead. "That should give us ample time, Sister, and we look forward to your return. I will make the arrangements personally, and he will be ready when you return. Travel safely with the God's and Goddess' blessings." He turned to Gregor as Tana waved a farewell, beginning to make her way back to the gates of the city. "I think you will find that though our cots are simple, they will be more comfortable than the forest floor. Let me show you to your place of rest." Gregor found his sanctuary was more than adequate to his needs. A rack had been provided to store his armor and weapons. There was also a small bookshelf near his bed that held several simply decorated leather-bound books. Gregor found a longing unlike he had ever known, eager to possess the knowledge and the wisdom they held.

***

Gregor found his tour of the city with Tana the next day enlightening and amusing. The tradesmen Tana chose to deal with were unique personalities the likes of which he had never encountered, yet each brought back memories of his home. Each man and woman seemed to possess a pure nature unspoiled by the life inside such great walls, and Gregor found it easy to understand why Tana trusted them, despite her strong dislike of all things civilized.

The baker, Master Regar, dealt in delicacies Gregor had never sampled until now. His ovens were easy enough to find because the smell of his goods drew you from blocks away. The scents issuing from the chimneys of his humble establishment made you hungry even after a meal, wondering what ingredients the cook had gathered to create such tastes. Gregor was sorry he lacked a cloth with which to dab his watering mouth as Tana and he entered the place. "Ah, the swordsman shares complements already, and you have yet to sample a morsel!" Master Regar handed Gregor a light, flaky item wrapped in parchment paper and a piece of rag for a napkin. "Have you eaten? Can't have a friend of Tana's going hungry in my home. Tana, would you like the usual, or are you feeling adventurous today? Got some biscuits for Fang. She should like these especially well. Soaked them special in some boar fat. The butcher has been favoring me with fresh meats of late. I suggested he might find a market for wrapping his meat in my dough, and business has been brisk for both of us since we teamed up. Nothing like one of my buttery rolls with a treat of meat baked inside." The laughter in his voice was contagious, almost causing Gregor to drop his first bite.

"Well, it is getting near noon meal. What do you charge for the new creation? I am sure Gregor and I would be thankful for the offering, once he finishes that glazed roll he has." Tana's hand shot out, as if she intended to take the rest of Gregor's treat from him. She pulled her hand back in mock concern when Gregor greeted the movement with a growl sounding much like Fang. "Have you come up with a name for them yet?"

The baker enjoyed the interplay between Tana and Gregor. Like so many of her friends in the city, he wondered often if she would ever find a human companion that suited her. The poor girl, in the baker's estimation, grew more feral each time he saw her. She spent too much time alone in her forest with little company outside her pet. "Watch your fingers, Tana. Looks like you would do better to snatch one of these biscuits from Fang than separate that handsome man from his pastry." The baker frowned momentarily in puzzlement before he spoke. "Well, the butcher is calling them traveling rations, as he is selling them mostly to the mercenaries and merchants floating in and out of Nactium. The name does not really do them justice, by my way of thinking. Why don't you and your friend try them and see what you can come up with that might suit them. Got a fresh batch, warm as you please."

Tana took the offered roll, biting into it with gusto. Her teeth carried through the light breading to find a well-seasoned hunk of meat inside. Tana's eyes opened wide in appreciation for the taste that blessed her tongue, savoring the mixture of buttered loaf and tasty meat. She chewed the first bite hungrily before giving her praise. "I recognize the deer meat, and the roll is definitely one of your best recipes, but the two combined is simply amazing. There should definitely be a name fitting it better than simply traveler's rations. Let me think."

The baker laughed as Tana resumed eating. "Well, the butcher has been seeing a lot of wild meats since the hired blades invaded the city seeking coin in service among the traveling merchants. It would seem there are some fair trackers among their numbers. Takes the butcher and me a day or two to prepare the loaves for the travelers, but they seem willing enough to wait since word has gotten around. You are enjoying softer bread than the merchants and their hired hands normally receive. It takes a stiffer loaf and a saltier bit of meat to serve for the trips of the tradesmen these days. They pay a fair price for these things, and I spend many a late night at the ovens meeting the demands of the market. The rolls like the ones you and the swordsman are having fetch a strong price. I have seen more than a few servants of the governor's house come right here to purchase as many as they can carry. It seems we have drawn the attention of a few stomachs among the more affluent. Still, I make a lot of it for the common folk, sending some to the guardsmen when I can. A lot of those guards are little more than boys summoned for the service, while their fathers try to keep the granaries full for the city. A man cannot forget where he came from when the Gods and Goddesses favor him, so I keep the militia in my favor with treats. Truth be told, I have already made more than any humble baker should, and could retire tomorrow if it suited me. Still, I cannot stand the thought of abandoning my ovens, and it looks like I will have no shortage of demand for my wares for quite a long time. Come up with a name for the finer rolls, and you can consider our debt settled, Tana." He went to get another loaf for Gregor to sample, while Tana finished enjoying her meal.

Once Gregor had a meat roll of his own, he wasted little time in making it disappear into his belly. He wiped the remains of it from his mouth and smiled brightly. "I have a name for it!" Gregor exclaimed around his last bite of roll. "You should call it 'the Baker's Secret.' I am certain you won't be sharing the recipe. Not too fancy, but I think it might serve your purpose."

"That is a great idea! We don't want to make it sound too high for the common people, and the wealthy sorts will feel it is more suited to them, with a proper name to distinguish it from common fare. I wonder what they would think if they knew the secret was common venison. Gregor, whenever you decide the adventuring life isn't for you, let me know. I could use a strong back and a sharp mind around here. The best part is, you get to eat all the breads and treats you want!" Master Regar patted his ample belly, causing a cloud of flour to rise as if to emphasize his point. "Now, you two get out of here. I am sure you have other places to show your new man, Tana, and I have more than a little to do, myself."

Gregor flushed red at this last remark, and stumbled over a reply to correct the baker's assumption. "Sir, I am not....well, I mean, Tana and I are not....she and I only just met and....I would not want you thinking....I mean, Mistress Tana is a fine woman...um, that is to say, I mean...."

Tana just put a finger to her lips, silencing Gregor, and gave him a wink. "Don't worry about that busy-body. No need to steal his gossip away. He won't be the only tradesman to make that mistake, and these old men thrive on the tales they carry to market. You can correct his error another time, but rest assured he will never believe you." Tana's warm smile was directed toward where the baker had disappeared into the back of his shop, but Gregor could not shake the feeling she was thinking about him. "We should go. There are several more people for you to meet."

with Tana and Gregor spent the rest of the day making the rounds at various other traders and artisans throughout the city. The huntress showed Gregor where to go, and nearly as important, where not to go. Tana was well known and equally well thought of among the people that Gregor met. The baker's misinterpretation of their relationship was repeated by several of the vendors, who felt compelled to mention it at all. It was an understandable mistake, since the men who usually accompanied her into Nactium were bound and unceremoniously dragged behind her. A few of the more robust gossips noted it was time that Tana had found a suitable male companion, considering her maturity. Tana corrected their mistake rather sharply, stating that she needed no protection from a man, and was by no means ready to settle in and bear children. That raised a few eyebrows, and brought chuckles from the bystanders, as she dressed down the offending parties. Gregor was certain he understood where Tana stood in regards to him, or any potential suitor, and was glad he had not taken to entertaining such notions. At least, that is what he told himself.

Tana had saved the best stop for last as they neared a simple stone building off the main thoroughfare. The sign at the front bore a large anvil and hammer, not unlike the other smiths in the city, and a single massive chimney billowed great clouds of black smoke.

Tana wrinkled her nose in disgust at the cloud, but opened the door for Gregor, motioning him inside. "Now, where is that man?" Tana looked around the neatly arranged rows of display cases, seeking the shop owner. A great hammering sounded from the rear of the shop. "Filcher, come here, you little weasel!"

Gregor was taken aback at the words Tana had shouted until he noticed there was a small, furry head that had poked up over the counter before them. Gregor's experience with the rodent hunters was limited, but, as the long, furry creature stretched across the counter, the warrior noted it was in fact a weasel. What it was doing here in this place, and why Tana was calling for it at all, was strange, to say the least. That Tana took the time to introduce Gregor to the animal was even more curious. "Filcher, this is my friend, Gregor. Gregor, this is Filcher. Filcher is in charge of guarding this humble establishment and making certain he is the only rodent that gets any part of the blacksmith's food. Go and get your Master, Filcher, and you can have a treat."

Filcher wasted no time scurrying down the counter and running through the opening that separated the work area from the front of the building. A bellowing voice replaced the steady hammer blows from the back. "What are you up to now, Filcher? It cannot be time for the luncheon yet. I am never going to get this forge hot enough with all these interruptions. Customers? Well, why didn't you say so?" The smith's voice shook the weapons and armor on display in the room where Tana and Gregor waited as he called out from the back room. "Be right with you!"

Moments later, the largest man Gregor had ever seen emerged through the archway between the two rooms, with Filcher perched on his shoulder. "Tana! Why didn't you tell me it was Tana, you little weasel? Probably because you can't talk!" The man removed his thick leather gloves and patted Filcher on the head. "Off with you, rodent!" Filcher took his cue, running up Tana's outstretched arm to retrieve the treat she had promised, a bit of dried meat. Moments later he disappeared behind the counter. "Well, I say the rodent can't talk, but he sure can beg. Damn good to see you, girl! Finally bringing a man around for the community's approval, I see."

"Gregor seeks the approval of only the God of Light, and perhaps the aid of a fine smith. I was wondering if you might be able to recommend someone." Though Tana's tone was serious, her smile betrayed her.

The giant smith's brow furrowed at her chiding. "Now, now. No need to get sensitive and question a man's worth at his own forge." He turned to smile at Gregor, extending a rough, thick-skinned hand that dwarfed Gregor's own. "Gregor, is it? A fine, strong name for a blade master devoted to the God of Light. I see by your grip you favor the right hand." The smith's eyes fell to the scabbards at Gregor's sides. "Good, good, but it makes me wonder why you would carry blades clearly weighted for one stronger with their left arm. Fine blades they are, too. Haven't seen their kind for a great many years. I used to number among the smiths who tended such fine weapons, when the Knights of the Golden Dragon still roamed these lands. May I see them?"

Gregor was happy to pass Master Silverwing's weapons to the smith for examination. "Gregor, Firebeard comes from a long line of oversized blacksmiths. His family has a very interesting history and in their time have served great kings throughout generations."

"Tana, your words honor me." Firebeard had turned to lay the blades across his counter for closer examination. "I am the fourth generation of smiths bearing the name Firebeard, after the giant who started our heritage. Way back in our family tree, there is one of the giants who live at the great Peaks of Flame. The first Firebeard was a wee one among his own people, but still a giant. Our family passes on the tale of his union with a simple human mistress of no small stature herself." Firebeard smiled as he related how the small giant and the tall farm girl, standing well over the tallest men in her village, came to meet. It was a story of love and heroism that rivaled the greatest stories of the land.

The original Firebeard had had to pass through many trials to win the Mistress Inania's love and the respect of her father, a father who was, to put it mildly, troubled by taking a giant as a son-in-law. No one could doubt Firebeard's love for the woman who would become his bride, and who would begin a line of great smiths that lived on in the master smith standing before Gregor now. The Lord he served so long ago knighted the first Firebeard, and though he never raised a weapon after he came into the Lord's service, his abilities at the forge were remembered in the Lord's house for generations. His hands forged the original weapons of the Knights of the Golden Dragon. These works of art, formed of steel and mystical alloys, had been blessed by the priests of the God of Light, and had brought down many evil creatures and men.

Master Firebeard scratched his chin thoughtfully as he finished his story. "I am glad to see Master Silverwing still possesses a pair of the originals, although that broken blade you bear on your back saddens me, Gregor. How did it come to be broken? I would not think it was even possible."

Gregor once more related the story of what had brought the blade to him, and in time to Master Silverwing. Firebeard was rapt as Gregor spoke, even as he examined the blade. "The Master of this weapon was well known to me, with my own hands having cared for this sword when it was whole. Would you allow me to restore the hilt? It is a terrible thing to know the weapon has been ill used, but some good should come of it yet. I cannot restore the full power to the weapon, only perhaps fashion a suitable hilt, but I am certain the temple priests guiding you now would have little trouble bestowing the proper blessings."

Gregor answered without a moment's hesitation. "I would be honored by your labors, Master Firebeard. Take whatever time you need. I will be deep in my studies at the temple, having little need for the weapon while I am there. I would also ask that you tend to Master Silverwing's blades. The fire of a proper forge has not touched them in some time, though the smith in Bella Grey, my village, did the best he could, and they are sure to need some repair."

"You honor me, Master Gregor. I will happily return a proper edge to Lord Silverwing's weapons, and fashion a proper hilt to the broken blade as well. I will not keep them longer than is necessary, and I have a very secure place to store them until you return." Firebeard turned and moved behind the counter, stopping in front of a massive metal carving depicting a giant, which must have been the original Firebeard, facing a massive dragon that dwarfed the giant by comparison. The blade the giant warrior wielded was a reflective black metal sword as tall as he was, that stood out against the steel surface where it was mounted. "Filcher! Make yourself useful!" The great wall hanging lowered to reveal an open space carved into the wall itself, forming a long table at Firebeard's waist. "Come around here, you two. I want to show you something."

Tana and Gregor stepped around the counter to join Firebeard on the other side. Filcher sat on his haunches inside the alcove, waiting for his reward. Firebeard tossed him a piece of dried meat from the pouch at his hip, and drew a great black sword resembling the one in the relief from its home in the wall. "The thing is much too large to wield properly, even by one of my size. The workmanship is amazing for something so dense. The metal is called Elenondo, or star stone, taking its name from the heavens of its origin. It takes a terrible heat to work the stone into any usable form, but there is nothing to match its strength that man can extract from the earth. The secret of working the metal has been passed down from generations since the first Firebeard fashioned this sword. You probably recognize the hilt. It is a larger version of the ones possessed by the swords of the Knights of the Golden Dragon. Firebeard's people held the great serpents in very high regard, and he was saddened to have to kill even a rogue one. The beasts generally keep to the volcanic mountains where they make their homes, and seldom come into contact with the civilizations of men. It is a beautiful weapon."

Gregor was moved to ask about the alcove itself, admiring the feat of craftsmanship. "That is my greatest construction of metalwork yet. The massive springs and lever bars keep the wall hanging from dropping too fast as it opens, and Filcher enters through a twisted tunnel to release the catch that opens it. There are other ways to open it, but I can't tell all my secrets now, can I? Your weapons will be safe within." Firebeard shooed the weasel out of the alcove and closed it once again.

Gregor and Tana left the smith to his work, and completed their tour of the rest of the city; she left him shortly thereafter at the temple to begin his training with the priests. Gregor felt an odd pain as she departed, a regret he had not experienced in his life. He missed his village and his parents, but this feeling struck him more deeply, though he could not say why. Tana would have recognized it, but much more time would pass before she felt the loss as strongly. It would be some while before they would see each other again. Duty called each to follow their own path, one to train as a knight of the Golden Dragon, and the other to protect the lands she loved.

6

To Catch a Thief

Boremac was angry. Travelflor did not number among the cities he favored, and for good reason. There were far too many guards and far too few marks, and the rogue had spent a fair amount of his visits here locked up in the local jail. Now the less than honorable elements that made a permanent home here had brought word that Boremac was being sought. He had followed the detailed instructions he had received to the letter, and here he stood in this warehouse of death. The smell of rotten meat and flea-ridden furs was nearly overwhelming, and the rogue found himself wondering what had happened to the previous owner. He had neither the time nor the inclination to dig among the rotting hides to see if the tradesman was still there. Boremac was right where he was supposed to be, despite the minor delay of casing the location. He was not about to take any chances with the finger of the Black Hand that had contacted him. The pickpocket ~~had gotten~~ was just about fed up with the whole mess, and was turning for the door, when a figure entered cloaked in black. "You came alone?"

"Your messenger insisted that I do. I won't even insult you by asking the same." Boremac practically spat the words out. "You have the coins and gems? I won't be handing my information over for free, and I expect to be paid before I leave here."

A slight, gloved hand bearing a small coin purse emerged from the folds of the cloak that hid the contact's face. "You will receive full payment once I feel certain you have information of value. You can count it at your leisure before we part company."

"Well, I am not happy about being kept waiting so long. I am a servant to no one, unlike you, and I have other things to do this night. Drinking and sleep number high on my priorities at such a late hour." Boremac grinned at his little joke, but the tone of the person with him did not show any sign of being amused.

"I would think securing one's place among the living would be a very high priority for one of your reputation. You should be glad I chose to pay you for your information at all. The others whom I represent have many ways to find out what they need to know that are far less comfortable. You just had the luck to come to my attention first, and I believe you are more useful to the Brotherhood alive rather than dead." This statement brought a light chuckle from beneath the man's hood that sounded like rough metal being scraped over the edge of an iron file. The man in front of Boremac did not wait for a reply before continuing. "What do you have to offer me?"

"I know the man you hunt has a student, and I know where he is headed. Silverwing will be leaving to pursue his pupil soon so as to retrieve his blades and complete the young warrior's training. The young one is already quite a talent, but the Black Hand should dispense with him readily enough. They would probably be paid his weight in gold for the elimination of the mentor and student. Yes, I know his name and where they can find him. Did you bring enough coins for that information? I doubt seriously the dead assassins the Hand sent for the ranger could have told you as much." It was Boremac's turn to chuckle, a cunning smile settling on his mouth as he decided to push his luck a bit. Boremac cocked an eyebrow at the individual before him. "Is there any reason for me not to see the face of the man I am dealing with? You have made quite an effort, and a successful one at that, to stay hidden from me in setting up this meeting. It seems only fair, since I am putting my life in your hands, and we will certainly be in touch again, that I know who it is I am trusting."

The figure before him seemed to consider the request. His answer came soon enough, as black leather gloves emerged from the cloak and pulled back the hood. Boremac smiled in appreciation of the man's little deception, noting the black mask that revealed only his eyes as the hood fell to his shoulders. "You are a careful bunch, aren't you? I can respect that. People in our line of work just never know whom they can trust. I took the liberty of writing the information down for you in case some unforeseen event prevented my arrival. I guess that is no longer a concern. If you don't mind, we can pass the coin and the paper at the same time with opposite hands. One cannot be too careful."

The masked figure nodded his agreement, and put out his hands, with one holding the coin purse and the other outstretched as a sign of good faith. Boremac reached out to take the coin purse, noting briefly that his new friend's eyes had darted upward ever so slightly before meeting Boremac's own intent gaze. "Oh, I wouldn't worry about your partner. He's dead. Nice dagger he had, though, seems a shame to lose it." The dagger appeared as if by magic in the masked figure's throat, neatly cutting off his ability to reply. The force of the thrust dropped the figure onto his back, and Boremac pocketed the coin purse before the dust had settled. "No, we can never tell who we can trust, and it doesn't pay to ask the wrong people the wrong questions. I am sure you would agree, if you were in any condition to talk. Oh well, best get your partner down here so you can look like you killed him. Won't matter much, and I am pretty sure you made certain no one will be checking this warehouse. Looks like it is time for me to be getting down the road again. See you in the lowest levels of hell when I finally make a mistake."

A hand grabbed Boremac's collar so quickly he didn't have time to react. "Damn. Silverwing I assume?" He did not even wait to be told, dropping his weapons to the ground.

Silverwing spun the rogue around to face him. The look on the ranger's face sent a shiver through Boremac. It appeared he had finally made that mistake. The knife under his chin only reinforced the thought. "Good, so I don't need to introduce myself. Who the hells are you and why have you been following me? Answer carefully."

"Opportunity." Boremac almost smiled... almost. "The hunter, Silverwing, and his student are now hunted by a very successful group of killers with only one known failure. That would be me." Now Boremac did smile. "I suggest I would be more use to you alive than dead. I know how they operate having been pursued for… some time."

"You appear honest enough facing imminent death. You may serve some purpose after all. Since you appear to seek any opportunity that presents itself, I will give you one suited to your skills. It might even give you some hope." The ranger's words caught Boremac unprepared, and once more his throat closed as if a hangman's noose were around it.

"You are not leaving without purpose, and do not make the mistake of thinking you are safe outside the walls of the city. The young man, Gregor by name, that I traveled with is the one they are after. You are going to make sure they don't harm him." Boremac noted it was not a question. "There is a weapon and armor merchant leaving for the port city of Nactium. He has found favor with the Temple of Light and is a patron of the temples where he travels. I will arrange for your safe passage aboard his ship. There will be a package of acolyte robes for you to use as a disguise in order to enter the Temple of Light where Master Gregor now trains. After arrival, find somewhere discreet to change into them and go directly to the Temple. Get word to Gregor that I am well, and I will contact him soon. You are to gather as much information as you can about the affairs in Nactium, and more importantly, make sure no harm comes to Gregor. Be ready to board ship without warning, and make sure your connection to my student is not discovered. If these assassins find that you are assisting us, I have no doubt your life will be forfeit. If you deviate from the path I have given you, I will hunt you myself. Do you understand?" Master Silverwing's hard features left Boremac no room for misunderstanding

Boremac smiled in spite of himself. He hated not being in control when his hide was on the line, but it appeared he had no choice. "So, I am to travel with a mercenary merchant and impersonate a priest to protect a fledgling warrior from a highly organized band of assassins. What could possibly go wrong? Let's not forget that I am supposed to do this for an indefinite amount of time, while trying to find out who hired them to kill all three of us, if I understand you correctly. Anything else I should know while you are being so forthcoming?"

Master Silverwing returned the thief's grin, and spoke with a softer tone. "Well, I am glad you understand your dire position."

The travel down the river was uneventful, and Boremac was glad to see the town of Nactium grow larger on the horizon. The river men had shown little interest in him except when he joined them in the games of chance that served to pass their free time. Boremac had acquired a small sum of coins from distant lands with only a minor exercise of his considerable skill at slight-of-hand. None of the river men begrudged him his winnings once he got word around that he would be supplying drink at the first tavern they could find. Boremac never cared for travel on the water, and the humid air wreaked havoc on his leathers. A proper tanner would be a first priority before he would be able to move fluidly again.

Boremac found the captain to be very accommodating as they neared the town. The rogue changed into clothes more suitable to the rest of the crew, proceeding to the shadowy inn nearest the docks with his new companions. The fact that the men were obliged to seek strong drink and soft women did not bother him at all. In spite of Silverwing's orders, he was about to enter the priesthood for a time, and he did not know when he might find opportunity for either of his favored vices again. Several days of shore leave ended with a rowdy brawl, indicating it was time for Boremac to move on to his assignment. He doubted it would serve him much to end up in the stocks. Boremac dodged a mug flung across the tavern, and slipped out into the streets of his new home and his new faith.

7

Books and Blades

Gregor took to his training with a conviction that was noted by all his teachers within the Temple of Light. His commitment was thought to be a great compliment to Master Silverwing. No one marveled at his studious behavior more than Father Havet, the tutor of languages both spoken and written, within the library. Gregor learned his basic reading and writing very quickly, and progressed into the ancient languages of the runic writings with unexpected grace. The more difficult scriptures took some time, as was expected, but Gregor's thirst for knowledge was unquenchable. It did not escape Father Havet's attention that even before Gregor had mastered the basic structure of language, he was captivated by the tapestries within the library and throughout the special temples of worship. These tapestries spoke of the miracles of the God of Light and the holy warriors of old who had destroyed demons by God's grace. Many of the statues and tapestries depicted the Knights of the Golden Dragon. Their greatest heroes and most terrible trials had earned sacred places in the blessed halls and sanctuaries throughout the temple grounds.

Gregor found purpose he had not known before among the priests. Their knowledge and teachings extended well beyond his expectations. He learned the healing arts, and how to channel the divine powers of the God of Light to knit the wounds of the people that seemed to constantly find their way to the temple's infirmary. He became a favorite among the sick and wounded, due to his story of coming to study at the temple and his simple nature, so much like the farmers he aided. The farmers from outlying villages had stories of their own to tell, and Gregor listened intently as they spoke of the ever-increasing goblin raids. Some spoke of the increased activity of wolves in the forests surrounding their homesteads as well, and Gregor found himself worrying about Tana with each new report. Even though the wolves were staying well away from the small farming communities, woodsmen who dared the forest to ply their trade found goblin corpses littering the woods as they trod carefully through the trees. The killing wounds on the goblin bodies were clearly inflicted by large wolves, although arrows were found in the corpses as well. The farmers had taken to leaving offerings in the forest to thank their unlikely aide, giving praise to the Goddess of Nature for her protection. With each bit of news concerning the strange happenings Gregor was glad to hear that Tana appeared to be well, but he wondered how long she would be safe.

***

Gregor was surprised to find his lessons included training with blunt weapons. He found an even larger surprise waiting for him at his first class in the form of the portly priest who was directing other acolytes. He was crowned with a ring of white hair, and wore his wrinkled features proudly. He shouted encouragement to the various young men and women who sparred with maces and staves, and he was even-handed with criticism to those not paying

96

attention. "Strike as though your lives depended on it! We may not seek the blood of those who strike at us today, but do not think the ones you will someday face will be subdued with the kindness of gentle swings." He harried one particular young man who was wielding a mace in a contest against a young woman swinging a staff. "She will knock you senseless if you do not parry her blows more energetically," the Father chided.

Father Wallin called to each of the remaining pairs, lining them shoulder-to-shoulder to present Gregor to the assembled students. Gregor was surprised to note that the number of male and female participants was roughly equal in the class. Obviously the God of Light made no distinction where the sex of his servants was concerned, and both men and women were called to serve as equals, or so Gregor assumed from the skills Sister Noria had demonstrated.

Gregor was taken aback with his introduction to the class. "Students, this is Master Gregor, who is to be a warrior of the God of Light. Those of you who have not had the opportunity to train with him in the library should take note, and study with him when you can. One can only marvel at his devotion to the study of our scriptures. He is a symbol of what one can accomplish with hard work and commitment to the faith we all serve." Father Wallin turned toward Gregor and bowed deeply. The class mirrored their tutor's gesture as one, and Gregor was overwhelmed with the show of respect.

"You all honor me too much. I wish only to reach my full potential in service to the God of Light, as do all of you that are assembled here and study within these blessed walls. My faith and understanding is only a spark when compared to the great fires that burn in the hearts of the priests and students that came before me." Gregor returned the bow of each of the people assembled in turn, noting the open faces of the acolytes as he did. He wondered briefly if he were up to the task that was before him.

"A knight of the God of Light transcends the powers of even the most studied priests, Gregor. You will become the first to stand against the great evil that threatens these lands in your time, and you will wield divine power in ways we cannot begin to comprehend. That is your destiny. That is why you are here." Father Wallin dismissed the class before turning to address Gregor again. "We should begin your blunt weapons training. You may favor the sword in battle, but one never knows when the weapon at hand may not be the weapon of choice."

Gregor found his weapon training with Father Wallin educational and painful. He had many opportunities to practice his healing skills and channeling on his own bruised body after each sparring session with the Master. Gregor mastered the heavy mace readily enough, and was able to best Sister Noria with the staff after multiple floggings at her capable hands. The weapon that perplexed Gregor the most was composed of a stout wooden handle with three iron chains extending from it. Each chain was capped with a weighty iron ball. This flail was unique to Gregor's experience with weapons, and the dexterity required to wield it effectively seemed outside his grasp. Father Wallin preferred the flail above all others, and demonstrated its disarming capability often, much to Gregor's dismay. The spinning balls could readily rip any weapon from his grasp, and the impact to his mailed hands caused Gregor to hold Father Wallin and the flail in high regard.

"Don't concern yourself overmuch with it, Gregor." Father Wallin smiled as Gregor rubbed his bare hands together. The latest flailing had proven most effective, and Gregor was practicing the healing touch of his shield hand on his bruised weapon hand. The mace he had been using hung from Father Wallin's flail, swinging gently as the priest moved to place it back in the practice rack. "I have a surprise for you tomorrow that does not involve stripping your defenses. You should take your rest early this evening. I took the liberty of canceling your class with Father Havet. He and I both know you are spending a great deal of time with books from the library when you should be resting, and Father Havet is very pleased with your progress; however, you will need all your strength tomorrow. I have arranged for some special guests to assist in measuring your weapon prowess."

Father Wallin's difficult training classes had honed Gregor's abilities, and the warrior found he favored the larger bastard sword, with its ability to be wielded with either one hand or two, over the shorter long swords with which he had originally trained. The weight of the weapon gave him stronger use of his cleaving attacks, and still allowed him to thrust effectively when needed. Gregor would normally have been very excited at the chance to test his mettle as well as his skill with his newfound weapon of choice, but he suffered some trepidation as Father Wallin turned to leave, chuckling to himself. Gregor was thinking a rest would certainly be welcome, as he walked to the main temple in order to pray for the focus he would no doubt need the following day.

***

The thief knelt before the great altar dedicated to the God of Light and wondered once more what exactly he had gotten himself into, or what Master Silverwing had gotten him into, anyway. Boremac had met with Father Oregeth, as Silverwing had instructed, and things had gone downhill rapidly from there. The good Father insisted that Boremac undergo the standard ritual of purification that all acolytes endured before being allowed into the temple grounds, assuring Boremac that he had had nothing to fear. "Nothing to fear?" Boremac thought, as he said his own version of the priests' prayers to the God of Light. Father Oregeth took a count of the sins that weighed on the rogue, and had determined a vow of silence was in order as penance. He explained this was as much to protect the sisters and brothers of the temple as to reconcile Boremac's eternal soul. So Boremac had spent the last several weeks in silence, except for speaking when called upon by the teachers in charge of his training. Father Oregeth had conveniently decided that Boremac should watch over Gregor as a fellow student and Boremac had learned a great deal about the holy swordsman. The thief was adept at listening through years of practice, and felt he knew as much about Gregor as the warrior knew himself, perhaps even more. Boremac was intrigued by rumors of a trial that would test Gregor's skill at arms. He had been impressed with the boy who had faced the two assassins a mere two cycles of the moon before now, but the word was that the final stages of his weapon training were nearing. If rumors were to be believed, Father Wallin had organized a special test befitting a fully capable holy warrior. More than skills with the shield and sword would be required, no doubt. Boremac wanted to contact Gregor more directly and open a dialogue with him, but that would wait for now. Tomorrow all the brothers and sisters were going to assemble at the city's arena to witness what Boremac was certain would be quite a show. "God of Light, please bless your humble servant, and allow him a draft most potent to slake his thirst once he is allowed to visit a most improper tavern again. Praise be to your holy presence."

***

Firebeard weighed the sword he had completed for Master Gregor and smiled with pride. It was a Masterwork of the Elenondo metal, that shining black metal that had fallen from the heavens as if it were a gift from the God of Light himself, and a perfect replica of the swords wielded by the Knights of the Golden Dragon he had once served. The weapon was forged as one piece, and bore the markings of Gregor's Master, lacking only the crystal centerpieces of Lord Silverwing's swords. The forge over which he labored to shape it had barely withstood the mystical fires that were needed to mold it, and it had cost him a fair amount of coin to recruit a mage capable of generating the flames, not to mention the diamond file and finely tipped chisel that had been needed for the detail work in the hilt, but it was worth it.

Father Wallin had noted that Gregor was favoring a bastard sword in his training, and the smith would be sure Gregor would have the finest blade the master weapon-smith could forge. Firebeard was unable to fashion a hilt for the blade Gregor had left with him. It would accept none other than its own original grip, the smith had reasoned, after many tries to seat it in a new handle. He could only assume that the divine power once present in the weapon as a whole was still retained, despite the nature of the creature that had torn it asunder. The master of the forge trembled, imagining what great evil could do such a thing.

Firebeard would have to hurry if he were to deliver the blade to Gregor before his weapons trial. The city was buzzing with the rumors of a holy warrior to be tested tomorrow at Nactium arena. Firebeard would be certain that Gregor would have a weapon befitting his station, though a proper shield would have to wait. The large smith hefted the blade, testing its balance, and giving more than one person in the lanes leading to the temple a moment's pause and a bit of a scare, as he trotted briskly through the city streets.

***

The aforementioned holy warrior received the weapon Firebeard had made with silence. Gregor was overwhelmed with the gift from the master of the forge. Sleep could not overtake him that night before his trial, as he weighed the sword in his hand and swept it about himself, taking care not to disturb the sleeping brothers near him. It felt like an extension of his arm, and Gregor marveled at its balance. The keen blade left no mark of its passage, as he inadvertently cut a nearby candelabrum neatly in two, scattering candles across the floor. He heard amused laughter quietly echoing nearby, and saw that his handiwork had not gone unnoticed.

Gregor realized the bald observer standing just inside the light cast by his scattered candles was a fellow acolyte from one of his many lessons. This particular brother stood out due to the close cut beard on his chin. More remarkably, the individual in question never spoke to anyone but the priests giving lessons, and spent a great deal of time in quiet prayer. Gregor had seen the man frequently when he was offering his own praise to the God of Light, and the mysterious figure was often in the main temple kneeling quietly as Gregor walked through the adjoining halls on his way to his other studies. Gregor hastily gathered up and extinguished the candles that had fallen to the floor, pausing briefly to wave in greeting to his observer. The acolyte only nodded, and disappeared into the shadows at the far end of the room.

***

Father Wallin stood on a large boulder at the center of the arena, wearing his battle armor, a pristine suit of chain mail bearing a prominent golden sun emblem on the chest. He held his preferred weapon, the oaken handled flail that Gregor had grown so wary of in his lessons, as he turned to the crowd of onlookers that filled the seats of the observation area. Gregor stood at the base of the great stone, flanked at his left by Sister Noria and at his right by Brother Findal, the three acolytes each clothed in suits of fine chain mail and bearing their weapons of choice. Gregor noted Brother Findal held a round wooden shield similar to the one he had been given in addition to carrying his mace. He found it curious that Brother Findal and Sister Noria were within the arena at all, and assumed they were present as protectors or healers if something went wrong, but he had no time to dwell on the development, as Father Wallin raised his voice to carry over the noise of the crowd. The audience packed into the arena seats quieted almost immediately, as the priest began speaking.

Gregor thought Father Wallin carried himself with remarkable grace, as he announced the event and named the participants, nodding to each in turn for the benefit of the audience. "I present for your approval the defenders of the God of Light in today's tournament! Sister Noria, master wielder of the staff, whose skills are unmatched among her brothers and sisters in the felling of foes. Her blessed hands turn the ash long arm with grace and precision. Brother Findal, master wielder of the mace, whose weapon of choice brings new meaning to the word dazed." The audience rippled with low laughter at the Father's jest. "Finally, the master of the bastard sword, Master Gregor, holy warrior and devout student of the faith. His skills in combat are untested, and so we have assembled here today. These three warriors of the God of Light will face overwhelming odds in the form of volunteers drawn from the finest veterans Nactium has to offer. Battle hardened warriors who know no fear and give no quarter!"

On cue, great doors were opened at the far wall of the arena by priests dressed in the same manner as Father Wallin. A score of warriors poured from the dark passageway beyond the great doors and lined up shoulder-to-shoulder facing the acolytes in a rough semi-circle. Gregor noted the men and women assembled themselves with military precision, although they seemed to be drawn from a wide range of organizations. Few of the adversaries had any insignia on their armor or shields, and there was a broad range of weapons mingled within the group. Some of the warriors bore tall metal shields bearing ornate carvings dented in places, showing they had seen their share of battles. Great swords numbered among the weapons, as tall as the men and women who held them at the ready. Armor plating ranged from simple suits of studded leather to complex plates of interlocking steel. Most remarkable were the two robed figures that stood at the farthest ends of the formation. The pair held long metal staves capped with orbs roughly the size of a fist. Two short, thin blades extended near the top of each staff, angled away from the orb cap. Gregor thought the formation resembled a figure with arms outstretched as if in supplication to the orb. He found the image unsettling, though nothing in the robed figure's demeanor seemed more threatening than the rest of the warriors assembled. In fact, the two men appeared disinterested in the whole proceedings.

Father Wallin drew the attention of all the people now present with a booming announcement, once the adversaries had settled into their appointed positions. "Now that we are all here, the rules of engagement are as follows!" Father Wallin turned to face the combatants, shouting over the heads of the acolytes below. "First and foremost, this is not a combat to the death! Any combatants who draw blood are required to allow for submission by their foe. Those participants who are wounded must acknowledge their wounding and either submit or continue in the melee at their discretion. Those sustaining wounds that draw blood should bring their weapon to their chest before reengaging. Those who determine their wounds are too severe to continue will immediately drop their weapons and proceed to the nearest of the priests that are scattered throughout the arena for healing. The aforementioned priests will collect anyone unable to do so. Any combatants that are knocked to their backs should use proper judgment and leave the combat area if they would not reasonably be able to regain their feet. Once again, you will indicate submission by disarming yourself. Master Firebeard has volunteered his services for evacuation of those combatants rendered unconscious." Father Wallin took a moment to acknowledge the giant smith before continuing to address the waiting combatants. "Use of missile weapons or long range channeling of any kind is strictly forbidden and will result in a forfeiture of payment to those being compensated for their participation. If I find it necessary to disarm or render unconscious any participants, all combat will immediately come to a halt and the offender or offenders will be jailed. Divine powers will be brought to bear without hesitation against anyone choosing to ignore these rules. The acolytes are encouraged to channel divine powers for defense or healing at their discretion and within the limitations of the aforementioned rules. Additional coin has been allotted to reward any hired warriors for exemplary acts of teamwork, and restoring your allies in the arena to combat is encouraged. Please acknowledge your understanding of these rules with a bow, and after a short blessing, we will begin."

The participants bowed as instructed, and a hush fell over the audience as Father Wallin blessed all those assembled. The crowds of people filling the stands sat quietly as coins changed hands, wagering on all manner of possibilities. Who would fall first? Odds were high that one of the acolytes would be mortally wounded while facing such large numbers, and even Boremac was tempted to wager on the strength of that bet. He scribbled a note to one of the arena's turf accountants, placing a significant sum against the staff-wielding sister. There were few among the onlookers that thought she would survive, let alone get out of the melee without injury. The strength of the two acolytes was known to most of the common residents of Nactium, though Gregor was a complete unknown. The rogue weighted his wager against Sister Noria with a vote of victory for Gregor. The odds makers may not have known his skills, but Boremac had little doubt that the sword wielder would be the last man standing, once the day was done. He recognized the two stave wielders opposing the trio as well, though he had never encountered a pair of the priests before. Their staves gave their affiliation away to one trained in observation. Boremac could not imagine why two brothers of the Order of the Crimson Night would even be here. Perhaps they had come at the invitation of the priest who was overseeing the event. Additional healers would have been welcomed, Boremac reasoned, and he was certain their skills would be necessary against the blade Gregor possessed. They would be the ones to watch.

The two robed figures facing the acolytes had not escaped Master Firebeard's notice. He was impressed with the craftsmanship of their chosen weapons, though they seemed ill suited to priests, and the smith could not imagine why wizards would have numbered among the challengers. The alloy that composed their weapons was not readily discernible at this distance, but Master Firebeard made a mental note to speak with the two men after the melee. It was time to get ready for his part of the event, and Master Firebeard had no doubt he would be busy. Many of the weapons and armor on the field were his work, and Gregor was certain to give the smith much repair work after proving his worth.

Gregor was terrified. He had a fine blade, and was well trained in the martial arts, and still he was terrified. It was Sister

Noria who took the lead in the trio, instructing her companions to spread out. "Allow enough space for your weapons to swing free. I should be able to protect your backs, so stay close to mine. Remember, they are only men." Sister Noria snickered in spite of the dire situation they faced. "Brother Findal, strike their heads and helmets, but remember to pull your strength. We only want to knock them out, not crush their skulls. Short measured strokes, and for all that is good and pure, do not over-extend. That has always been your weakness!"

Gregor felt strengthened by her faith in their abilities. Her rapid instruction to him bolstered his own faith. "Gregor, remember the shield, and wound the shoulders of your attackers when you can. Disarm their weapon arm and focus on the softer targets. The ones that carry tower shields will no doubt cause you the most trouble, so move away from them to allow Brother Findal or myself to dispatch them. Keep moving in a circle, and do not try to take more than two at once. Ready, and go!"

The trio spaced out as planned, and waited for the twenty warriors to make the first move. The wait was brief. The opposing forces split into three groups of six, taking up position around the three acolytes. It appeared there had been some planning on their part as well, and the group facing Sister Noria moved in first, rapidly closing the space between their weapons and her staff. This was their first mistake. Sister Noria drove the first ones rushing toward her to their knees with rapid twists of her staff. A groan of sympathy escaped Brother Findal, even as he neatly knocked out the two kneeling figures. "That was most unkind, Sister Noria. I know the fury of that strike all too well. Better they are unconscious, I think."

The attackers were a bit more cautious as they more fully took the measure of the acolytes. The men and women still moving toward Sister Noria gestured to the other warriors facing Gregor and Brother Findal. Moments later, the air was filled with the howls of rushing warriors. They must have determined that attacking the holy warriors one at a time was not going to work, and a full attack was the best course of action. This was their second mistake.

Sister Noria barked orders to her brothers, as the men and women encircled them. 'Spread out! Brother Findal, heads! Master Gregor, weapon-bearing shoulders, and keep moving!"

Sister Noria fought with a grace Gregor had never witnessed, and the stands surrounding the arena swelled with the sound of the audience drawing a deep breath as one. She used the staff as an extension of herself, and vaulted behind the remaining four opponents who were charging where she had just been. The ripple of hesitation she caused with this maneuver coursed through all the remaining foes, giving Gregor and Brother Findal the opportunity they needed to strike.

Brother Findal lacked Sister Noria's grace and style, but he more than made up for it with sheer strength. Three of the six that charged him fell to rapid strikes that knocked them backward. Weapons littered the ground from those that Master Firebeard had already carried away, and priests ran out to tend other wounded and unconscious attackers as the melee charged through the inside of the arena. While the other two acolytes were handling their respective groups, Gregor discovered the gift bestowed by his sword; true unhindered penetration. Gregor parried the weapon strikes brought against him, and used the shield to block his undefended side, searching for opportunities to strike. The aggressive pursuers were shocked as Gregor cut the handle of an attacker's mace in half while deflecting the blow of another attacker's great sword. Gregor was overwhelmed, and almost struck down, as he looked at the remaining pieces of the handle in the large man's hand. A great gasp issued from the crowd in the arena, as once more, all eyes seemed to focus on Gregor. He had no time to feel the weight of their attention. The woman wielding the sword that narrowly missed him had lost her footing as the sword completed its arc, and she began to fall toward him. Gregor pointed his sword at her reflexively. The black blade of his weapon passed through her chain mail armor at the shoulder, cutting into her, as momentum carried her forward. Her body temporarily blocked the remaining attackers, and Gregor pushed her off the blade with his shield. Two of his three remaining foes fled as she dropped her weapon and fell to her knees. Bile rose into Gregor's throat, as blood streamed through the fingers of the hand his victim had brought up, covering her wound. A pool of blood formed around her, as the priests hurried to her side, preparing regenerative prayers even as they ran across the ground to aid her. The blade had gone all the way through, leaving a large gouge in her shoulder at the front, and a clean tear also pouring out blood at the back. None of the assembled witnesses had ever seen a wounding such as this.

Brother Findal was still engaged in a desperate melee with one seasoned attacker wielding a club and heavy shield. The two men exchanged blows with fevered intensity, each trying to undo the other with the heavy strikes. Sister Nadia had borne her attackers to the ground, delivering stunning blows to each as they struck the hard dirt. She swiftly brought her staff to bear on Brother Findal's final opponent as her incapacitated victims were dragged out of the arena. Even as she disarmed Brother Findal's attacker she noted that two of the mercenaries who had been advancing toward Brother Findal were now focusing on rapidly shortening the distance between Gregor and themselves. The heavily armored warriors moved to join the remaining opponent already advancing on Gregor. Three hardened fighters formed up as one, creating a wall of tower shields with just room enough between them for the use of their deadly blades, intent upon forcing the young warrior to submit.

Gregor would not submit. He knew he had to end the contest before someone was killed. Gregor let his own shield fall from his hand as he lowered himself into a sprinter's stance. His now freed fingers wrapped tightly around the hilt of his sword as he launched himself across the distance between himself and the three men approaching him. There was a pause as if time had stopped. Every person in the arena seemed to be holding their collective breath as they wondered what he could possibly be thinking. They would have been even more astounded if they knew the truth of the matter. Gregor was not thinking at all but acting as he had been trained, and on a much deeper level, he was praying to the power that had saved him so long ago.

Reflexes stopped Gregor short with the mercenaries just within reach of his blade. He pivoted on the tip of his boot with the art of a trained dancer as his blade cut neatly across the tops of the tower shields just at the level of the necks of the men bent on his defeat. Each man in his turn dropped his sword and the remains of their shields, and knelt before Gregor in submission to his prowess. The men then rose as one and lifted their heads to the sky before nodding to Gregor. All three of them bore an open cut that trickled blood down their throats. Gregor bowed his head before genuflecting briefly to honor the combatants that had all performed so well in the rite of combat. The acolytes assumed the trial was over. They were wrong.

***

Boremac watched the melee with interest. Despite his loss when Sister Nadia had not been overcome, the contest held his attention until the last. The rogue would make a healthy donation to the temple when the coins were counted after his finder's fee was taken. Unlike the rest of the audience who were following Gregor's every move, Boremac kept his eyes on the robed figures he had noted earlier. Their movements had escaped notice once the fighting had begun in earnest and the rogue doubted anyone else was paying any attention as the pair positioned themselves behind the large boulder near where Father Wallin perched. He knew shadowy tactics better than anyone, and those two were definitely up to something.

***

Master Firebeard had a secret. He had planned on returning the blade he could not repair to Gregor when this last test was concluded. That wasn't the secret though and the large man

112

practically hopped from one foot to the other with excitement as the last combatants knelt before Gregor. The smith had been commissioned several weeks ago, in anticipation of this final test, to fashion the armor Gregor would wear when knighted. The smith had scoffed at the head priest when Father Oregeth had asked him what payment would be required. "You cannot price the honor bestowed upon me with this commission, good Father. The sweat of this labor is given of love and respect for the man that will wear it and the God that he serves." The master smith would hear no more talk of payment from the priest at the time and had shooed him out of the shop with a smile while the contest progressed. Here in the arena, Master Firebeard had imagined sunlight glinting off the armor befitting the knight that Gregor would soon become. The twinkle few had ever seen in the smithy's eyes turned into fire brighter than his hair when he was roused from his revery. His services were still needed within the fighting grounds.

Priests bustled around the arena, directing carts that were collecting the unconscious and tending the wounded. Gregor took in the remnants of the battle, glad that the trial was ended and no one had been mortally wounded. Shock froze him as a robed figure mounted the great boulder where Father Wallin stood. He only had time to take in the danger as the metal staff the man held glowed with a deep crimson light and swept toward the back of Father Wallin's skull. The Father must have seen the fear etched in Gregor's features and he reflexively turned to meet the unseen threat. Father Wallin's flail wrapped around the glowing staff with practiced skill but his opponent had obviously anticipated the countering maneuver. The staff was pulled away from the priest even as the light surrounding it brightened. The balls and attaching chains of Father Wallin's flail took on the~~ir own~~ brightened glow of the staff they had trapped. Moments later Father Wallin's weapon exploded, throwing him off his perch. The Father's face was covered in weeping wounds, and holes in his chain mail emanated tendrils of smoke where he lay. Brother Findal and Sister Nadia ran quickly to tend their fallen teacher. They dropped to his side, divine light enveloping their hands as they prayed over him. It was all the opportunity the other robed assailant needed as he moved to flank them. His staff was glowing with the same queer crimson light as he touched the unprotected heads of the distracted acolytes almost gently. The effect was immediate as the pair of healers fell at Father Wallin's side, the healing light extinguished even before they came to rest.

Any fear or doubt Gregor had entertained once the strange mages had revealed themselves was gone. Gregor was a fury, moving with purpose toward the attackers, released from his stupor by the assault. The sun's radiance began to diminish as the priest who struck Father Wallin began to speak rapid, brutal words, raising a hand toward Gregor. "Move further one step and their souls will weigh on yours alone. There is no need for them to die, knave. Give us the broken blade and we will spare them."

The fledgling holy warrior answered with peace and purpose, seemingly startling both the individuals he now addressed. "The God of Light protects this arena from power-wielders such as you. Any magics you hope to use to escape will unravel even as you think of them. Your threats are in vain. I do not have the blade and would not give it to you if I did. These servants I call kin are all servants to the God of Light as am I, and their souls will be called at his time, and be at peace when they are. There will be no such peace for the two of you. Agony you cannot imagine will be yours to bear for all eternity once I separate your tainted souls from your bodies. Kill them if you must, but know that they are all that stand between you and the bite of my blade."

The robed figure on the boulder hesitated, absorbing Gregor's words. His mouth formed a sardonic grin, but it was not the man who felled Father Wallin that broke the silence. The silent smith who watched as the exchange unfolded could hold his tongue no longer. "Gregor, they must be spared! I have the broken blade with me now and it is of no use to anyone!" Firebeard's voice trembled with anguish. "Let these fiends take what they have come for and be gone. I cannot bear the weight of the loss of these innocent souls if I have the power to prevent it."

"So there is wisdom here after all." The priest turned to address Firebeard directly. "Bring me the blade and they shall be spared." He turned to sweep his eyes around the arena. "All the other priests will leave now, or the innocent within these great walls will know the fury of the Abyss. Come to me with the blade in your hands." Master Firebeard held out the blade and walked toward the man at the stone. Gregor nodded to the priests scattered throughout the arena and the healers moved out of the center ring through the great doors that had admitted the challengers. The holy warrior's hands tightened on his black sword as the master smith drew near the boulder. His body tensed in preparation to strike down the priest near the bodies of his fallen companions. No one was prepared for what happened next, except Boremac.

The priest watched the large man approach as he was instructed. The plan had worked perfectly and his Master would be pleased. "The people assembled now know the strength we wield. You owe your lives to this humble servant, and you should enjoy each breath you draw from this day. The end is com..." Blood spouted from a ragged hole that appeared in the man's throat, cutting his words short. A long handle protruded from the back of his neck where the balanced dagger had entered. Boremac broke the silence with his words to his brothers and sisters of the Temple that surrounded them, compelled to explain his actions." Someone had to do something. That man was really starting to chafe me."

The remaining priest's reaction was immediate." So the choice is death!" His body drew into the robes the figure wore and his staff disappeared with it. All that remained was a pile of cloth near the three unconscious bodies. The mortally wounded priest on the boulder knelt with his staff in his hand as he was suffused with crimson light that was so dark it appeared to be black. The sun's rays disappeared and the arena was dropped into twilight. Unlike his companion's, this figure's robes ignited, and the staff he held dripped and melted into a molten pool at his knees. A great column of fire burned at the top of the stone, giving birth to a terrible creature Gregor had never seen before.

***

Boremac held out his hands as the two guards came to collect him. The priests of the God of Light chanted as they rose from their seats around the rock. His work here was done, and he was prepared to pay the cost of his actions, unwilling to flee. Even as the demonic form emerged from the flames at the boulder, the guards remained focused on apprehending the man of the cloth who had slain the robed figure. Boremac did not blame them. They had a responsibility to the people in the arena, though they could do nothing to protect them from the hideous creature that had appeared. This was the province of divine powers, and though Boremac was immediately concerned with his own predicament, he knew that Gregor would be the one to pay most dearly for the rogue's actions. The thrown dagger was guided by skills well-honed in a life spent committed to self-preservation, but the motivation behind it went against everything the thief had ever done. Boremac brought his eyes to meet the two guards as he spoke," I submit to the will of the God of Light. I trust in the wisdom of the power that guided my actions and will deliver us from this evil." Boremac allowed the guards to take him, quietly adding his voice to the chanting of the men and women of the faith. It was then the rogue discovered peace he had never known, even as the jailers led him out of the arena.

***

The creature had flesh the color of obsidian covered in a fine coat of fur. A thick white mane dominated its head and back. Four grotesquely powerful arms that were layered with muscle sprouted from its torso, the top pair tipped with pincers instead of hands and the lower pair ending in claws with razor-sharp nails. Its head was a blending of a humanoid skull with an elongated muzzle similar to a giant wolf. Although many people in the arena viewing area fled at the sight of it, most were mesmerized by its smooth animal grace as it charged from the flames toward Gregor.

Gregor planted the balls of his feet, ready to receive the beast's attack. Moments stretched into hours as the demon closed the distance between them, efficiently pumping clawed arms and legs to increase the speed of its bounding gait. The pincers extending toward the warrior snapped repeatedly as if anticipating cutting Gregor's flesh. The swordsman realized too late that he had tossed away his shield during the previous melee and would be sorely pressed to face all four appendages with only his sword. At the last moment, Gregor moved toward the demon. He dodged to one side as his black blade swept in a downward arc, severing one of the vile pincers. The creature ignored the wound as it pivoted to face him, digging the razor-sharp claws of its undamaged appendage into the dirt as the beast came to its full height within arm's reach of Gregor, drawing back its remaining limbs and pointing its muzzle down at the warrior. The demon seemed to take real notice of the warrior for the first time, rapidly barking at him and snapping his remaining pincer in a warding gesture. The wounded arm was already regenerating, and Gregor had to wonder what exactly this creature was capable of as a soft growth of flesh began to harden. He moved backwards out of reach and tried to think. In the brief time the demon was replacing its lost limb, Gregor heard a soft chanting start in the seats of the arena.

The twilight enclosing the arena was filled with white light emanating from the followers of the God of Light. It was a sign of faith that would conquer the darkness, and Gregor felt his despair leave him. He knew it. He what he needed to do. Gregor turned from the creature and fled toward the boulder. The beast pursued him immediately as the reforming pincer became fully functional once more. The game was over, and the beast moved with remarkable skill, ready to devour its prey. Gregor leapt into the air to take the high ground the boulder provided, and turned to meet his attacker. A small prayer was all he could recite as he threw his legs out over the shoulder of the beast and extended his sword to his side. As Gregor felt the tug of the earth, the creature's head fell from his shoulders, but the struggle was not over yet. The demon flailed its arms, blindly seeking the holy warrior who had removed its head, which was already beginning to reform. Gregor had precious little time as he moved to strike the final blow.

"The God of Light will endure you no longer, and as his sword and protector, I banish you to the Abyss from which you came!" As Gregor spoke these words, the blade of his black sword absorbed the white light in the arena and burned with the divinity of the God of Light. Gregor plunged the sword into the center of the thrashing arms, causing the demon's body to convulse and shooting its limbs outward to the sides of its torso. The form dissolved into a cloud of acrid smoke that smelled of brimstone, and the beast was gone. Gregor fell to his knees and wept.

Chaos swept the arena as the unnatural darkness gave way to the returning of the sun's light. The brothers and sisters of the God of Light moved into the arena grounds where the battle had taken place, rushing to see to the fallen. Divine healing knitted the weeping wounds sustained by Father Wallin as the priests stripped away his damaged armor, inspecting his body. Remarkably, only his leg had been broken by the fall from the boulder, and the minor bruises would heal in their own time. Sister Nadia and Brother Findal were unaffected by the magic that rendered them unconscious, though they could not be awakened. Father Wallin was also trapped in the sleep, marked by shallow breathing and the slow beating of his heart. None of these three figures could be roused and were gently carted to the infirmary at the Temple.

Firebeard moved to the top of the boulder, intent upon examining the pool of metal that formed where the priest's staff melted. The metal had hardened where it laid and still glowed with the same the deep red that suffused the staff as it had struck Father Wallin. "Strange. I should chip away some of the stone and examine it if I can." Firebeard mumbled to himself, his curiosity and professional interests held in check only by his good sense. Too many unknown powers had been revealed to risk touching the metal directly, and it would be some time before the smith could determine anything about the alloy's creation.

Channeling the forces that Gregor had used against the demon had taken its toll on the holy warrior. He remained on his knees, offering thanks to the God of Light for the power to overcome the creature. Slowly, Gregor felt a measure of strength return to his limbs and was able to shakily regain his feet. His eyesight had darkened, and even as he stood the area around him appeared to be no more than a brightening haze filled with shadows of movement. He felt hands take his arms to steady him as he swayed on wobbly legs, wondering where his weapon had fallen. "We have you, Gregor." Gentle words touched his ears. "Are you all right?"

"I think I will be fine. The power has taken my eyesight but light returns. I cannot see much more than a bright blur." Gregor blinked his eyes rapidly, trying to clear his vision.

A light chuckle came with the reply. "It is a wonder you can see at all, Master Gregor. The prayers of at least a hundred brothers and sisters poured through you. I would not be surprised if the God of Light himself empowered your weapon. The power that flowed into the sword you wield certainly appeared to be a direct intervention."

"We should get him to the infirmary before he gets any heavier, brother. It will take more than the two of us to bear his weight if his legs give out. Walk as much as you can, Master Gregor, but we will carry you if we must."

Gregor did as he was told and focused his concentration on remaining conscious and upright as he was led to the Temple grounds. He barely heard the cheers that filled the arena as the priests led him out the great doors. Word spread through Nactium, and the streets were lined with people struggling to catch sight of the new champion. Such a blessed warrior had not been seen in the streets of Nactium for quite some time. No one could know the true destiny of this young squire who was yet to receive knighthood, but many of them, while recounting his victories in the arena, could not help but think he would be the one to rebuild the Knights of the Golden Dragon, those chosen Knights of the God of Light whose order had been wiped out so long ago.

8

New Assignments

Boremac had spent an interesting night in the confines of Nactium's jail. Numerous visitors had stopped in to share words of support and assured him that the merit of his deed would grant his release once his actions were weighed at trial. Only one visitor had caused the rogue to reevaluate his actions, and this man had given Boremac a great amount of food for thought.

The man had been clothed as a myriad of other commoners that had filed through the rest of the day and into the evening. The first words this newcomer shared let Boremac know this man was here on business. "We don't take to assassins coming within the walls of Nactium without paying proper respect, brother. Don't know how you got yourself into the Temple but I doubt you'll find much sanctuary there now. Won't take much to have you dangling from the gallows by sunset tomorrow. Anyone who tosses a dagger so well is probably traveling with a hefty price on his head. I would advise you to take advantage of the time you have and make peace with whichever God you follow. One way or another, you will be meeting them in person. By the time night falls."

Boremac kept his tone even and low as he answered the man's threats." My reasons for being here are my own and the killing of that priest held no profit for me, at least not in coin. You would do well to choose your enemies with more care."

"You speak boldly for a dead man. If you find a way out of the cell and beyond the walls of the city, don't let your shadow darken these streets again. Sounds like there might be a bit of brains in that shiny head of yours. Heed my words, brother, because the next time you know we have found you, you will be dead." The man turned away with a quick word to the guards watching Boremac's cell, "better keep a close watch on this one, gentlemen. Never know what those shady types might try." And he was gone.

***

The visitors at dawn took Boremac unaware as a guard banged on the bars of his cell. The thief rubbed the sleep from his eyes and turned to address the offending jailer, only to have harsh words resting behind his lips quickly swallowed. "Father Oregeth and the robust smith from yesterday's event, Master Firebeard if I recall correctly. What brings you to visit this humble servant of the God of Light? Imminent release for me, I hope. I received word yesterday that I have pressing business to attend to in another city far from this one."

Father Oregeth frowned deeply before speaking, "It gives me no great pleasure to speed your release as I am certain any time spent here would be well-earned for past sins. That is not an immediate concern to me, and you have been called upon to serve Master Silverwing more directly at this time. Arrangements have been made for your immediate discharge into our care until local constables are able to sort everything out. It is difficult to hold a man on the charge of murder when there is no body or weapon to be found. As I explained to the governor, there are far more terrible forces at work here as indicated by the demon's manifestation in the arena yesterday. You will accompany Master Firebeard and myself to the Temple grounds." As Father Oregeth turned to speak with one of the nearby guards, Boremac noted that the huge smith carried a long wooden case roughly the length of a great sword and two hands wide. The rogue's curiosity was piqued, especially after the role the master smith had played in yesterday's events. "The papers should be in order, guardsman. Please verify the governor's seal and release the prisoner into my custody." Boremac thanked the God as the cell door swung open and the three men left for the Temple of Light.

***

Gregor followed as Father Havet led him into the part of the library forbidden to all but the most senior priests within the Temple of Light. The books within contained all of the acquired knowledge the library held of the darkest Powers identified and cataloged over the centuries by the servants of the God of Light. Father Havet was explaining that the books were kept from most eyes to prevent possible misuse, but Gregor's attention had been immediately drawn to an ornate tapestry hanging at the far end of the room. "Who is he?" Gregor cut Father Havet off to make inquiry, never taking his eyes off the figure pictured in the tapestry. The man represented wore dark crimson robes and held his hands out before him as if he were receiving a gift of some kind. The figure's deep eyes were set amid a narrow face that was framed by long black hair. Something in the way the priest stood called to memories deep in Gregor's mind.

"That is Father Tur'morival, Master Gregor, and once he was known as the greatest demonologist to ever study within the Temples of Light. Father Tur'morival gathered many of the books in this room, and authored some of them as well, with the knowledge he collected. It was a sad day when he left the Temple, but the head of the church at the time had been left no choice. Father Tur'morival held the belief that the only means to defeat the powers of the abyss was to find a way to control them. The church has very strict guidelines in place regarding the use of knowledge concerning demons and their progeny. When encountered, they are destroyed, and if a person suffers from possession by these forces, the spirit is cleansed and the evil driven out, but Father Tur'morival argued against these practices. He felt the church was limiting its ability to fight the creatures and would ultimately be unprepared when the Crimson Night came to pass."

"What is this Crimson Night, Father?" Gregor's head swam as Father Havet related the divine prophecies predicting the night of the Blood Moon. The more he learned, the more certain Gregor became that this was the same man that had invaded his sleeping mind that night in Dakin's cabin.

"It was predicted over 1000 years ago that a blood red moon would rise in the night sky, and a gateway to the Abyss would stand open until the dawn. Chaos would pour out of this gateway, and mankind would either be enslaved or destroyed by the legions that would come forth. Father Tur'morival argued that controlled summoning of the demons would allow the brothers and sisters of the Temple of Light to undo the armies of demons and seal them in the Abyss for eternity. You see, Gregor, the manifestations of the demons we encounter in this world are only shells, physical forms assumed by the creatures from the Abyss when they make their way here. That is why when you cut away the limbs of the demon you faced in the arena, it was able to reconstruct itself so rapidly. Pieces of these manifestations can be damaged by cold iron and blessed silver, and some minor creatures can even be destroyed by these weapons as well as other alloys created for that purpose, but the demonic soul remains in the Abyss, and only the physical form is dismissed. Father Tur'morival committed the later years of his life to studying means of a more complete summoning, wishing to draw the souls of the demons into their physical manifestations to destroy them utterly."

"His secret experiments resulted in the death of one of our adepts and he was expelled from the Temple. The story is that Father Tur'morival had gained a great deal of support among the priests closest to him, and began minor trials summoning imps and other diminutive demons in an old tomb the families of the city no longer used. Once he had mastered the smaller creatures, he gradually graduated to summoning larger beasts. There is much debate to this day as to what exactly went wrong, but it appears that some more intelligent and infinitely more powerful demon in the Abyss had taken note of Father Tur'morival's experiments. All that is known, largely from the books Father Tur'morival wrote and the Journal that was found secreted in the tomb where he worked, is that Father Tur'morival had decided to contact an infernal broker of a sort. Certain demons called Wethrin'draug sometimes acted as intermediaries between summoners and the powerful Tharnorsa, who are the main powers within the Abyss below their Princes and Kings. With the information he had gathered, Father Tur'morival reasoned a Wethrin'draug would be an excellent test of his theories regarding the demon's soul paired with the flesh in this world. Somehow the demon was aware of Father Tur'morival's manipulations and escaped the restraining divine powers that had been prepared for the experiment. One of the first acolytes to arrive when the demon was clawing its way from the tomb where Father Tur'morival performed his experiments was slain immediately, and several other priests were wounded before the Wethrin'draug could be banished. Father Tur'morival was later found in the tomb, clutching his journal to his chest within the confines of a protective circle composed of runes and wards, narrowly escaping death himself. The journal was seized for evidence, and Father Tur'morival was later excommunicated after his trial. Several of his stalwart supporters left with him and formed the Temple of the Order of the Crimson Night. There is a book here written by Father Tur'morival himself detailing their founding principles and the requirements for the priests to join their number, many of whom are very well thought of demonologists in their own religious orders. It was established not so much as a religious group but more as an information collective, and the members with a variety of religious backgrounds take advantage of the focused collective's libraries and knowledge. I have visited their Temple here in Nactium on numerous occasions."

127

Gregor absorbed all that Father Havet had said before speaking." I have seen this man, or at least I believe I have. It was a dream, a nightmare really, but I'm sure it was Father Tur'morival."

Father Havet cocked an eyebrow and frowned. "Master Gregor, I assure you that is quite impossible. Father Tur'morival left the Temple over 200 years ago."

***

Boremac took only enough time to suit up in his leathers and secrete his weapons on his person before joining Father Oregeth and Master Firebeard in the main Temple. He could not help feeling a bit out of place garbed in his usual attire, and the sour look Father Oregeth wore as the rogue approached did nothing to ease his mind. "I see you have made yourself ready. It gives me no peace of mind to entrust you with the task set before you, Boremac, but I must believe Lord Silverwing's faith is not misplaced. There is to be a gathering in the woods of Zanthfar. Lord Silverwing is making his way to the druid's grove there as we speak and has requested his weapons be delivered to the city with haste. Master Firebeard has readied the weapons and will escort you to the stables where a fast horse is waiting. You are familiar with the city of Zanthfar?"

The rogue could not help smirking as he answered. "Oh yes, I am well thought of among my peers within those walls. It will be good to meet with some of my old acquaintances there. I have had a brush with the local... guild... and remaining in Nactium is not in my plans."

"Yes, well, it does appear that fate does favor the foolish and the blessed in equal measure." Father Oregeth is smiled for the first time Boremac could recall. "You will find your mount is tireless in service and will bear you to the city within a relatively short time." The Father turned to Master Firebeard, "Take him to the stable and make sure he makes the gates without pause. The stable master has the horse ready and adequate foodstuffs and supplies have been packed in anticipation of your arrival. You can bring Master Boremac up to date on the way but do not tarry. There is no time to waste." Father Oregeth made rapid hand gestures blessing the pair as they left the Temple.

"Come on, Boremac. The priests and I have labored through the night during your stay in the jail. We should hurry to be sure our labors were not in vain. There is much Master Silverwing needs to know." Firebeard took long strides as he hurried out into the city streets and Boremac marveled at the huge man's speed, jogging along beside him as the master smith related the discoveries of the priests and the produce of his night's work.

When they reached the stable, Boremac bent forward with his hands on his knees to catch his breath. Master Firebeard stood in front of him with a boot tapping as the smith impatiently waited. Boremac regained his composure and frowned at the blacksmith as he began to speak. "Good Smith, I am glad to have the knowledge of the demon in question to share with Master Silverwing. I'm equally certain that said knight would be more than pleased with the additions for his quiver you have produced. There is one bit of crucial information that seems to have been missed by all of you in your efforts to prepare. I know who was responsible for the

129

appearance of the demon that was so intent on Master Gregor's undoing. It was the staffs the errant priests possessed that gave name to their affiliation, Master Firebeard, though I would not have expected you or the others to recognize them. The order of the Crimson Night is somehow involved in the recent events, though even I cannot imagine why. Only the highest-ranking members of the order possess such staffs.

Firebeard stared at the thief in disbelief. "How would you know that and why would priests committed to protecting the lands from demonic forces have reason to bring one against brothers and sisters of the Temple of Light?"

"That would be the riddle, wouldn't it?" Boremac paused before continuing, measuring his words. "I know who bear the staves because there is a man with only one hand on my list of acquaintances who had both before he tried to acquire one. Where my information comes from doesn't matter, it is more important what is done with it. Father Oregeth needs some priests and guards to hit the place where the students of the order gather now. It is probably too late, but go and make Father Oregeth aware so some guardsmen can be rounded up." Boremac pulled the long narrow wooden case from Master Firebeard's hands and turned to secure the package to the horse's saddle. He jumped up onto the horse with the practiced grace of a man used to mounting walls quickly and smiled as he watched the smith's large form disappear around the corner. "That might have bought me time for a drink. What do you think, boy?"

The horse shook his head by way of reply and cantered rapidly toward the city gates nearby. It appeared this steed knew where he was going and Boremac would have a dry throat until they got there. "Water it is then, I suppose." He dropped his hand to the water skin hanging at his leg and held the horse's reins with the other as the pair raced down the road to Zanthfar.

***

Gregor made a home among the books in the secured area of the library Father Havet had shown him. There was less than a week until he would be keeping Vigil in the main temple, awaiting the touch of his God. Gregor absorbed as much as he could from the most complete manuscripts. Father Tur'morival's personal works were as educational as they were obscure, filled with a great deal of theories and assumptions that seemed to be contradictory to most of the other assembled works. Father Havet lent his assistance when Gregor needed help translating some of the dark passages found in Father Tur'morival's personal journal, although the priest was loathe to do so. Gregor could not imagine what could possess any man, let alone a servant of the God of Light, to perform the rituals detailed throughout the priest's personal text. The certainty Gregor felt when he first saw the tapestry only deepened. Father Tur'morival was the figure that had wanted the broken blade despite Father Havet's insistence the priest had died long ago. What possible use he had for it, Gregor could not imagine. The holy warrior refused to think of the apparition as a man, though he was at a loss to define the creature that had stood before him in his dream.

9

Drunkards and Fools

Boremac's trip to Zanthfar had been uneventful, which was a pleasant turn of events for a change. The roads were thick with the cities' militia along his route. The rogue took a measure of comfort in this, despite his usual feelings for peacekeepers. He was happy to stable the horse and carry the heavy wooden case for Master Silverwing to the nearest inn. He felt his relief diminish only slightly as he entered the tavern proper. The ranger was waiting at one of the tables in the tavern, and Boremac could not even secure much-needed refreshment before Master Silverwing motioned to him. "So, Silverwing, you will be buying the rounds this evening? Your kindness is noted and appreciated."

"All you need should be well provided for with the winnings from Gregor's challenge." Silverwing's furrowed brow told the thief all he needed to know about the ranger's feelings concerning those events. "You can tell me exactly what happened later. Right now we will relax and share a cup."

Boremac waved over one of the barmaids, placing an order for the strongest brew they had and instructing her to keep his mug full. He dropped a few coins in her outstretched hand, turning his attention back to Silverwing. "No need to get upset. You knew who I was soon after we met, and I did save the boy a bit of trouble in the process of protecting my own interests. I would think a bit of betting would be the least of your concerns."

"Yes, your talent is put to good use even though I must wonder at your intent. Still, Father Oregeth sees something in you that I cannot. His faith in you is the only reason you're here now. You would be wise not to forget that." Master Silverwing's words stung the thief, but Boremac could not deny the truth of them. "He chose to release you from the jailers in Nactium for his own reasons. Reasons that disagree with what I know of you, although it appears you gave the church at least a nodding respect while you were there. Father Oregeth said you spent a great deal of time at the main altar communing while you were maintaining a vow of silence. Your prayers never fall on deaf ears, so I hope you were not too flagrant in your language." Master Silverwing smiled.

Boremac returned the smile with a grin of his own. "My prayers are between me and the God whose service I have been pressed into. I am sure you can respect that. You should open the package. Truth of it is, I've been wanting to know what was so important to worry my butt for so long on that horse."

"You know the blades I wield from the encounter in the wood where you discovered Gregor and me. Is there more here than that?"

"Yes, the fine blades will bite all the deeper for the care of Master Firebeard. He sent along something more to win your favor, as if his name were not enough. Come on now and open it."

"Master Firebeard; there is a man I've not seen in too many years to count. Did you have time and chance to visit his great forge? The skilled hands of that smith forge many of the lands' greatest weapons and armor. It is a sin to see Nactium and not see that giant of a man at work." Master Silverwing rested his hands on the case as he spoke, taking pleasure in Boremac's discomfort. "The stories that man could tell. Many heroes known throughout this land would have fallen without the labors of that smith. No other smithy served the Knights of the Golden Dragon within the walls of Nactium as well, or as long. I wonder what possible gift he would have sent. You know, the last time I was in his humble establishment, he offered a shining suit of plate armor befitting a king. Perhaps we should drink his honor before opening the case." Boremac felt as though he were watching from the shadows as brave adventurers fought against terrible creatures, waiting for the great treasures that would be his should they fall. Silverwing's fingers drummed lightly on the wooden box before him as the ranger lost himself in thought.

Boremac's reaction was immediate and abrupt. "Drink, wench! Get over here and bring my friend a mug! What kind of place is this where man has to lose himself in thought, instead of drink? Come on and be quick lest old sorrows take his tongue before we can drown them!"

The barmaid bringing the ranger's drink took her time going to get a mug of stout ale. Something appeared to be in the works as the first server passed a mug intended for Silverwing to one of the other barmaids. A decidedly unpleasant smirk appeared on the new server's full lips as her eyes met those of the rogue, and Boremac could not help but think he should remember her. The mug sloshed as she slammed it on the table near Boremac's hand, a bit too near, he thought. "Your friend been right nice to be serving. You, we could do without. Don't go making trouble for yourself. You'll find you and that mouth of yours out the door before you can wiggle that tongue." Her finger was wagging in time as she spoke, a sneer bending her lips. "Do not go thinking I don't remember the last time you was here, Boremac. You best tip better this time, you rotten scoundrel, and be glad me sister isn't working."

Boremac was caught off guard by her words, but not for long. He had thought there was something familiar about her face. "Aye, I see the resemblance now. She was a fair one, to be sure, with quick hands." The rogue smiled, lost in memories of his previous visit. The barmaid returned his grin with an innocent upturn of her own mouth. Her hand swept tightly in a practiced motion, raising a warm welt on his cheek.

"Red suits you, Boremac." She tapped his bald head as she spoke, admiring her hand-print where she had slapped him. "It wasn't my sister that you gave that pitiful purse, it was me. All she got was the pleasure of your company." The barmaid turned on her heel with a quick, "begging your pardon, sir," to Master Silverwing as she moved to see the other patrons. A low rumble of laughter coursed through the tavern, with a number of patrons rubbing their cheeks in sympathy, as she sauntered away.

Boremac's features reddened deeply as she moved away from their table, as if to disguise the new mark on his cheek. "A man meets all sorts of lasses when he gets in his cups. Seems I made quite an impression on two of the ladies of this house last time I passed through."

Silverwing cocked an amused eyebrow at the thief. "Well, it would appear age has not affected your abilities in this area, at least. Pity the drink clouded your mind or you would have remembered her sooner. You might have saved your pride a wound, at least."

The rogue rubbed the marked side of his face gently. He was grinning as the thief realized Silverwing's mistake. "I think you read too much in the lady's words. She came upon her sister and me while we were sharing some time." Boremac dragged his hand over his face as if trying to clear the memory of some unpleasantness. "The tumble she gave me was not of the same kind as her sister, if you follow. She caught me unaware with a clubbing and when I came to consciousness, half my gear and all my coins were gone! I later learned that the lady who had shared my bed was supposed to be wed soon to a noble of some wealth. Well, needless to say, rumors of her involvement with myself and some other patrons were not well-received by her suitor, despite his desire for her hand."

"Sounds like she is still serving tavern patrons. You probably saved the man trouble down the road."

"That's the rub, Ranger! I tried to explain that to the men he sent around to collect me, but they were hearing none of it. That sot was really taken with her. Can't say I blame him. She was definitely not hard on the eyes." Boremac rubbed his shoulder as if tending to an old wound just remembered. "Took me a time to heal up after that trouble. Good to know he left her to tend her own bed, so to speak, for all the suffering I had on her account."

"It is a shame you haven't learned anything from borrowing others' troubles, though I should be glad of that to some extent." Silverwing lowered his eyes to the case in front of him. "Let us tip our mug to Master Firebeard, the greatest smith in all the lands, and take a look at what his latest labors have wrought."

The two men clinked their mugs in honor and at last Master Silverwing revealed the contents of the long wooden case. The twin swords, masterfully crafted works of the descendant of the original smith who served the Knights of the Golden Dragon so skillfully, were no surprise. Their keen edges and glimmering hilts had been restored to the condition they had possessed when these weapons first left the forge. The additional space within the case was nearly full with other gifts as well. There was a fine leather quiver nearly filled with arrows that a first glance seemed unremarkable, though the nocks were formed of some metal unknown to Boremac. The rogue noted the fletching as Master Silverwing drew his fingers lightly across each bit of feather. The Ranger drew forth one of the arrows and admired the workmanship of the shaft and point. "Magnificent work! He once again combines form and function as art in order to maximize potential."

Boremac looked at the arrow, wondering what was so special about it. "Forgive me, Ranger, but it's an arrow."

"Yes, a wasp and a bee are both insects with wings and stingers, but the wasp brings the anger of its sting many times while the bee may strike but once. These fine arrows are wasps, my friend, and are a most damaging kind to the demons that roam these lands." Silverwing handed one of the arrows across the table to the rogue. "See the twisted head? The Smith has grooved them slightly so they bite deep. These are no ordinary metal tips. They are silver and steel alloy, not unlike the blade of my sword."

"Seems to be a waste of precious metal to me." Boremac could admire the penetration potential of the points but saw little use of the softer silver alloy.

"Yes, I can see that it would be to one unfamiliar with battling demons. Silver weapons are the most potent against the inhabitants of the Abyss. Mere contact with unblessed silver boils the blood in their earthly forms. Metal that has felt the infusion of the light carries a much greater threat, as you witnessed in the arena where Gregor faced the Raukohaun. No such creature can stand before the power of the God of Light, or weapons suffused with said power."

"So it was the blessing of the blade Gregor carried that destroyed the creature?" Boremac puzzled over the memory briefly. "That would explain why the beast took no care in its attacks, even as Gregor carved away its head."

"The demonic creatures that managed to infest this land fear nothing within it, even the weapons that can destroy the shells they possess here. The only thing they really fear is failure to cause appropriate amounts of chaos while they are here. Lower demons answer to greater powers in the Abyss. My guess would be that the Raukohaun that faced Gregor and failed to destroy him has had his form reduced in the Abyss to that of an imp. The lords of the Abyss are not nearly as forgiving as the God of Light and the Goddess of the Land." Master Silverwing's features darkened. Memories of death flooded his mind. The Golden Dragon's history was tainted by failures of this kind, though they were rare. "I have seen brave knights torn asunder by evil that you could not imagine, Boremac. Skill at arms is no measure against demon kind where faith lacks. I hope the greatest evils you face are those of mortal men."

Boremac returned Silverwing's stark look with deep concentration painting his own features. "The evil of mankind is trouble enough for me. I have encountered it often in my line of work. It is the nature of the business, you might say. I can't help but think my luck in the past brought me to this present." Boremac stared intently into the depths of the ranger's eyes, the rogue's hands clasped as if in prayer before him. "You believe what you like, Silverwing, but the time among the priests taught me a bit about myself. Can't say I am proud of my past. I look to a different future now."

"It is not my place, nor my intention, to judge you. I will not bind you to any path. You may go as you please with the blessing of the God of Light for your service, if you choose." Silverwing's eyes dropped to the contents of the case, hidden from the rogue by the broad wooden lid. "Master Firebeard seems to think there is work for you in service of the God of Light, judging from the other items he sent."

Boremac cocked an eyebrow at the ranger's words. "Master Firebeard must have been very productive to take my needs into account. We hardly spoke and he made no mention of anything in the case for me when I took possession of it."

"Well, a man of your questionable nature would have been hard-pressed to deliver the case without opening it if you knew its contents. Certainly you can understand his desire to speed delivery without any unnecessary complications." The ranger grinned at his own words, softening the affront to the thief. "He does not know you nearly as well as I do, though the items he forged show he is not against you, at least."

Boremac looked hungrily at the case's open lid, making no attempt to disguise his interest. "I think you need to let me know what you're asking of me before I go taking gifts from strangers. No doubt the price of the items within will be paid in full for the trouble bearing them brings me. Since we met, I have not had the chance to suffer from boredom in pursuit of your labors."

"I cannot deny the truth of that. You have gone well beyond the limits of your nature. The task before you is the same as it has been since you left for Nactium. Wait here for Gregor and gather what information you can about the powers that move against him. Your knowledge of the priests working to undo him at his weapons trial will no doubt prove invaluable. The Order the Crimson Night obviously play some role in recent events. Their desire to acquire the broken blade that Gregor carries is strange. The blade would serve them no purpose if they are consorting with demon kind."

"What is it that makes the blade so important anyway?" Boremac had thought about the little information concerning the Order of the Crimson Night and could find no connection.

"It is half of the sacred sword always carried by the leader of the Golden Dragon. It was broken in the body of the last remaining leader of our order, Lord Clamine. Gregor witnessed the Tharnorsa, who killed Lord Clamine, wield the blade against our old leader as if the God of Light had stripped the sword of its power. The hilt disappeared with the demon when Lord Clamine gave up his body to save Gregor." Master Silverwing frowned deep in thought for a moment before continuing. "I know of nothing in my experience that would allow such a demon to wield the weapon. It is terrible to think that such a force exists. Even an Abysmal leader of demon kind should have been dismissed from mere contact with that sword. It has been passed from one leader of the Knights to the next for 400 years and never has it failed, until now."

Boremac pointed at the ranger. "Who are you?" It seemed a simple question that should have had a simple answer. The rogue felt he knew but he wanted to be sure who this man was before he willingly pledged his life.

"I am the last Knight of the Golden Dragon, save Gregor, Once the chosen archer and faithful servant of the God of Light." Lord Silverwing thought that would be obvious to one as observant as the thief had proven himself to be. "We were broken apart when our Captain failed in his faith many years ago. Lord Clamine, the

Knight who gave his life to save Gregor's, would have rebuilt the order, given time. We both assumed there was time and we followed the paths laid before us in service to our God. Often I have questioned the wisdom of our parting, I left to learn the ways of the Goddess and Lord Clamine established the Knights of Bella Grey."

Boremac brought his hands together once more, as if in prayer. If he were to serve the God of Light, he needed to understand why. "There is a good reason to question the logic of the God you serve. Faith is one thing; foolhardy risk with little profit is another entirely. I have relied on luck and skill with a sure gain in sight, but what you're asking of me surely holds only death as it's reward. A blessed soul parted from a sinful body is still a fate that holds little value for me."

"You are not bound in body or spirit, master thief. The God of Light only offers the path, our God does not force you to follow it." Lord Silverwing reached into the case, placing two daggers and a belt of throwing blades before the rogue. "These are one path. You may choose to take these gifts and go. Master Firebeard had some insight into your nature, judging from the arms I lay before you now." Four long hilts protruded from the belt and all of the hilts were intricately carved in a fashion Boremac felt was familiar, but he could not immediately place the runes. The two daggers were also decorated with the same runic symbols, carved into gilded grips. The blades of the daggers were formed of the same metal gracing the tips of the arrows that the master smith had made for the ranger. The daggers' hilts were mirror images of the hilts of the throwing daggers in the belt, except for the distinctive pommels that gave rise to Lord Silverwing's rub concerning the master smith's thoughts on Boremac.

Boremac had to smile in spite of the reference the pommels of the daggers conveyed. He ran his fingers over the small heads in appreciation of the workmanship, admiring the smith's jest at his expense. "Indeed, he appears to know more of me than his limited exposure would allow. I think Father Oregeth might have played some part in these little faces." The pommels were carved in the form of two tiny jesters' heads with the three-pronged caps favored by court fools. One bore a broad smile, while its companion possessed the exaggerated frown of one conveying deep dramatic sadness. Each tip of the hat's ears on the miniature fool's heads held a different tiny symbol. The sides were tipped with a tiny moon and sun opposite each other, while the center held a slightly larger star-burst shape with small spikes coming out as if it were glittering. "Yes, I am a fool to take the path laid so neatly before me, but what is the meaning of the symbols on the tiny hats?"

Lord Silverwing laughed openly at the inquiry. "I would think it was obvious! Those who choose to serve the God of Light are watched over by him day and night. You are right to assume that Father Oregeth had some role to play in their design. The runes are ancient carvings dating to the first Communion of the first priest called to the God's service. You are honored. I think the fools show Father Oregeth's sense of humor as well as Master Firebeard's desire to make the weapons unique to you. The good Father was not always the leader of the God of Light's faith and much of his wisdom comes in the form of a light heart in even the darkest times." Boremac thoughts were lightened by the knight's laughter. He placed his own worn blades on the table and sheathed the blessed daggers at his sides. The rogue drew one of the balanced daggers from the belt alongside the other that had served him so well. "Is there some ritual to be performed now that it seems I am to join this foolish enterprise?"

"You have completed the test set before you and in doing so have proven your worth. There is no need of Communion for you. Only those chosen to bear the burden of faith and carry the light into the darkest places must seek the touch of the God of Light." Lord Silverwing ended their time abruptly, rising from the table and beckoning Boremac to do the same. The rogue rose and secured the belt of throwing knives to his waist. "I will be leaving soon. You will stay within Zanthfar and await Gregor's arrival."

Boremac's curiosity pushed him to keep the knight a bit longer. "Two questions I have for you, though one might seem a simple boast. Why would I have need of so many throwing daggers? One has always been ample in the past. More importantly, what makes you think Gregor can make the journey here safely? He has increased his skills since he faced the assassins on the road to Traveflor, but I doubt he would pose much challenge to assassins of the Black Hand if they were to find him alone."

A strange smile bent the knight's lips before he replied. "I will answer the second question first. He will leave Nactium alone, but the God of Light, who has prepared his path as well, guides him. Another will aid him should such aid be required. There is another power that is served by his destiny. The Goddess will keep him as she sees fit." The Ranger motioned toward the belt of throwing daggers as Boremac reflexively placed his hands protectively on his new implements. "I trust you have mastered your foes in the past before releasing the single dagger you possessed. Service to the God of Light is not always so readily prepared for, except to keep faith that the one that watches over you will deliver you from evils. I cannot say where your path may lead, but I am certain you will find use for all your skills, all your luck, and doubtless all your weapons."

Boremac wondered once more at the wisdom in following this man. Faith in powers outside his own was not something he had experience with, and despite his time in the Temple, it was not something on which he was ready to rely. Boremac shrugged and turned to go, somewhat reassured that his luck would carry him through if the God of Light should forget which side the thief was on.

10

Destinies Intertwined

"Yes, I miss him too but there is nothing to be done about it."
Tana patted Fang lightly on her head as the pair sat near the
campfire. They were well into their month-long journey to the grove
of druids that watched over the wild lands near Zanthfar. Tana had
regretted missing Gregor's weapons trial but she had duties of her
own to attend. Word had come to her mother's grove that all
available followers of the Goddess were being sent to Zanthfar. The
creatures within the lands had grown progressively more
aggressive, and strange unnatural predators were being reported as
well. Great horned bears and massive wolves with elongated fangs,
clearly outside the Goddess of nature's realm of creation, had been
wreaking havoc among the villages scattered throughout the wilds.
The Lord of the local lands had sent his militia into the woods to
investigate and, after much loss of life, the few creatures they were
able to slay had been delivered to the druids for study. Fear held
sway over the villagers, and the people within Zanthfar, as one of
the largest river-bound cities leading to the sea, were beginning to
feel the loss of grain and fresh meat from the outlying settlements.
The Lord's personal coffers were being drained with the cost of
mercenaries hired to secure passage of the trade flowing into the city
gates.

Time had passed quickly, too quickly for Gregor to feel he had learned enough from the library. There was nothing to be done about it. And truth be told he had studied the demonic forces as completely as he could. The holy warrior had gained many insights into the one called Tur'morival, though what could have driven a priest so committed to his faith and his brothers so far from the God of Light was still a mystery. His journal gave little meaning to the fall from grace, and Tur'morival seemed so bent on his own path to destruction that the death of the acolyte at his hands appeared to have made no impression on him at all. What wicked taint could drive a man to such madness? Gregor was certain Tur'morival was driven insane by the very powers he proclaimed to have learned to control.

The creatures of the Abyss were ruled by chaos and madness, that much Gregor was sure of, and in that lay their greatest weakness. Demons were so driven to cause destruction and havoc that they felt no remorse. There was no honor, nor even a hint of organization, in the actions of such creatures. They gave their power over readily enough to those who foolishly summoned them to this world, all the time seeking to break free of the bonds of their masters. Gregor could not fathom the minds of those sorcerers who would risk their lives, and worse still, their souls, to bargain with the infernal creatures.

Tur'morival had to be the one responsible for the demons that had infested the home of the Knights of Bella Grey, of that Gregor was certain. No other being could have harnessed such power and so willfully sought the destruction of the knights Gregor had served. Why? It did not make any sense. The Knights were committed to peace. There had been no open effort by Lord Clamine to rebuild the Knights of the Golden Dragon, and those warriors who chose to train with him and the small group of standing regulars with him were dispersed to the four winds once they were considered capable. They kept the roads safe within their homelands, using the knowledge they had gained and the aid of the local priests to combat infrequent incursions by Abysmal evils. The Knights of Bella Grey did not even maintain an altar to the God of Light within their stronghold. The sanctuary there was open to the practice and worship of all faiths of the training Knights. The answer to his questions was right in front of him; Gregor was sure if he had more time he could find it. Unfortunately, his time within the great shelves of books was over.

Father Oregeth personally came to escort Gregor from the tomes collected for demonic research. "Gregor, you have devoted yourself to these books long enough, and it is time for you to make the last step into the light of our God." Gregor could not help but sense there was sadness in the Father's tone despite his gentle smile. "You will take your Vigil with the God of Light tonight in the Great Temple. I have no doubt our Master will favor you and elevate you to knighthood. Master Firebeard has fashioned a wondrous suit of plate mail for you for your communion that will serve you well in your travels as a symbol of your rank. The brothers and sisters of the Temple, and throughout the lands in service to our God, look forward to His divine grace accepting you into the place that is your destiny."

Gregor accepted the words though his mind was clouded with his own thoughts. "I accept the call and welcome it. Only by moving forward in faith can I accomplish the deeds that the God of Light has had the wisdom to set before me. Will I be alone in the Vigil, Father Oregeth?"

Father Oregeth smiled at the earnest question as if he had anticipated it. "No, my son, you will not be alone in the Vigil and you will truly never be alone again though no footsteps will mark the passage of the company you keep. Three have been chosen to witness your induction into knighthood. I believe you will be pleased with my selections. Come to the main Temple with me where you are to make your communion. The others await our arrival."

Gregor's heart leaped at the sight of the three that waited near the altar. Joy overtook his good sense as he spread his arms wide to embrace the three figures as one. "You are alive! God of Light be blessed and save us all, you are alive!" Father Wallin chortled at Gregor's display and announcement of the obvious while Sister Noria and Brother Findal flushed deeply at the open affection. "You slept so deeply. Forgive me for not visiting you. I've been so caught up in my own studies. It is a sin that I was not present when you arose." Gregor dropped his hands to his side and stepped back as he lowered his chin, clearly ashamed for forgetting his friends. "I beg your forgiveness. I cannot believe I've been so poor a servant to you in your time of need."

Father Wallin was the first to speak, causing Gregor's eyes to meet his own. "There is nothing to forgive, my son. You were doing what you must to prepare. Only death would have kept me from witnessing this day, and the God of Light has more time allotted for me yet." Brother Findal and Sister Noria nodded their agreement. "Nothing you could have done anyway, Gregor. The priests in the infirmary kept us as comfortable as they could and prayers swept our unconscious forms day and night."

Brother Findal laughed now as he spoke. "We must have put quite a scare into them. When we did awaken, they were clucking around us like mother hens. I doubt you could have seen us anyway with the crowds of brothers and sisters coming in constantly to see if we were really awake."

"I was longing for my staff to sweep them away so that we could come to you, but Father Oregeth forbade it. He said we needed to rest so we would be ready for the Vigil." Sister Noria did appear ill at ease without her trusted staff.

Father Wallin's face became serious as he looked at the holy warrior before him. "I would be honored to suit you personally for the vigil if you would allow me, Gregor. Master Firebeard has outdone himself in fashioning the armor that you are to wear, though I do not envy anyone kneeling in it for the hours of the night to come."

Gregor answered without a moment's hesitation. "The honor would be mine, Father." He lowered himself to his knees before the companions he had thought were lost.

Father Oregeth touched the bowed figure, bringing Gregor again to his feet. "Make ready and prepare your body and soul for the Vigil. Father Wallin will prove an appropriate guide. He has prepared many that have come before you. Brother Findal and Sister Noria, prepare the altar. Gregor, I look forward to seeing the Knight you have become in the morning. There will be a great feast to celebrate your becoming a Knight of the Golden Dragon in the main Hall tomorrow. It has been too long since such a celebration has taken place, but I have faith it will not be the last."

Father Wallin presented the plate mail with the grace and respect befitting the master smith that had fashioned it. The armor shone like a glimmering sun in the candlelit quarters where it rested on a post in the center of the room. Gregor's time as a weapons page gave him a full appreciation of the steel plates intricately layered that would cover him from shoulder to boot. Master Firebeard had duplicated the twisted dragons that formed the hilts of the swords of the Knights of the Golden Dragon, the heads forming a "T" at the breastplate under the chin guard. The shoulder guard at the right was adorned with a black sun formed of the same material as his personal blade, and a full moon made of highly polished silver shimmered at the left shoulder guard. The center held a shining golden orb that radiated small slivers of light, slender fingers of gold, that at the bottom of the orb almost touched the heads of the dragons carved below them. The spine of the armor held the broken blade that was Gregor's charge in a gilded sheath befitting its importance. As Father Wallin dressed him in the armor, Gregor noted it was much lighter than he would have expected. He flexed his metal gloves easily and was able to bend the elbows and knees unimpeded. The plates allowed for a certain amount of air to pass through them as he moved around the room and the supple leather straps that held the plates in place allowed him to move as fluidly as if he wore no armor at all. Gregor found the arming doublet beneath the armor was a thin but sturdy material unlike any he had ever felt, and said as much to Father Wallin.

Father Wallin laughed at Gregor's observation before forming a delicate reply regarding the nature of the cloth. "Few men ever feel the touch of such fine linens without the leave of a noble born woman. The arming doublet is made of silks of the highest quality. Air must pass freely through the cloth to cool the skin it protects. You see, Gregor, a woman of quality simply cannot sweat. You will find this particular silk cloth does not tear easily, which is why the noble houses that prize the wedding dresses made of it are able to pass them from one bride to the next. The men of nobility are not known for their patience after a long courtship and a trying wedding. Gowns of this material enclose the treasures of the bride, much like the complex locks that protect the valuables of the noble families in their vaults, serving to dampen the fires of men and teach them appreciation for the gifts women bestow."

Gregor turned crimson as the question he posed to Father Wallin rushed past his lips. "Are Knights in the service of the God of Light allowed to wed?" He bowed his head even as his hand moved to touch the heart that beat rapidly beneath his breastplate.

Father Wallin weighed his answer to the question carefully before replying. He was certain there was more than idle curiosity at work. He thought to himself that young men were incorrigible. "It is an interesting inquiry for one about to become a Knight, Master Gregor, and unexpected to say the least. The holy warriors are not restricted from taking a mate should they choose to do so, though it is a rare occurrence. Men and women who serve the various Gods and Goddesses as weapon's bearers have wed one another, and even taken partners outside the orders they serve. It is a rare companion that can devote their life to those who stand so close to death so often. More often than not the one who would wed the servant of the God of Light suffers long years of anguish until the object of their affection retires, or passes into their final rest." Father Wallin's voice took on a solemn tone that seemed out of place with his nature. "It is not a burden one should place on those whom we might love without much meditation."

Gregor brought his eyes to meet Father Wallin's and replied simply. "Yes, Father Wallin."

"Do not trouble yourself with thoughts of what may be, Master Gregor. The time at hand should be your focus, and there is much you need to know. My long sleep was not a peaceful one, and I fear it is my duty to share knowledge of my dark dreams without the benefit of wisdom. A great demon is at the heart of the evil that has infected this land. This particular demonic power is rarely encountered within this world without being summoned, and only the most powerful summoners know the means to control one, though control is a strong word in this case. You encountered one of the Tharnorsa as a weapons page. It set you on the path that brought you to us. These terrible demons are feared even in the Abyss for their limitless cruelty and cunning." Father Wallin dabbed sweat from his forehead before continuing. "The Tharnorsa appeared to me as I slept, telling me of things to come. Terrible things, Gregor, where the very gates of the Abyss opened into the lands, and demons of every sort poured into the world. It knew you, Gregor. I am almost certain it was the one you encountered so long ago, and there is something else. It was not alone. A robed figure stood near, surrounded by the fires and bloody mists that emanated from the demon. I felt as though I should know the figure but..."

Gregor knew the figure and could hold his tongue no longer. "Tur'morival is the name of that escapes you, Father Wallin. The priests believe the leader of the Order of the Crimson Night is no more, long since dead due to the passage of years. I know he is not. I, too, encountered him in the realm of dreams. He is a man no more, though I cannot say what he has become."

Shock silenced Father Wallin for a moment as he considered Gregor's words. "Why would even a fallen father of the God of Light seek to doom his soul and the lands which he sought to protect? Why would he seek to bring the Crimson Night that was foretold to pass? What could he possibly hope to gain? Is he mad?"

"Only he knows the answer to those questions. I have every intention of finding him to stop whatever it is he thinks he is planning. I can only hope that the demon aiding him is the one responsible for the slaying of the Knights I served. It will feel the full wrath of my heart and purity of my soul. I promise you this, Father Wallin; the demon will not come to this world again, even if I have to follow it into the Abyss to destroy it."

***

The two great wolves ran through the wood taken by the will of the hunt. Prey was near and though there was hunger in the pair, there were two individual passions that drove the wolves; one propelled by feral instinct and the other by a need for the freedom of the animal form. Fang and Tana had hunted together often since their lives interlaced so long ago, but somehow this time was different for the huntress. She had taken to the trees of the unknown forest with Fang to disrobe and change into the form of the animal Tana called kin, as much to escape the press of their journey as to leave the thoughts that clouded her mind so much of late.

The Goddess she served gave little counsel despite the entreaties Tana voiced in prayer. She grew more certain of the link that bound her to Gregor with each passing day. Tana feared for the innocence the young warrior possessed. One could not be thrust into the world and not be corrupted by the forces that surrounded them, even in the sanctuary of the Temple of Light. Evil of many forms tainted the natural places and the cities were filled with dubious men at the best of times. These were not the best of times. Gregor's simple nature had awakened desire in her to protect him, and she felt the loss of his company with so great a distance between them. There was another feeling her travel down the road to Zanthfar had brought to the surface, one Tana could no longer brush away. She felt the pull of desire for the man he was to become.

Scents and sounds of the deer the pair tracked drove thought from Tana's mind. She gave herself to the hunt and kept pace with Fang as the two wolves neared the kill. Instinct was so much simpler to understand than emotion.

Fang tore at the deer, eating her fill of the first fresh meat she had taken in quite some time. Her mistress was captured by the fire before her, staring into the dancing flames, deep in thought. She was enveloped in the sounds of the forest as her mind kept taking her to the first time she had encountered Gregor, long before the careless swordsman had entered her home.

The dream had been as real as the flames that flickered before her now, though the place she had found herself in had been very different. She was trapped in a rocky valley shadowed by two great mountains. Little vegetation was visible, and what trees and grasses there were struggled to retain their normal forms. The sparse growths were twisted by a pervasive evil that hung over the landscape. Tana felt weaker with each breath of tainted air that stank of sulfur and brimstone. She stared into the darkness where the valley's entrance was lost around a natural bend in the rock, sensing more than seeing the vicious forms that would soon enter the narrow stretch of land where Tana found herself.

The swordsman had appeared halfway down the rocky wall of the cliff to Tana's right, kneeling on one knee with his head bowed and a black blade held out before him. The dim light of the valley made the glowing weapon all the more remarkable, burning away the darkness near the man and making his plated armor glow. Gregor had lifted his head and pointed the sword to something behind Tana, nodding as he looked beyond her. Tana tore her gaze away from the warrior to see what he was acknowledging. The avatar behind her was as wide as the valley and as tall as the mountains it floated between. The Goddess of Nature extended her arms as Tana watched, restoring the plant life below her outstretched hands. The avatar nodded to Gregor and then to Tana as the druid huntress knelt to honor the vision. Tana had no fear as

156

the avatar disappeared, and she turned to meet the creatures she knew would flow out of the darkness in moments.

The holy warrior appeared at her side. "We must not fail." The words were the last thing she had remembered before Tana had awakened from the dream, and she had known Gregor was that the warrior the first time he spoke. Tana had not been able to decipher the vision despite turning it over in her head often, but she knew in time they would stand together in battle. Their destinies were intertwined and victory would be a matter of faith.

**

Gregor knelt before the great altar in the main Temple, clearing his mind of all thought. He offered up prayers as instructed by Father Wallin and focused on opening his body and spirit to communion with the God of Light. A multitude of candles drove the shadows from the circle of light in which he knelt, illuminating the form of the God he served that towered over the altar. Gregor gazed openly upward into the stone eyes of the statue that seemed to contemplate the faithful warrior. He could not help feeling his worth was being measured as the words of faith and commitment passed his lips.

Hours passed before the final judgment of the God of Light came. Gregor felt an undeniable force draw him to his feet as the statue before him was enveloped in light, pushing away even the glow of the flickering candles surrounded him. Father Wallin had prepared the warrior for this moment, and Gregor unsheathed the black blade of Elenondo, bringing it up pointing it up pointed to the God of Light as he had been instructed. As if in answer to the gesture, light

157

poured from the statue's stony eyes and engulfed Gregor in divine power. Nothing could have prepared the warrior for the sensations that flooded into him as the God of Light set his entire being aflame with energy. There was no pain, only the complete understanding of the divine strength of the God that had chosen him. Gregor knew now that he had been chosen to serve the light long before he understood such a faith even existed. A final surge of divine power ignited his sword, much as it had done in the arena. When the light diminished, runes remained near the base of the blade on either side of its flat surface. Gregor stared at the markings, at a loss for comprehension.

"You are complete, Master Gregor, and the God of Light has titled you well." Father Wallin looked at the runes carved into the blade of the knight's sword. "The markings are an ancient tongue that is all but forgotten, except for those of us who serve and study within the great library. They spell Onmea, the Sword of Light, and that is how you shall be known. Lord Gregor Light-sword, I bow to the Knight of the Golden Dragon."

11

Meetings

The last days of the journey had been uneventful as Tana and Fang neared Zanthfar. The road was well patrolled several days' march from the main city and wooden towers manned by standing garrisons dotted the road. Tana encountered frequent patrols of well-mannered soldiers that kept merchants and travelers safe as they neared the city. These men and women carried stories of orc raiding parties that appeared to have driven the rogues and bandits from their usual hunting areas. The soldiers were not pleased by this new development, but they had been able to kill or drive away the new threat so far. Each of the orc parties was led by a creature similar to the one Tana had encountered in her own forest, and it was these beasts that had caused the most loss of life among the travelers and patrols. The beasts could not be captured and there were no remains when they were killed, so the soldiers were at as much of a loss as Tana to determine their origin. All of the roads that led into Zanthfar were plagued by these frequent attacks and the war party sent out by the city to locate their source had not returned.

The pair had bypassed the city to take the more direct path to the Grove that oversaw the wild lands of Zanthfar. The forests surrounding the central meeting place were full of makeshift camps, and more rangers and druids of the Goddess were arriving daily. Tana made her presence known to the high Druids overseeing the gathering and offered what services she had to provide food and shelter for the multitudes. Mithirina, the leader of the Grove, assured her that the villagers protected near the Grove had provided for the gathering long before the calling went out, and all knew the true bounty of the Goddess. "You should take counsel with your brothers and sisters. We shall share our knowledge soon and we must all learn what we can as the rest of those sent for arrive. I imagine there are many here you have not seen for some time. Share the peace of this Grove and rest while there is still an opportunity."

Tana moved through the scattered camps and was warmly greeted by strangers and old friends alike. The forest dwellers shared stories similar to Tana's own, colored by their perception and the lands from which they had come. Tana noted the men and women who protected the mountainous northern lands had been sorely tested with the incursion of the brutal orc tribes. These humanoids, though primitive and savage, had never been a direct threat to the mining camps located throughout the rocky terrain until recently. Some orc groups had even taken slaves and begun extracting ores from the tunnels. Rangers who tracked the ore laden caravans of these orcs noted that they were moving into the barren wastes that were shunned by the hardiest plant and animal life. They could not fathom what power could coordinate such organized movement among the savages. The beasts of burden that were loaded with the bounty were a mystery in themselves. "Lizards wit' thick 'ides an' t'ree pair of legs endin' in clawed feet. Th' creatures be as long as two horses an' stand 'alf th' height of a man. Th' beasts were driven forward by th' constant crack of a t'ree-pronged barbed whip wielded by 'andlers that took their lives into their 'ands with every step. Th' lizards seem to 'ave little need o' food. Their meals are comprised of slaves brought for that purpose, or th' corpses of their orc 'andlers that are caught nappin'." The mountain ranger describing the lizards took a moment to poke casually at the fire before him. "They kill 'em orcs when they can and, more often than not, th' lizards drag off th' wounded ones after a battle before fleein' deeper into th' mountains. Makes it difficult ta interrogate th' bastards when th' wounded are taken by their own pets."

"They might have been trained that way." Tana interjected the thought that seemed to be shared by many of the others around the fire. Nods of agreement were seen as the ranger made to answer.

He shook his head before replying, his gruff voice tainted by despair more than a desire to disagree. "These be sad times when even th' barbarian orc tribes would rather be ate alive than caught. It mus' be sumthin' terrible that would make any creature choose death from th' rippin' jaws of one of those lizards over th' punishment of their master. Dark times."

***

Two days after Tana had arrived, a gathering of all those assembled was held. The sheer number of people that had come made it necessary to send various animal companions away, and still the open center of the Grove was filled with tight groups of rangers and druids from all across the lands. Each group was notable by both the markings on their armor and the various leathers that composed said protections. Tana recognized many of the groups from her studies but, even among her peers, there were markings that predated written languages; ancient tongues and insignias unknowable to outsiders. Every size and shape of man and woman was represented, from the thin delicate tree dwellers of the great forest, rumored to have distant connections to the long forgotten elves responsible for training and educating the earliest druids, to the stout, broad men and women who watched over the deepest caves and tunnels that wound through the mountainous areas.

Tana had never seen the tree dwellers before though she had heard stories of them as a child. Many simple people thought of them as fey creatures born from the hearts of great old trees. Even other rangers and druids rarely saw them, and Tana could easily understand the mysticism that surrounded these people as she looked at their delicate features and the gentle point of their ears, so like the red foxes'. Each of the three that had come had long flowing hair with intricate braids held by links of thin vines and leaves. The forest they called home was an ancient one, full of creatures considered rare and magical, (that no hunter dared enter) Anyone seeking to pillage that bounty would rarely escape the creatures within, and never made it from the wood without the aid of its protectors.

The mountain people were another story. They were well respected among the miners they kept safe. Gifts of strong drink and fine mining tools were often left for them in tribute before ore was drawn from a new shaft. These mountain rangers often set markings for the miners to guide their picks and keep them from dangers like faults in the stone and hidden underground riverbeds that could collapse tunnels on the unwary. Some of the hardiest mountain people even took brides from the family they protected, and this was considered a high honor for the family of the lass in question. The miners prospered, and the mountain rangers and druids kept their numbers growing, which was crucial in light of the latest developments. Despite the welcoming nature of the rocky mountains' protectors, Tana found their stories the most terrible. It was their people who suffered the most at the hands of these new threats, and there was no end in sight.

Mithirina brought her hands up to quiet the murmuring gathering, and silence, broken only by bird songs, enveloped the Grove. "Let me start by thanking all of you who have come. The numbers who have responded to the calling far exceed our greatest hopes. We have much to review with you, and there is much to accomplish before the light of the sun passes away today. There are a few I wish to introduce before going any further. The sturdy gentleman to my left is Fasurel Stonecutter, a man well known to the people who call the mountains to the north home." Several cheers broke from the crowd as Fasurel raised a rough, callused hand in greeting. "His knowledge of the great mountains of his people is matched only by his bravery when defending them. Mistress Alunia joins us from the ancient forest to the east. As many of you know, the Ardataure peoples keep constant vigil over the mystic beasts within their forest, creatures that once roamed all these lands in the ancient times. Mistress Alunia's sharp eyes have already brought us much information about the problems in the wild lands where this Grove makes its home. Last, I present to you, Lord Galant Silverwing, ranger, protector, and the last Knight of the Golden Dragon. This man dedicated his life to the destruction of all manner of evil forces throughout these lands before being called as a ranger of the Goddess we all serve. He is a servant of two faiths, a bridge between the natural and the civilized world. Each of these three representatives brings their special gifts to us, and hopes that we can together find a way to end the troubles that have come to our lands."

The lead druid paused for the spontaneous applause that could not be contained. Tana was shocked at the sight of Master Silverwing standing among the various people's leaders. His appearance as the representative of the civilized human settlements, and being noted as a bridge between the keepers of nature and the same, would have been curious enough when Tana considered what she knew of the man. It seemed to Tana that Master Silverwing had long ago turned his efforts to the protection of his remaining brothers in arms and away from the general population. His appearance was surprising enough, but the twin blades hanging at his sides brought up a number of other questions. These were the twin blades which Gregor had put into Master Firebeard's care, showing signs of work that could only be attributed to him as they glowed in the sunlight, fully restored. The myriad questions in her mind would have to wait, and with effort Tana pushed back the two most immediate ones: where was Gregor and was he safe?

"We have become aware that the curse shrouding this wild land is a disease that has spread to all corners of our world. There is still little information to illuminate how or why these things have come to pass, but I wish to share what we do know." Mithirina waited for silence to retake the Grove before continuing, "Many of you here have noted the appearance of the demon blood orcs, or Nilorque as they are called, leading aggressive bands of raiding parties into the lands of men. Until recently the orcs were a minimal nuisance easily dealt with by the militia of the cities, requiring no intervention from the peoples that protect the wilds. The Nilorque have changed that, and we fear that they are only the outward sign of a much greater evil. Mistress Alunia will now share her observations since arriving here."

The Ardataure stepped forward, speaking in a light voice that carried over the Grove. "Many of you know the border plains in this area are home to the largest concentration of orc tribes in the lands. The hardy wild men and women who share hunting grounds with these barbaric tribes have always formed a buffer between the settled lands and the plains, even trading with the more civilized orc tribes. Nilorque, who have never in the past been encountered more than one at a time, have begun entering the plains areas in groups as large as twenty within the past few months. They are strong orc warriors imbued with power by their tribal shaman before taking on the role as chieftain in a group, and they have steadily grown more powerful than has been witnessed in the past. Something is driving them to bring together their tribes, testing the strength of this new unification with the massacre of human tribal groups also living in the plains areas, wreaking havoc and causing bloodshed with no discernible pattern or reasoning. It is as if the Nilorque, previously only honored and recognized by their individual tribes for their battle prowess and hunting abilities, have somehow been called upon by some outside power. The seeds of power planted by their tribal shamans appear to have been manipulated and multiplied tenfold by this unknown power. We have reason to believe that the power in question is either a mage or priest of some great strength in this land, who has somehow managed to take control of a Tharnorsa from the Abyss itself. The Tharnorsa, a demon lord within the Abyss rarely encountered on this plane even in its incorporeal form, is for all appearances somehow in thrall to its summoner. Word has come from Lord Silverwing that brings us to this conclusion. Lord Silverwing?"

The knight stepped forward into the spot Mistress Alunia had left. "A student of mine, Master Gregor, was completing his training in Nactium at the Temple of Light with a weapons trial. It was a standard test of arms that all knights face, and the Governor was kind enough to allow the final test to be held in the arena of the city. A witness reported to me that during the melee, two priests of unknown faith took control of the arena and, though one was slain, a Raukohaun rose from the body as the other priest disappeared. The witness described the creature quite thoroughly. It was little more than a demon whelp, spawned of an unholy bond in the Abyss, but no less a demon that required very little of its summoners. Master Gregor was able to slay the beast, and faith prevented any further deaths in the arena. There were no protective symbols or circles noted in the arena itself, indicating the summoners had not prepared the arena grounds before the creature was brought forth. Such blatant use of the summoning magic with complete disregard for the safety of the summoners is unheard of even among those misguided souls who worship the creatures in the Abyss. Master Fasurel Stonecutter has made some troubling discoveries in the barren mountains near his home lands as well. Master Stonecutter, if you will."

Master Stonecutter stepped forward to relate the discoveries of his people. He was a short, sturdy man with long reddish hair drawn back in a rough braid. His face was dominated by a broad, grizzly red beard touched with gray. Large, piercing, ice blue eyes, clearly meant to see in the caves where light was sparse, appeared to be protected by eyebrows that stuck out like ledges over them. He surveyed the large crowd uncomfortably and then looked down at the handle of the pickax on which he rested his hands, as if it would provide a better audience.

"My people have experienced loss of lives and territory in huge amounts since these damned orc tribes started unitin' under one banner. I never seen them so organized. They are usin' beasts of burden that resemble our own companions, only a lot bigger and a lot meaner! Instead of jus' eatin' plants and small animals, these things are vicious meat eaters that'll turn on their own wounded and would just as soon tear apart their orc masters. Only a swift blow to th' skull will take th' fight out un th' creatures." Fasurel's eyes flashed as he brandished his pickax as if to drive home his point.

"So far th' orcs that have taken over mines have stayed up higher, and mostly to themselves, in th' lesser-used tunnels. A few of my brave brothers and sisters who watched these camps closely have survived to report. They've seen ore laden caravans headin' deeper into the mountains toward th' volcanic craters, where we got no interest in goin'. Our people explored them sometime in th' past, but they be too hot to mine. They found giant lizards, hearty mosses, and smaller cave dwellers that fed on th' mosses in some of th' cooler caves. Nothin' can live up on those fiery peaks." Fasurel looked up and across the crowd as he warmed to his subject, losing his shyness as he gave as much detail as he could.

"Someone or somethin' has found a way to breed a creature that can endure th' awful heat and carry great loads." He spat on the ground and continued. "We noticed that after some days th' minin' camps held by th' orcs stop producin' and th' caravans stopped as well. Th' orcs must've found a way to use th' creatures to tunnel deeper into th' mountains and make shafts comin' out closer to where they be taken th' ore, as we keep seeing orc drivers and lizards goin' in while only big huntin' and raidin' parties are comin' out. We tried to send in some trackers to find out where they be takin' th' ore but no one returned. We figure, with as much time has passed, we have to count them among our dead." Fasurel lowered his voice in obvious pain as he continued, "we pray their end was swift and th' Goddess showed them mercy in their passin'."

"We been trying to take some of th' orcs alive to question, but those damn lizards tear 'em apart before we can get to 'em. Soon as those lizards get loose and fill their bellies, they take off. I thank th' Goddess for that as their hides are so tough nothin' gets through 'em except for th' sharpest minin' picks!"

Suddenly realizing he was the center of attention, Fasurel blushed and looked at his feet again. "That's all I got." Master Stonecutter waved Mithirina forward while he moved back near the others. His withdrawal demonstrated such unexpected speed and agility that it drew a small ripple of laughter from the crowd.

Mithirina spoke almost immediately, as if to draw the attention from Fasurel, quieting the crowd. "Many have died to gather the knowledge these people bring to this gathering, and no doubt many more will sacrifice their lives before we are prepared to face the unknown evil that has come to this world. It falls to the protectors of man and beast alike to uncover the forces against which we stand. The council of few becomes the trial of many, which is why we have gathered you here. Drawn from different faiths, we must unite for the good of our lands and the peoples we serve. Many of you have protected these lands as individuals. That time is past. Before night comes, you will be brothers and sisters moving as one and guarding each other as we decipher the mystery set before us. Master Fasurel Stonecutter has spoken with many of you individually and chosen the most seasoned and gifted to travel into the barren lands of his home. The greatest responsibility will fall to this group of rangers and druids. We must know what evil has been sown in the mountains, no matter what the cost."

***

The deep red stone glowed in the Overseer's hand as he sat at his obsidian throne. He preferred the darkness of the sanctuary to remain unbroken but there was no way to block the glow of the orb when it was used. Tur'morival had sent the stone with the payment for Silverwing's death and insisted on using it for contacting the Overseer. The master of assassins could find no reason to deny the request at the time. The direct communication simplified things for them both, and the contractor had good reason for secreting himself far from prying eyes. The Overseer could respect that.

His assassins had failed to kill the ranger despite months of observation. The Overseer was not used to failure. The fallen killers had displeased the master before and had taken the responsibility for slaying Silverwing in an effort to regain faith. Their heads should have been placed with the others in the main Hall but the Overseer found pity for them and let them rot where they lay. "Perhaps I am getting weary of the blood; time wears the soul even when the body does not age," he mused in in the deep quiet that surrounded him.

You would prefer to join the dust of your mentor, Overseer? Death is only the beginning, and I am certain you know there is a special place in the Hells for your eternity. Tur'morival's contact rang in his head like a bent chime, with warbling notes and a tinny, low clanging that defied music. *We have known each other a long time, brother, and it would sadden me to no longer have you as counsel.*

The Overseer sensed no threat in the words that rang in his ears. Mocking words had become little more than an expected greeting from the dark priest, and the Overseer treated it as such. "You had some trouble acquiring the broken blade from the boy I understand, and one of your trusted priests is dead. The Order will no doubt be exposed. Why would you take such a chance?" The Overseer awaited the demonologist's reply. Incautious words would tell him what he needed to know.

Tread carefully, master assassin. You should focus on the task set before you. The boy and Silverwing would be of no concern to anyone if they were dead. I am willing to forget the failure, but I require something in return.

"The broken blade and the boy, no doubt. Do you care if he lives or dies? I doubt you have much use for him, and the blade is easily taken from a corpse."

I want the boy alive and my reasons are my own. I sense you're not telling me something. Would you prefer I dig it out of your mind? As if to make the priest's point, the dark red stone warmed in the Overseer's cold palm. The old killer tightened his grip in response.

"You might find that more difficult than you think, Tur'morival. You would be unwise to test the extent of my reach." The Overseer waited for the warming in his palm to dissipate before continuing. "Good, I'm glad we understand each other. It seems Lord Silverwing is coming to you. Do you want us to kill him, or would you prefer the pleasure?"

Leave the old ranger to me and capture the boy. Bring me that blade and do not underestimate Gregor. He will only grow stronger. The Overseer felt fear with the last thoughts and regretted he could not see the priest's face.

"As you wish, Tur'morival. We have already made preparations to take the boy, and I will have my people move ahead. Still it is a shame not to just kill him." The stone darkened in the Overseer's hand, plunging him into a comfortable absence of light. His words echoed through the chamber, disturbing the quiet of the tomb. "Pity we missed the first time."

***

Gregor took his gauntlets from his hands, wishing to feel the warmth of the fire against his skin. A shroud of thick clouds hid the light of the moon and stars. Gregor mused over the journey to Zanthfar so far, remembering the morning after his vigil. The great feast of the Temple of light had been filled to capacity with peasants and nobles alike when Father Oregeth announced Gregor. It had been all the newly knighted young man could do to not be overwhelmed. Applause and cheers had flooded the great Hall, causing the walls to tremble with their force as the assembled raise their voices in praise and hope. The streets had filled with those waiting to catch a glimpse of the first knight to emerge from the Temple of Light in years beyond recall, and Gregor had felt the touch of thousands of hands before mounting the horse assigned for his journey. He had been glad to bring the stallion to the road and begin moving toward Zanthfar; the air of the road hit him like a much needed taste of freedom.

Only two days from Nactium, the horse began to favor his left rear foot. Upon inspection Gregor discovered that he had thrown a shoe, and unfortunately there was no blacksmith anywhere near. However, there was an encampment of city militia nearby, and Gregor was able to leave the horse in the care of a young man in the service of the city's patrols. The poor young man was ill-equipped for such duty and appeared to be younger than Gregor. As the boy stared wide-eyed, listening intently to the holy warrior's instructions concerning the horse, Gregor had once more realized the burden he

171

carried. So many young men and women just like the boy before him were conscripted into the militias across the lands to fight against forces they could not possibly defeat. The boy's face swam up in the flames where Gregor now warmed his hands, serving as an odd reminder of what was to come if he failed. The people of the lands would be enveloped in chaos and death if Gregor could not stop Tur'morival, of that he was certain. through it,

Great guttural howls broke ~~the knight from~~ his thoughts. He reflexively secured his plated gauntlets and rose to his feet. He drew his sword, noting that it was glowing with a steady luminescence. Gregor turned away from the fire, forcing his eyes to adjust as he searched the darkness within the trees surrounding him. There were shuffling noises from all sides and he caught sight of small pairs of bloody glowing orbs that appeared to be floating in the blackness. The strange apparitions winked out as quickly as he spotted them only to reappear elsewhere. Gregor kept his back to the fire until it was uncomfortably warm, hoping to force his attackers to come at him from the front. Every nerve in his body screamed in alarm as he planted his feet in a combat ready stance. As if in answer to the glow of the sword, a crimson mist came into being and moved toward him from the trees. "Who walks these woods? Show yourself!" Gregor kept his voice steady and his sword arm at the ready though his mind filled with fear. The mist was not unfamiliar to him. It was the same light that had surrounded Tur'morival when the priest had presented himself in Gregor's dreams so long ago.

"Sheath your weapon, Master Gregor. You will find little use for it against me." The voice emerged from a robed figure clothed as Father Tur'morival had been in Gregor's dream. The priest bore a staff like those possessed by the summoners from the arena that emanated the light coloring the mist surrounding him. His voice was at once mocking and respectful, and Gregor could sense no threat in it as the man continued to speak. "You know why I have come. Give me the blade desired by my master and we can return to him in peace. There will be no escape for you this time, Knight." As if to demonstrate the truth of his words, several large wolves emerged from the darkness near the figure.

Gregor was torn by anger and pity as the creatures came into the circle of light cast by his fire. The beasts barely resembled the noble hunters they once were. The glowing orbs he had seen in the trees dominated their faces. Unnatural power had swollen their bodies to obscene proportions, tearing the hides where pulsing muscle was now exposed. Deadly thick claws shredded the flesh of their paws and a bloody grimace haunted their maws, forced into being by a protrusion of grotesque fangs. There was the sound of tortured growls emerging from the space beyond the fire at Gregor's back as well.

The knight tightened his grip on the hilt of his sword, readying to spring at the priest even as he answered. "I doubt these poor creatures would trouble me if I drove my blade into your heart. One who would corrupt such noble animals deserves no more, and I can find no reason to hold further counsel with you, demon servant."

The vile laugh that emerged from the hood made Gregor cringe in disgust; it was so much like the cursed voice of the priest's Master. Only the flesh of a man on the hand that held the great staff made Gregor certain it was not Tur'morival before him now. "You'll find there is much you can learn for me, young one. You will serve the Father Tur'morival, one way or another. Would it not be better to go to your Master freely? Your God has forsaken you, giving you faults possessed by so many that have fallen before you. The beasts in my service are but a taste of the power wielded by Father Tur'morival, and the forces of good make no move that he has not foreseen. Do not dismay, master Gregor. All those who serve our

Master once labored in vain against the darkness. There is only one end to that path. A meaningless death that changes nothing."

Gregor stepped a pace closer to the priest. He found his movement matched by the beasts near their dark creator as the threat in the wolves' voices deepened. "You are bold and full of deceit, priest, but do you really think these animals will save you? You speak as though I am alone even as Divinity infuses my blade." The knight angled the blade towards the priest's head to illustrate his point. "Do you think the powers of the Abyss will prevent a stab deep into your heart? You should welcome my strike. Perhaps the God of Light will take pity on your tainted soul and guide you to the divine power you have forsaken. There is no salvation for those who accept the Unnamed One, who holds sway over the souls in the Abyss, in exchange for power in this world. Do not deceive yourself even as you weave the web for me. Go back to the darkness and release these poor creatures. The only hope for you is to relinquish the hold of your master and pray to the divine power you have forsaken. I will take no pleasure in killing you if that is what I must do, except that these poor beasts will be welcomed into the arms of a loving Goddess."

There was no note of pleasure in the priest's words as he called for Gregor's doom. "You speak well for a blind servant of a meaningless God. What can be expected but empty words from one who struggles so hard against his true destiny? All mankind craves the power we possess. The Order of the Crimson Night alone is blessed with the ability to bend this world to our desires. Serving the powers of the Abyss with the promise of immortality is more than a reasonable sacrifice to make. You will know the true power that Father Tur'morival possesses soon enough. For now know that my pets will tear the armor plates away that cover you one by one until I grow weary of your pleas for death. The powers I have at my disposal will be more than adequate to sustain you. Father Tur'morival has

174

such plans for you, such plans." The priest waved dismissively towards Gregor. "Take him now."

The first strike came from the rear, nearly knocking Gregor to his knees and causing him to stumble forward toward the beasts in front of him. He felt some small relief when the four wolves to the front of him did not immediately attack, choosing instead to gnash their great jaws at him and growl deep in their chests. It took him a moment to figure out what they were doing but it became apparent soon enough. He sidled quickly away from the stalking wolves nearest the priest but found he had been pushed away from the limited protection of the fire that had been at his back. Two pairs of wolves came around the fire, positioning themselves so that the animals were able to encircle him. They had shut down any means of escape with the efficiency of the pack hunters they were, and would begin their attack in earnest soon. For the moment, they seemed content measuring their victim and looking for the best place to strike. Gregor felt certain if one of the creature struck him fully from the rear, he would be borne to the ground. He had no desire to rely on the mercy of the wolves if they knocked him down. Gregor turned with practiced skill, his eyes never coming to rest on any one beast, as he waited for them to make the next move.

The wolves circled as Gregor turned in the opposite direction, matching their pace. The knight was fairly certain the animals would get the best of him if he were caught in a melee for too long. He decided the best course was a direct approach in hopes of scattering their number, even though that would mean exposing his flank. Gregor only hoped the steel plates covering his back could resist the claws of the wolves that would take advantage of the opening. The pack showed no sign of fear as he turned, his blade waving around the circle. There had to be a weak link in their formation, though all the predators seemed equal in size, and space between them was almost nonexistent. While making a third turn, Gregor spotted it. One of the wolves had only three full paws. It held as steady a pace as it could, but would just slightly miss a beat as it went around with the others, leaving just the room Gregor needed to break free of the trap. Gregor passed his eyes over the creature once more and knew what he had to do.

As his target drew near where the circle passed closest to the fire, Gregor dropped to his knee without warning. His sword swept low, carving away the rear legs of the wolf positioned ahead of the limping wolf and arcing up, as Gregor used the counterbalance of the swing to roll him back to his feet outside the circle. The three-pawed wolf turned to snap at him and was cut off by the fire itself, its body forming a block in front of the wolves nearest it. The block being temporary, Gregor knew they would leap over the fire soon, and there were still three others that had no impediment. The wolves that had been moving behind Gregor when he struck were already charging around their downed companion. Gregor saw his advantage immediately and took it. He slipped fluidly around the wounded creature and stabbed at the great maw of the wolf at the front of the group nearest him. Even before the creature realized it was dead, its body ignited as the blade of the sword brightened, emerging from the back of its splintered skull. Gregor withdrew the bloody, shining sword and moved toward the next tainted wolf. Some survival instinct still lived in the minds of the creatures, and the next beast withdrew as Gregor brought the brightly lit sword to face it. Gregor was sick with the thought of killing the creature, and he threw his heavily booted leg out to make solid contact with its muzzle. The strike was answered with the sound of splintering bone and tearing flesh. The animal was turned away by the impact and stumbled out of Gregor's path. Only one more animal remained between the priest and himself; the priest realized the danger of his position only moments before was too late. Dark words began to flow from the priest's black tongue even as Gregor raised his sword over his head. Ignoring the last animals that were preparing to launch their grotesque forms at him, Gregor asked for one bit of aid from the God of Light he served. "Let my blade strike true and release these creatures from their binding." The sword leaped from Gregor's hands, spinning through the air as it closed the distance between the knight and the priest. As if in answer to Gregor's prayer, the blade's flight straightened as it struck through the priest's robes. The summoner's words were silenced by the penetration of the blade, and blood ran over the hilt of the weapon as the man fell to his knees. "Pray now, priest, and hope there is time for a reply."

Even as the priest fell to the ground, one of the demon wolves pounced. A glimmering white suffused its form, as a much smaller creature than the one that had jumped at Gregor glanced harmlessly against Gregor's chest plate. Upon finding themselves so near man and a fire in their normal state, the other remaining creatures fled into the woods. Only the body of the slain remained, or so Gregor thought at first. The wolf that had suffered the abuse of his boot emerged from the trees where it had retreated, its broken jaw dangling from its snout. A wave of pain swept over Gregor at the sight of it, and he moved to kneel in front of the wolf, laying his gauntlets to one side as the animal sniffed tentatively at Gregor's now bare hands. There was no threat in the wounded beast, and the knight spoke gently to him as he moved one hand to cradle the broken jaw. "Goddess save me. Tana would have my head if she could see such suffering. We will put you right." The wolf's eyes stared into his own as Gregor drew energy into his hands, knitting the bone and restoring the flesh. The wolf barked loudly to show that its muzzle was quite functional, and ran off into the trees to join his remaining companions.

A wet nose nuzzled the still kneeling knight's back as Gregor watched the wolf go. It appeared he was not alone. The warrior turned slowly, not wanting to alarm his remaining companion, and once more extended his hands. Three-Paw, who it seemed had been watching over the healing of his pack mate, sniffed at the offered hand and sat on his haunches in front of the knight as if waiting for something. "My powers are not so great that I can restore your lost paw, my friend. Old wounds are beyond me. Still I owe you my life, I think, and though it is a poor payment for such a deed, let me see what I might have." Three-Paw cocked his head at Gregor and limped to the smoldering remains of the dead wolf, prodding it gently with his muzzle before sitting on his haunches again and turning his head to stare at the knight. "Ah, I think I understand now." Gregor rose and stood next to Three-Paw, offering a small prayer over the fallen wolf before carrying its body to the fire. This seemed to satisfy Three-Paw, and he took up a position near Gregor, lying down and watching the flames as the fire consumed his dead friend.

***

The mood was light in the Grove after long days spent hunting. The rangers from various lands had blended well and no one could doubt their effectiveness. Tana's group included one of the mountain guardians as well as an Ardataure that was a very capable scout. The slight female remained high in the trees every night, keeping a constant vigil as the others slept. Sephia rarely spoke to the rest of the group and preferred to use simple hand signals that were readily understood by all. The scout's falcon companion had also proven invaluable.

Dramor, the mountain warrior her group had drawn, had proven very aggressive in the pursuit of his duties. He definitely seemed to enjoy running headlong into every group of orcs they encountered. Tana had somehow fallen into the role of leader, and she felt this was in no small part due to her ability to explain tactics to the stout, broad-shouldered mountain man. "If I be in the middle of the bast... orcs, beggin' your pardon miss... Why can I not jus' tear em all new ones?" The puzzled look on his rough features made Tana smile, in spite of her mood.

"If they have one of the demon bloods with them, Dramor, you would be killed. There is no reason to think they wouldn't have a leader with them, and you have not seen what those creatures can do." Tana kept her face deadly serious while Dramor turned her words over in his head.

"Ya got me there, I must admit it. I hadn't laid me eyes to 'em biggun orcs and jus' got to the trust those that had." He thought a bit longer, then his heavy, dark eyebrows shot up. "I gots an answer to the troubles I be thinkin'. I can make like runnin' to em and the rest all hold there in the trees. If'n I see a biggun in the bast... orcs, I mean... then I can drag 'em chasin' me up to ya here. Yup, that'ud work!"

Tana had been unable to argue with him once his mind had been set. She cringed every time he shot out of the trees, bellowing like a grizzly bear, but she could not deny his effectiveness. For a person whose legs were so short, he was fast and no one in the group could match his strength. He had happily hollered out a warning when they encountered their first large group. "Got a bunch of em! Took two out on me turn! The biggun is mine!" Dramor was as good as his word and the demon blood orc had indeed fallen to his pick. Once all the orcs had been slain, the mountain man stood a long time staring at the ground where the demon blood had fallen. "Don' know what to make of it, Miss Tana. Drove me picks home and the darn thing just blew away like there weren't much to hold it together. Don' know what to make of it a'tall."

Tana's group was in charge of patrolling the forest near the plains. The first few days brought them into contact with as many as two or three raiding parties, but the wood had grown quieter recently. Tana largely attributed this to the more concentrated efforts of the rangers. The reports that came in from other groups agreed with what her party was finding. The remaining orc war parties were larger and always had a demon blood leader with them. Once the leader was slain, the remaining orcs fled toward the plains. The forces that had drawn them together as one tribe were diminishing.

Tana had chosen this evening to learn more about her companions. Many of the rangers and druids told stories similar to hers. There were a number of interesting animal companions in the group, though most of the local rangers and druids traveled with wolves like Fang. There were, however, exceptions like the large wildcat accompanying one of the other druids.

One of the other rangers had been rescued, and subsequently befriended, by a weasel that reminded Tana a great deal of Filcher, Master Firebeard's pet. The ranger in question had been captured by a poacher whose knot tying ability had given him no end of trouble. The weasel had come along while the poacher slept, and gnawed away the ropes which bound the ranger. The ranger had fed the weasel and then had tried his best to gently shoo him away into the woods, but the little rodent had refused to leave him. The small, slender creature stayed mostly at his master's side, though it did have a tendency to explore other people's packs. Curiosity had almost been the end of it when it made the mistake of assuming Dramor's companion, a large reptilian creature, slept while it scurried over the reptile's back.

"Dramor, is that beast of yours always so nasty?" Tana asked in a huff after the lizard snapped its jaws behind the frightened weasel several times. It never moved, it simply twisted its neck, tracking the rodent, before bringing its scaly head to rest again near the fire pit.

Dramor turned to look at her, petting his creature lightly on its head as if he had not noticed. "Eh? You mean Carver? He wasn' gonna eat that stretched little rat. If he'd a' been hungry, he would' a caught'im. He was only funnin', weren' you, Carver. He didn' mean no harm. Just watchin' the little bugger didn' get our stuff. No harm, Miss Tana. He wasn' meanin' no harm. Carver jus' a bit away from his home and it's makin' him a bit edgy. Know what I be meanin'?"

"Yes, I do understand that. We are all a long way from home. We should be able to make our ways back to our homes soon, if things keep going the way they are going. It won't be long until the trouble here is done." She was hoping as much as any of them for that to be true. The reply that came from just outside the light of the fire surprised them all.

"We will be leaving these wild lands soon but not to go home, I fear." Sephia's soft voice emerged from the shadows as she stepped toward the fire. The large falcon she called Keen was perched at her shoulder, its eyes scanning the darkness beyond. "The demon blood leaders that remain have abandoned the orcs. They travel as one group to the north, to the lava mountains. Keen tells me the creatures move quickly. Their work here is done."

Tana turned to address Sephia, "What do you mean, their work here is done?"

"We have been distracted, as was the intention of the one who guides them. I cannot say what purpose was served when the demon bloods were sent here, but it is not their losses that make them leave now. Whatever power guides them is calling them home." Sephia's placid features remained unmarked by emotion as she continued. "There is something else. Keen has seen men moving through the forest. He cannot say how many. They are hiding their number."

"Ah, prolly jus' poachers or maybe robbers stayin' off the roads. The local militia have been jus' about all o'er the roads wit' the trouble." Dramor waved at Sephia dismissively. "You gettin' all in a twist o'er nothin'."

"No, Dramor, these are hunters of men. They move like snakes in the night, hiding in the trees during the day. No broken branches or matted grass gives hints of the path they have taken. These hunters are watching and waiting for... someone. Some are near the road from the southwest. There are others in the wood but I know not where. They move constantly at night, searching."

Tana's mind raced as she considered Sephia's words. Nactium, the killers were watching the road that came from Nactium, but why? First, Master Silverwing's weapons turn up with news of the demon trying to kill Gregor. Now assassins lay in wait on the road from Nactium. What was happening? The only thing in common was the city of Nactium. Tana realized there was only one person she cared about in that city who might leave it, Gregor. Gregor would leave to find his Master once he was knighted, and the same path that brought Master Silverwing his swords would lead the young knight to Zanthfar. Tana had to find the assassins before they found Gregor.

12

Heads or Tails

It had been three days since Boremac's meeting with Silverwing, time enough to start feeling his appetite for trouble. Tavern wenches to the left and alcohol to the right... what was a respectable scoundrel to do?

He woke, if you could call it that, with a pounding head and teeth that felt like they were wearing dirty socks. The bed was shaking and seemed likely to splinter apart. Groggily, he reached out to the warm body next to him. "Mornin', love," he said thickly. "You feeling frisky again?" "BAAAAAAA," was all the answer the rogue got before his bedmate resumed struggling.

Boremac's eyes popped open, coming fully awake. "What the hell???"

Lurching out of bed, he took in the situation in an instant. The goat, unwilling as she had been to share his bed, was trussed at her front and hind legs and attempting unsuccessfully to escape. The animal protested loudly now, ignoring the bit of rag that had secured her muzzle and focusing on the leather lines binding her legs. He wondered how he had managed to sleep through any of it at all. Well, on second thought, since he had been more comatose than asleep, it was entirely possible.

"Just wait 'til I get my hands on that wench...she will pay for this!" he muttered darkly, as he clumsily attempted to untie the goat, dodging the nipping teeth intent on the same purpose. "Be still, you damned animal!" Finally, he managed to disentangle the leather bindings, receiving a startling knock to the head for his efforts. As if this indignity were not enough, the creature paused briefly to kick its rescuer squarely in his nether region before bolting out the open door to the rogue's room. The distraught nanny charged out of the bedroom, down the inn steps and into the common room. There was a great commotion below filled with shouts from the afternoon's patrons and the sounds of broken crockery. Boremac knelt hard on the wooden floor, gently checking his wounded pride for any permanent damage as the pulsing in his head continued to intensify. Another sound, this one all too familiar to the thief, brought him to his feet.

Quick as a snake, Boremac's hand shot around the corner toward the source of the shrill laughter penetrating his skull. Luck smiled on him as the offending female turned to flee, knowing she had been discovered, and he caught a full hand of her hair. The rogue was pleased with his first catch of the day despite his pain. "OWWWWWWW, stop that!!"

"AH HA!" Boremac dragged the girl into the room to face him and pushed her roughly up against the wall. "You better speak quick before I share the wealth of pain that nanny gave me," he growled ominously from under lowered brows. The girl quailed under his hands, a pained look coloring her features. Boremac wondered at her response. He was sure he wasn't holding her that hard, considering his current condition. His eyes swept around the scene of destruction that had been his room, and noticed that his blades were missing. Returning his gaze to the girl, he raised his eyebrows questioningly, "Well?"

"It were just meant to be a bit of payback for ruinin' me and me sister's chances of gettin' out of this tavern. We made sure you

184

had enough to drink and more before we brought you up here last night to tuck you in." The girl wiggled as if she were trying to find a more comfortable position. Boremac pressed her a bit harder. "And?... I am sure there is more you are not telling me." The girl gave a little gasp as he pressed. "What's the matter? Is there a nail poking your backside? Or maybe my blades?" He said with another abrupt push.

"OWWW! All right, I took' em. I admit it. They looked like they might bring a pretty price. Stop mashin' me and I'll give 'em back!" The barmaid relaxed visibly as Boremac took his weight off her so he could retrieve his belongings. "You ought to know that what goes around comes back to ya, Boremac. Seemed rather fittin' for an old goat like yourself to wake with a nanny fit to be tied." Once more her laughter pummeled his aching skull. "For all your carousing of late, I am surprised you haven't had that lass sooner."

Boremac secured his belt and turned to meet her chiding with a laugh of his own. "I supposed there is more truth in that than I would care to admit." The rogue stepped to the center of the room where the barmaid now stood with his daggers in hand, points out, he noted.

"Take the daggers, but you might do well to pay me first. What is that narrow hide of yours worth to you?"

"Fair enough." It was her turn to grin, and Boremac extracted coins from his pouch before taking the offered blades. He didn't like being at her mercy without knowing what to offer, but he tossed a gemstone in with the coins to be certain the barmaid shared what she knew.

"Nice! Might take some time from tables with that bit." The barmaid tucked away the payment and put on a mask of concern for his benefit. "Tough figures looking for you in the city of late,

Boremac. Should be glad I like you or they would have picked you up already. You wouldn't be wise to be hanging around the inns so much anymore, I think. These aren't the usual roughs that come by making inquiries, and definitely not the local constables so far as I can tell. Asking a lot of questions and not real happy when they don't get quick answers. I would take your blades and go, Boremac. Come in when there isn't so much trouble."

"Well, I guess it was just a matter of time, but I have to remain here in the city a bit longer. Promises to keep, love. Unless you might take to the tables a bit longer and help me save the world?" There was no indication that he was speaking in jest, and the darkness in his eyes piqued her attention and curiosity. "A price much greater than those meager coins would be yours if you could keep my confidence. Of course, you might just as likely be killed for associating with me if what you say is true."

His last words made her reconsider the wisdom in protecting the thief. "What have you gone and gotten yourself into now, Boremac? Some fool has filled your head with importance, I am thinking. Still, you have my attention. Tell me what you would have me do and I will tell you if I can do it. Don't see any profit in being dead."

Boremac sheathed his daggers as he suited up in his leathers and chucked her lightly under her chin. "Your part would be simple enough. Just keep an eye out for the knight that will be coming to the city, and give him a message for me when he arrives. Think you can manage it? In return I will give you enough coin and gems to get you half an interest in this tavern."

She winked at the rogue coyly and answered with a singular affirmative. "Done." She extended her hand to seal the deal. As Boremac reached out to take the offered hand, her eyes left his to rest at his waist. "Do those daggers always glow like that or are you just happy to see me?"

"What?" Boremac was taken aback by this new development. He too looked down at the two dagger hilts that glowed with a soft white light where they protruded from his belt.

13

Shadows and the Light

It had been several days since Gregor had placed the stones over the dead priest. The knight had regretted not being able to commit the body to the ground properly, but there was nothing to be done about it. Despite the man's misguided path, Gregor had prayed for the fallen one to be united with the true God he had once served. Three-Paw kept pace with the warrior as he reached the outskirts of Zanthfar. The odd behavior of the wild animal puzzled Gregor, but he was glad for the company. The knight felt certain the beast would make its way home once the pair made their way into the heavily patrolled lands of Zanthfar itself. Three-Paw had taken up the habit of wandering off into the woods whenever Gregor took to the road to check his path and exchange news with the militia of the city. The watchers of the road told Gregor that there had been rumors of a great counsel among the druids who watched over the woodlands near Zanthfar. Since that time, many groups of rangers and druids had taken up patrols, reporting many strange things at the outlying posts along the roads. Large orcs that dwarfed the other humanoids and the raiding parties they lead were becoming more and more common. The brutal tribes of orcs seemed to be pressing their way toward Zanthfar itself, though at this point they had had little success breaking through the patrols of rangers. Gregor could not help but wonder if Tana were among them, and prayed for her safety.

He was still a day's hard travel from the city when he decided he would take the road on the following morning. The desire to find his teacher pushed him, though he was uncertain why. Gregor could not shake the feeling that his mentor was in danger. The young Knight had learned to trust his instincts as well as his training, and he made the last camp that would be outside the reach of the city's walls with much trepidation. The cause for his alarm became evident soon enough as he returned to his fire with an armload of fallen wood.

No twig broke, no shadow shifted within his limited view. Gregor had just enough time to place his hand at his sword hilt before several webs the breadth of his height fell from the trees and pinned him face down to the ground, leaving the wood of his load scattered in every direction. The weighted nets were well placed by his attackers and he could not budge. It appeared that the men that had sprung the trap saw little need of stealth, as Gregor twisted his head to see the men emerging from the wood in a rough circle around his prone form.

"Ha, well that was easy enough. You two to go and get the cart. We will drag him to the road." The coarse female voice seemed to belong to the leader of the group. "Damn shame we cannot just kill this one. Club him and secure his arms and legs. Be quick about it!"

Several grunts of acknowledgment sounded as the way-layers went about their tasks. A shout drew Gregor's attention. "Who the hell are...?" The challenge ended with a fluid gurgling followed by the reply of the new arrival.

"What is this about? Seems like a lot of trouble for so little a reward. Certainly the lot of you can see the waste of time in taking this prisoner." Gregor caught sight of a glimmering white light at the corner of his eyes though he could not see the source.

The female's voice rose in a clear challenge to the unknown killer. "Show yourself, bandit, and maybe you can make your way out of this wood alive! We have no patience for rogues, even talented ones. You're clearly outnumbered, and there is no profit for you to take for interfering here."

Two more of the brigands dropped near where she stood, throwing daggers protruding from their necks. The silky voice had moved while she spoke and emerged now from behind her. "Ah, I disagree with you there, mistress of the Hand. Yes, I know who you are, and I know your kind never labor for free. Give your prize to me and leave here before I have to do something nasty. I can assure you, your parcel will be delivered to your master with much haste. I have been seeking an audience with the Lord of assassins for quite some time."

"You slay mere pawns, fool. It is better that you should cull the unprepared from the Brotherhood. Do not think you have any chance of surviving my blade." Her voice was light and it appeared she was glad to have the chance to shed the blood of a worthy challenger. "Come out of the darkness and face me." She waved a hand toward the shadows. "No one touches him but me! This one is mine." The reflection of firelight on metal was little warning as once more a throwing dagger tumbled out of the darkness as if in reply. Even as she returned the blade to her assailant with a flurry of motion, she smiled. This would be fun.

Boremac stepped into the firelight, dropping the dagger intended for the leader back into its sheath. "Can't blame me for trying, Sgiana. It has been too long since our weapons crossed. Let us dance." The rogue and assassin each brought their weapons into their hands with the economy of movement that was the mark of their craft. Boremac noted the pommels of the twin blades of the assassin and grinned. They bore the prestigious skulls that were granted to the brotherhood's elite killers." Is your master still mounting skulls of the fallen assassins? I bet your pretty head will be worth quite a bit." He began to circle her, with Sgiana matching every step.

She took her time measuring her foe, noting with pleasure that the throwing dagger she had returned to him had made its mark. The assassin nodded slightly to the thin line of blood tracing its way down the torn leather at the rogue's left shoulder. "If I remember correctly you favor your right hand, fool. It would be a shame to kill you too quickly."

Boremac feinted rapidly, stepping toward her in reply. The attack caught her slightly off guard, allowing his own left-handed dagger to penetrate the light protection at her right shoulder. He glided backward as she moved her own daggers to cut him, the jagged blades narrowly missing tearing his stomach open. "Nice move, my lady. You will find my blades are equally effective no matter which hand they are in." He nodded lightly to the wound he had opened at her right shoulder. "Looks like we are even now."

Her eyes narrowed at the rogue's words. She had underestimated him for the last time. The movement of the two combatants was remarkably similar as their blades clashed and withdrew, each in their turn. Something in the way the rogue moved tugged at Gregor's memory, though it took him some time to think why he knew him. This was the acolyte that had seen Gregor slay the candelabrum so long ago when he first held his black sword. The blessings of the God of light truly took strange forms. The knight would never have known him except for the bald head once more glimmering in the firelight and the unmistakable close cut beard that he had found so curious when last he had seen the man. Despite the man's skill, Gregor saw little reason to think he could undo the assassin.

The killer was learning more of her challenger with each thrust and parry. He preferred a quick strike that would kill his

191

opponent, and each stab he weaved beyond her blades was easily countered with a backward step or slight twist. Each time he cut her leathers or punctured her flesh, the rogue was paid double for his efforts. She was in no hurry to kill him; she found so few real tests for her vast skills of late. The marks of her efforts wept openly, painting Boremac's leathers from his neck to his waist. No one among the onlookers, or the two figures engaged in each other's destruction, could have known what was going to happen next.

Gregor heard his companion before the others and shouted. "No!"

It was too late. Three-Paw crashed into Boremac, spinning him away from the assassin as the first arrow appeared in her chest. The sound of splintering bone and the rushing air forced from her open mouth were the only sounds for a moment as Sgiana fell face forward toward the ground. A frightening bellow erupted from the trees as the whisper of arrows was suddenly everywhere at once. Gregor had never seen anything like the man charging out of the trees, holding a giant pickax over his head, intent upon killing Boremac. Bodies fell from the trees, clothed in black leathers, with arrow shafts protruding from various body parts.

Despite his prone position, Gregor raised his voice over the thunderous hollering of the short, broad figure nearing Boremac's kneeling form. Jumbled words poured forth as he sought to save the rogue. "Stop! You there, do not harm him! Get down or lose your head, rogue!" As it turned out, the knight's words were all but wasted.

Boremac dropped to his back, shooting his legs upward to take the new threat high in the chest, easily throwing the thick man over his body. Despite the short, heavy figure's considerable girth, the man landed a few feet from Boremac flat on his back with a ground-shuddering thud. Boremac began to throw his legs forward, intent on regaining his feet, only to be struck in the chest by a gray wolf considerably larger than Three-Paw. The beast pinned the rogue to the ground, its paws resting on his shoulders as it drew its muzzle close to Boremac's nose. The animal let out a growl that let the man know that trying to move would be a very bad idea.

Gregor's voice once more shouted out in confusion and alarm. "Fang?!? Fang! Where's your mistress? Tana! Get Fang off him! He is one of the good guys! By the Light, someone get me out of these nets!"

Dramor sat up, still gripping his pickax, and shook the lights dancing in his eyes from his vision. " What'cha want me to do, Tana? Thump the thief or free the knight?" There was no doubt which of these two actions he would prefer, judging from his tone.

The voice that answered the mountain man's inquiry made Gregor's heart leap for the sound of it. Despite the current predicament in which he found himself, the knight flushed deeply as Tana emerged from the wood with an arrow nocked and pointed at the rogue. "This one is well in hand, I think, Dramor. Get Gregor out of those nets so we can sort this mess out." She shifted her arrow to line up properly with Boremac's nervous gaze. "You won't give Fang any reason to tear out your throat, will you? Be careful how you answer, she is a bit high strung with all the excitement." Boremac's nearly imperceptible shake of his head seemed to satisfy Tana. "Good, we will get to you in a moment. Fang, make sure our friend stays comfortable." Fang barked her response, the wolf's eyes never leaving the rogue's.

Dramor busied himself with first pulling at the tangled mass of netting before giving up and cutting through the individual strands. "Rest easy, boy. We'll have ya outta here before ya can spit." He yelled over his shoulder to the leather-clad figures that began emerging from the trees. Gregor was thinking that this man could do nothing else, he excelled at bellowing. "Could use a 'and over 'ere!

Damn nets is tough! Can one o' ya or a pair lend a blade?" A few figures that were checking the bodies of the slain assassins moved to help the mountain man. Dramor appeared to be well on his way to joining Gregor in the interlocking nets before he was finally freed. Gregor brushed himself off, trying to make himself presentable while Tana stood near the center of the encampment, giving directions to the assembled rangers and druids. Boremac seemed to be all but forgotten.

Gregor's next action went against all he knew to be proper, but he never regretted it, even as he begged Tana's forgiveness later. The knight came before her as the druid warrior hung her bow at her back and replaced the arrows she had collected in her quiver. Impulse drove away good sense as he threw his arms around her. "I have missed you so much, Tana. I'm glad you are safe. Many things have happened since I saw you last and I feared I would never see you again. I..."

She silenced his words with a light touch of her finger to his lips. Tana backed away from him, fighting her own desire to be near him, but knowing now was not the time. "You seem to excel at finding trouble, Gregor. Let me have a look at you. So what is all this? The work of master Firebeard is unmistakable; however, the meaning of the symbols your armor bears is unfamiliar to me."

Gregor could not hide his disappointment at her withdrawal from their embrace though he recovered quickly, relating his acceptance by the God of Light at his vigil. He briefly touched on the meaning of the symbols he wore and told Tana of the path that brought him to meet her once more. She nodded, listening intently, and did her best to hide the feelings she had herself so recently discovered. The man that then stood before her now was still a boy in so many ways, yet it had been all she could do not to return his innocent embrace moments before. The forgotten rogue brought the pair out of their preoccupation.

"If it's not too much to ask, could someone get this animal off me?" Boremac had lain quietly beneath his keeper throughout the exchange between Tana and Gregor, but enough was enough and he decided if the wolf meant to eat him, then so be it.

Tana turned to the rogue, smiling. "Sorry about that. Fang, come!" As the man rose to his feet, he was aware of a large number of arrows nocked and pointing in his direction. There was also the matter of the mountain man that still held ill feelings for the tossing the rogue had given him. "I guess we should give you a chance to tell us who exactly you are and how you came to be here. The words between you and the assassin give me little hope for your redemption."

Gregor spoke in the rogue's defense before Boremac could get his tongue moving. That probably saved his life, as certainly as Three-Paw had by knocking him out of the first arrow's path. "He is a friend to Master Silverwing, and to myself as well, though I do not know his name. He spent a great deal of time at the Temple of Light, with instruction to watch over me I suspect, though we never spoke. Gregor turned to Boremac. "You were the one who killed the summoner at my weapons trial, am I right?"

Boremac bowed with a flourish to the knight before him. "I am that man, master Gregor. Boremac is how they call me and I am at your service. Master Silverwing sent me to watch over you until you were knighted at the Temple though an enforced vow of silence restricted my contact with you. Father Oregeth insisted I hold my tongue and focus on my past sins while I was within the Temple. The priests are very sticky about certain rules where their faith is concerned, and I was treated as any other acolyte. Still, when there was a need for my skills, I was able to do what was necessary to protect you."

Tana narrowed her eyes at the rogue. "A saint in a snake's skin. Care to explain the exchange between yourself and the assassins that lie strewn about us? There seemed to be only a minor difference in each party's intent until we started shooting."

Boremac had anticipated this line of questioning, considering the first arrow had clearly been intended for him. "When one comes upon a nest of snakes, it is safer to assume the guise of the slithering creatures than to bare your flesh to their fangs. I was saddled with the protection of Gregor by Lord Silverwing himself, and guided to the young Knight by the God of Light. Divine guidance does not give me divine insight. I proceeded in the best manner I knew how without knowing the numbers I faced. You cannot deny the end justified the means in this case. Despite the danger to my person, I can assure you Gregor's safety was foremost in my mind. Are the marks on my body not proof enough for you?"

Gregor spoke up with the last statement, noticing as if for the first time the multiple bleeding wounds and tears in Boremac's leathers. "Lower your weapons or be ready to bury me beside him!" Gregor moved between the archers and Boremac, examining his wounds. Blood painted the rogue's leathers and many punctures still bled freely. Gregor remembered the wound Lord Silverwing had sustained so long ago and he feared for the rogue now. "I thank you, Master Boremac. If you had not come when you did, I would certainly have been overcome and the loss of life among these protectors of the wood would have been terrible. Please rest yourself and allow me to tend to your wounds."

Boremac raised his voice to the assembled rangers and druids. "Finally, a voice of reason among the accusers! You would do well to learn from the actions of this Knight among barbarians!" The rogue raised a fist in defiance before collapsing to the ground in a heap.

***

"I don' know what'cha thinkin' trustin' his kind. No sense in it, none at all." The mountain man's words were the first thing Boremac became aware of after he awoke. The rogue could feel the warmth of a fire nearby and a heavy gauntleted hand resting on his chest, protectively monitoring his steady breathing. He decided to keep his body motionless a bit longer. The group that had come upon his attempt to save Gregor appeared to be in deep discussion concerning his fate.

"I cannot disagree with Gregor's measure of the man at this point, Dramor, though I am not real comfortable with the bandit. He stinks of lies." Boremac flinched inwardly at Tana's biting words. There was little doubt that she was in charge of the group, and her decision would carry a great deal of weight.

Gregor's reply to her vitriolic statement brought the rogue little comfort. "I sense no threat in the man and his actions, though questionable, do stand up to his explanation. If Master Silverwing has seen to call on this man to protect me, I can find no reason to distrust him. My mentor's wisdom is far greater than mine, and he has taken the measure of this rogue."

A new female voice entered the counsel. The lilting tone of this one's words spoke of ethereal beauty, almost forcing Boremac to expose his conscious state. "Your mentor's sight may have been tainted, Lord Lightsword. These are evil times. One should take nothing for granted. We should bind the rogue until we are able to take proper measure of his intent. He clearly voiced his intentions concerning you before he was aware of our presence." Boremac did not like the way this conversation was going, not one bit. He cursed silently as once more the naive knight attempted to come to his aid.

"Mistress Sephia, I appreciate your concern but I think you go too far. The divine gifts that restored his flesh would not have flowed into my hands so readily to save one bent against the powers that grant him life. The knitting of his wounds only reinforces my beliefs where the rogue is concerned. Who are we to bring harm to one the God of Light has seen fit to heal? If we are to question him so be it, but you will not bind my charge."

The delicate voice answered with her even tone, though Boremac sensed more than heard her disgust. "Do what you must, Lord Lightsword. You should be aware that your charge has awakened and has been listening for some time. Even now he deceives you."

The hand resting on the rogue's chest came up abruptly and Boremac's eyes sprang open to find Gregor's own looking into his. Boremac felt it was time to come to his own defense. "What? A man awakens to people discussing how best to undo him and you think I was going to spring up and announce my awareness?" Boremac sat up, pushing Gregor aside, as his eyes filled with the flames before him. "My thanks you Gregor, or Lord Lightsword or whatever they're calling you now, for your faith in a misguided soul trying to make up for poor choices. As for the rest of you, if my options are arguing with you for acceptance with the promise of being trussed up and sent to the local constables, or giving over my charge to you group of tree dwellers and making my own path, I will bid you farewell and hope your Gods and Goddesses give you strength enough in your quest. Gregor, your God chose me, not the other way around and I do not pretend understand why. Take my words for what you will and decide what you want to do because you are wasting time." Boremac then cast a withering gaze around the fire, daring each person in turn to meet his eyes and finding few that would. "Time is not something you can squander, and you would do well to take advantage of the aid offered, no matter what you think of the source."

Tana's voice lifted before another could object to the rogue's speech. She brought her hands up to signal her desire for silence as Boremac set his arms across his chest, feigning objection. "Your twisting tongue holds just enough wisdom to keep me from cutting it out. Answer me this, bandit, and make it quick. How did you come to find Gregor? The obvious answer would be that you were lying in wait with the others. If I can find no other reason, I will cut your throat myself."

Boremac took only a moment to consider her threat before deciding that honesty was the best course to follow at this time, though he was not pleased with sharing the truth of his journey. The path that had led him here seemed ridiculous even to his own ears as he related it. "My blades brought me here, though not in any manner you would expect. Trusting any higher power, outside that which governs my luck, has never meant much to me in the past. A low glow came to the hilts of the daggers I was gifted from Master Firebeard, the master smith from Nactium, and I could find no reason for it save a sign from the God of Light whose priesthood blessed these weapons. I acquired a horse and rode hard down the road toward Nactium. Master Silverwing charged me with waiting for Gregor in the city of Zanthfar at our last meeting, but it took no leap of faith to think the young Knight might find trouble making his way to the city. My assumption seemed to be confirmed the farther I got from Zanthfar, as the light from the daggers intensified the closer I got to this place. Seeing no point in announcing my presence, I cloaked the daggers within my leathers and pointed the horse back towards its home stables in Zanthfar before I made my way into the woods where Gregor had been captured. I assume you were present when I arrived, though I cannot say why you did not engage the assassins before I did." Despite his desperate situation, Boremac could not resist the smirk the ~~bent~~ his lips.

"Cepheid noted your arrival and chose to have us hold, bandit. Whether you like it or not, we saved your life. Three-Paw, the Wolf that knocked you out of the path of my arrow, was guided by my words." Her sharp tone softened before she continued. "Dramor took matters into his own hands and decided to be sure you had no chance to threaten the other members of the group. He has a certain determined logic that sometimes puts him into conflict with my direction, especially when he senses a threat."

Dramor interjected his own comment at this time, so moved was he by her words. "I'da had 'em, quick feet or no, if'n the knight hadn' drew me attention. Save me ears burnin' now if'n I had."

Boremac prepared to reply but Tana cut him off with a sharp look. "Dramor, still yourself for the time being." The huntress turned back to Boremac with a brief nod that he could not decipher. "You are lucky the mountain man was not more focused, bandit. Dramor knows only one way to dispense with threats. As for your story, I did note the glowing daggers you wielded against the leader of the assassins. That is part of the reason you still draw breath. It would have taken no effort on my part to let her kill you. We had marked all the other targets before my arrow penetrated her chest. We owe you some small debt for distracting the killers, but they were doomed from the moment we arrived. Would you turn your daggers over to Gregor for examination?"

Boremac felt the fact that she was asking him for permission showed definite improvement in his current standing with her. He turned to extend the daggers' hilts to Gregor as he answered with a single word. "Gladly."

Gregor took the daggers to examine them and get a better sense of the divine blessing that would give truth to the rogue's words. The intricate runes traced on the blades were clearly the marks of the Temple of Light, and the symbols that graced the odd hats that adorned the two jesters capping the hilts matched the design of his own chest piece. The work of master Firebeard was unmistakable, as was the guidance he had no doubt received from one of the more highly placed Temple priests, though Gregor was at a loss to decipher the meaning of the pair of fools decorating the pommels. He was moved to say as much as he handed the blades back to the rogue.

Boremac grinned at that knight's questioning gaze. "Clearly Father Oregeth questioned the wisdom of me joining this quest to set the world back to rights. I can only hope that my face more closely resembles the smiling one at the end of my days." Boremac grew serious before he continued. "I've never been one tied by my word in the past. Honor means little to a man that is surrounded by thieves most of the time. Still this much I can promise you, Lord Lightsword. I have given my word to an honorable man and he has shown me nothing but trust in all our dealings. You will not fall as long as there is power in these quick hands to prevent it. I am figuring between your faith and my luck, we should do well. Of course, we can't forget these graceless bush beaters that would see a man undone over his misunderstood intentions."

Gregor's hands shot up in a warding gesture to the others around the fire, hoping to stifle the flurry of curses the rogue's words would no doubt bring. "We have all made errors today, Master Boremac, and increasing the animosity within our number serves no purpose. Despite the rangers' handling of you, I am certain you can see they had my safety at the front of their minds as you did. Bickering accomplishes nothing. Please choose your words more carefully, if only out of respect for me."

Dramor's loud voice broke the moment of silence observed after Gregor spoke. "I got nothin' but respect for ya, Lord Lightsword, but this man needs to air out 'is voice. I wan'ta give ya my respec' for tossing me, Master Boremac, and I 'ope ya can see me wantn' to give you a what fer of yer own." The mountain man struggled to his feet, clearly still affected by Boremac's abuse, and bowed to the rogue. "I cannot rightly speak for all of us, but me, I welcome ya. We gonna need all the 'elp we can muster 'fore this is over wit'."

Tana stood beside Dramor and the others around the fire. There were looks of concern, and a few smiling faces that shook their heads as they rose, but together they bowed to their leader's judgment. "What a day has come that brings the valiant to lie down with the serpents! The Goddess and God must bless us all to suffer this fit of madness. We will follow you, Gregor, into the Abyss itself should that be what is required, just do not ask me to follow the words of this most questionable individual. His tongue twists like smoke in a whirlwind."

Boremac decided to accept the compliment implied in Tana's words, no matter what her intention had been, and he laughed openly for the first time he could remember. "We are not so different, huntress. I would say that of the two of us, my game is far more dangerous than yours. Ever had a rabbit scar you for turning your back to it? Those assembled here would do worse than to have me to guide them in a pinch. At least I know enough to keep my enemies in front of me." The throwing dagger leapt into his hand before Boremac had made his feet and the blade spun through the air just past Tana's ear. Five bows, including Tana's own, were nocked and at the ready as the sound of breaking limbs drew Gregor's attention beyond where Tana stood. A thud sounded in the darkness outside the light of the fire, and a misfired crossbow bolt angled out from the ground near where Tana stood. Boremac moved to retrieve the bolt, staring intently at the tip. "Looks like we're even, huntress. Good thing none of you tree dwellers got hold of this. You would have gone ahead and tasted the point to test the poison. Would've killed you so fast, you would not have had time to flop." He tossed the offending bolt into the fire. "Contact poison, and a rare one to be sure. Someone really wanted to break up this little party. Wonder why the assassins haven't killed you, Gregor? No offense of course."

Tana relaxed her drawn arrow and placed it into her quiver as the other archers followed her lead. "Why would a lone surviving assassin take a shot at me?" The question was rhetorical judging from her tone, but Boremac was moved to answer it anyway.

"Well, he identified the leader of the group easily enough. You may as well have put a bull's-eye on your back when you shot the assassins' leader. They do not take kindly to outside interference. The killer no doubt saw an opportunity to gain favor with the Master of these bastards if he could have taken you down before retreating. He probably hoped to secure his departure in the chaos created by your demise." Boremac shrugged as if what he said should have been obvious. "That brings us back to the question of why Gregor was not slain. These Black Hands are killers, not kidnappers, at least not without a damn good reason, and highly skilled professionals besides. Given time and inclination the lone remaining hunter would've slain you all."

Gregor spoke up before Tana could reply, though he seemed to be sorting his own thoughts as well as addressing the others. "He wants the blade I carry, and it appears he wants me as well, though I cannot say why. If master Silverwing were here, he could shed some light on the motivation of the dark priest. Boremac, you said you spoke with my mentor recently. Where is he now?"

"Well beyond our reach I'm certain, Gregor. I remained in Zanthfar at his request before he left to go into the mountains, though

I am unsure why. Can I see the blade of which you speak? Lord Silverwing told me you bear part of the true sword that has honored the leader of the Knights since it was first created." Gregor reached behind his back to pass the blade to the rogue, the hesitation in releasing his grip on it nearly imperceptible. The rogue noted his reluctance and kept the blade held before Gregor as he examined it. "Never held a blessed artifact before. Can't say I see much to it, though it has a keen edge. It was finally crafted to be sure, but is useless without a hilt. What are these runes tracing up the blade?" The rogue handed the blade back to Gregor's waiting hands.

"I cannot say. The runes are ancient and their meaning is lost to all but the one that crafted the weapon so long ago. Long study in the Temple of Light brought me no closer to deciphering them." The knight turned to Tana to explain the importance of the sword. "This sword is the weapon passed from one leader to the next throughout the history of the Knights of the Golden Dragon. The will of the God of Light himself was brought to bear against all manner of evil in the time since its initial blessing, when the first Knights were called. Somehow the blade was undone when the Knights I served were destroyed. A power infused the blade which allowed a great demon to take possession of it as it was turned against the last leader of the Knights of the Golden Dragon,. I think now that I know why the blade was broken even as Lord Clamine sacrificed himself to save me." Understanding lit Gregor's features as he stared into the flames, remembering that terrible night so long ago. "The God of Light kept the blade safe in the flesh of his holy warrior as He dismissed the demon that would've killed us both. The sword hilt was lost in the Abyss with the dismissal of the creature, carried away with the Tharnorsa."

"Who is the priest? Who could wield such power? Evil of this nature is surely beyond the grasp of mere mortals." Tana's matter-of-fact statement drew Gregor's eyes to meet her own.

"Father Tur'morival is no mere mortal, at least not anymore. He once served the God of Light and formed the consortium of priests drawn from many faiths to create the Order of the Crimson Night. The Order's purpose was to prepare the followers of true faiths for the Crimson Night that was to come, and for many years they stood at the front of the battle against Abysmal incursions into the world. I believe Father Tur'morival was tainted by the forces he sought to defeat, though I cannot say why this came to pass." Gregor shook his head as broken images invaded his mind from his encounter with the demonologist in his dream. "He is no longer a man. Some form twisted by the demonic forces he has chosen to ally himself with is all that remains." Gregor related his encounter with Father Tur'morival as well as what he had been able to learn studying the priest's written works in the Temple of Light. The knight also shared his recent encounters with the priests of the Crimson Night, answering a few questions offered by the rangers and druids as he progressed, though few interrupted his discourse, content to learn what they could from his words.

"Your encounter with the cursed wolves shows the priest's power to twist simpler beasts, but we have not encountered any of these Crimson Night staff wielders within the wilds near Zanthfar. Do you think they have the power to create the demon bloods we have seen leading the orc tribes?" Tana looked at Gregor with many questions poised behind her eyes, choosing to save the others until they were safe.

"Demon bloods?" Gregor was caught off guard by the question. "What are you referring to as demon bloods? Have you encountered twisted humanoids as well as animals? I've seen no such creatures, but there was little news delivered to the Temple in Nactium concerning Zanthfar while I was there pursuing my training."

Tana shared what she knew of the demon blooded orcs that had until recently caused so much trouble in the area. Gregor's face became more troubled the longer she spoke. He felt sure that the manipulation and creation of such creatures was beyond the powers of even Father Tur'morival, and he said as much. Gregor could find no logic in the creation of such a force, even if the dark summoner could control such numbers of the creatures. Something else had to be behind the demon bloods.

The young knight's attention was drawn to Tana as she finished addressing Gregor and Boremac. She was talking low to Three-Paw while examining his maimed paw. As the huntress spoke a few reassuring words to the wolf, she enclosed the damaged paw in her hands and closed her eyes as she meditated, communing with her Goddess. When she drew her hands from Three-paw a moment later, his maimed paw was restored. Three-paw seemed to be as amazed by this as Gregor was, and the wolf let out a bark as it touched the renewed paw to the earth. Tana shooed the animal toward the forest with a few words of praise and a wave of her hand. Gregor found he was wondering just how much power Tana had over the natural creatures, as the lame wolf that had kept him company bounded into the woods toward its pack, once more whole.

Boremac began addressing the group. "Not really all that hard to figure out once you have all the pieces to the puzzle laid out before you." Boremac shook his head. "Of course, extracting things intentionally hidden is more in my line of work than the rest of you. Two motivations come clear if you look at it properly. The two most basic motivations of all mankind amplified to the level of power said man, or demon in this case, wields. Fear and revenge, Lord Lightsword, are as old to our people now as to the ancient ones that first emerged from the wood to conquer the lands. Your Father Tur'morival fears that sword. That is obvious from the lengths he is going trying to obtain the blade. What reason would he have to fear the weapon, you ask? Simple enough really, so I will let you puzzle that one out on your own. I will tell you this. The hilt is not lost, and I suspect it is much closer to Father Tur'morival than one might think. So who has the hilt? The same demon who took it in the first place, no doubt, and he still hungers for the flesh that escaped him. That would be you, holy warrior."

"I can find no argument with your reasoning, though how Father Tur'morival is able to exercise his will over the demon is a mystery. It gives me no pleasure to know that the Tharnorsa has returned to this land, even bound to the demonologist. He will pay for the blood of the Knights I served." Gregor grew silent for a few moments as he considered the rogue's words. "Is the true blade the only thing that can slay Father Tur'morival? Why would he allow the hilt to remain so close to him, as you suggest, knowing the demon he controls would destroy him at the first opportunity? The demon must seek a great prize to be at the mercy of any mortal. Lord Silverwing is heading to face father Tur'morival and knows nothing of this. We have to find him before..."

"Yes, before the trap is set." Boremac finished the knight's thought. "Unfortunately, Master Gregor, Father Tur'morival seems to have put everything into motion quite well. Lord Silverwing is the bait."

14

Into the Unknown

Lord Silverwing was already far from Zanthfar as his messenger set out to rescue Gregor from the Black Hands. The last remaining original Knight of the Golden Dragon found the company he kept was well chosen for their task, and the journey into the mountains had gone largely without incident. He could have had no way to know his destiny was laid out before him long ago. The knight had departed the gathering accompanied by the strongest and most resourceful rangers and druids that were available. Thirty-five strong men and women were now part of this largest incursion into the forsaken volcanoes. Soon the sturdy trees that dared the ragged mountainside would give way to the scrub brush and hardy grasses of Master Stonecutter's homeland.

Silverwing took some time to review the composition of the group he and Fasurel led into the mountains. Fasurel was still a mystery to the knight. He spoke little, favoring action over the broken words of his people, to demonstrate his capabilities. The mountain man was well thought of by the others of his clan that traveled with the mixed band of warriors and priests. Three mountain rangers that had accompanied Fasurel to Zanthfar spoke of him in a way that bordered on reverence. They said that many of their clan would join them once the party drew near their homes. Fasurel only shrugged when Silverwing questioned him about this, saying that he would take no more than the villages could spare. Master Stonecutter saw no reason to diminish the numbers of protectors that were still in the mountains. "We be strong in spirit and arms, Lord Silverwing, an' those with us will serve." Fasurel's words echoed now in Silverwing's mind. The statement left no room for discussion at the time, reinforcing Fasurel's reticence.

Fifteen forest dwellers filled their ranks as well. The woods rangers' weapons, which consisted of short, well-tended swords and longbows, were in sharp contrast to the heavy picks and axes favored by the mountain rangers. The sturdy, broad mountain men wore the only heavy armor among the members of the group, each suited in loose fitting chain mail. The chosen protection of the others ranged from light leathers to the heavily studded leather plates Fasurel himself favored. The two Ardataure, the long-lived people that were the protectors of the Ancient Forest, were the ones that Silverwing found the most curious. Each was armed with a longbow that measured his full height and were made of a wood that Silverwing could not identify. The pair also carried small daggers, little more than keen knives, for close confrontations, however Silverwing doubted anyone or anything ever got very close. They moved with no more sound than spirits, disturbing nothing where they passed. Each kept a falcon as a companion, which made them excellent scouts. Few creatures escaped their attention, and they interpreted the movements of the natural beasts well, allowing the group to have a good deal of warning concerning potential threats. Silverwing had found it curious at first that the pair of Ardataure sent their companions back to the woods before entering the forsaken mountains, however their reasoning soon became clear. One Ardataure explained that there was little use in putting their companions at risk within the harsh lands that were their destination. Silverwing had seen the wisdom in that and suggested that the mountain men might release their charges as well. Fasurel had only laughed before giving an answer to that thought. "Ya thinkin'? That be something ya not likely see. Lizards tha' follow us built a' hardier stuff and not likely ta go without a boot.

209

Las' one tha' got a boot took a leg wit' the boot, so don't wait ta see that."

Silverwing nodded in understanding and posed a question to Fasurel that had tugged at his mind for some time. "Why do you not have a companion, Master Stonecutter?"

Fasurel's smile faded, his eyes wet as he turned to the fire, avoiding Silverwing's gaze. "No, no companion fer some time. He was a terror, he was. 'Fraid a' nothin' an' sadly that was what undone 'im. Kilt a bunch a' orcs 'fore they had 'im. Poor Claw, 'e never knew wha' hit 'im and I should be glad for it. The one tha' put the bolt in 'im paid tho', be sure a' that. Kilt the ones tha' Claw didn' then tracked that bastard three days and nights till I tore 'im apart. Didn' bring me Claw back ta life but I keep 'im 'ere." Fasurel tapped his chest as Silverwing brought a hand to the mountain man's shoulder. Silverwing found tears of his own tracing down his face as his new friend finished speaking. The knight would not fully understand the meaning behind Fasurel's words for a few more days.

***

Master Stonecutter joined Lord Silverwing at the fire. His concern was evident as the mountain man dropped his solid form next to the ranger. "We 'ave no words from the tree dweller gone scouting. Don' care for the lack, knowin' those demon bloods were so near last word. The one bein' in camp gettin' jumpy too as his partner hasn' come back. No good us staying 'ere so long. Goin' need some ground under our feet soon. Jus' what I be thinkin'."

Silverwing had hoped for better news but the mountain man's words were no surprise to the knight. "We cannot commit more scouts to find the others. Break up those that remain into small groups and have them spread out in a rough perimeter. The demon bloods behind us have the numbers on their side, but I do not think they are pursuing us. We need to take them off guard and destroy them before they reach the mountains. Too many innocents will be sacrificed if they do."

"Whatcha thinkin' to do for yourself, Lord Silverwing? Don' want you going off by yourself and get yourself kilt now. We fall as one or not at all, and I prefer not at all." The strength of conviction in the man's tone made Silverwing certain there would be no arguing with him.

"I am going hunting, my friend, and it would appear from your words that you are, too. Disperse the others and meet me back here at the fire. You and I will find the demon bloods and draw them within range of the rangers' bows. Tell them to watch for a signal before they move to strike. I want the creatures well within the circles of light cast by our fires before the first arrow flies." Lord Silverwing stared into the fire, waiting for Master Stonecutter's reply.

"An' what signal you wantin' them to look to?" Master Fasurel was more than ready to take the fight to the creatures that threatened his homeland. Still this knight was a mystery to him, and for all the time they had traveled together, the mountain man had yet to see the ranger draw his weapons. Some things one just accepted on faith, he reflected as Lord Silverwing answered his question.

"They will know it when they see it. Just tell them to be ready and move as one when they do. Fasurel, I need you to restrain your vigor once we meet these creatures. I should have little trouble drawing their attention from range. You should not engage the demon bloods until we know how many they number." Lord Silverwing's eyes studied the flames before him as he prayed in preparation for the fight to come.

***

"Strike now, Fasurel!" The small number of demon blooded orcs felt the bite of Lord Silverwing's arrows as they scattered from the bonfire below. The silver tipped points struck true, and the demon bloods burst into flame before collapsing in a pile of ash. His quiver grew light with the speed of his shots, and Lord Silverwing quickly secured his bow at his back before drawing his blades to engage the creatures. Fasurel ran from the trees, flanking the creatures and swinging his double-edged ax in wide circles to kill the demon bloods as efficiently as possible. The sturdy mountain man was surprisingly able on his feet, dipping below the long claws that appeared to be everywhere at once. The brutal creatures' arms swept harmlessly over his stout form as Master Stonecutter cleaved away the limbs of his foes. Lord Silverwing had little time to admire the mountain man's skill. He faced an assault of his own as the darkness nearby swelled with the sound of inhuman howling, and more demon bloods flowed from the tree line.

His powerful thrusts did little to turn away the first wave. Lord Silverwing realized his error soon enough as his arcing blade tossed one of the creature's heads into the air, dissolving the charging demon blood's form before its skull struck the ground. Silverwing spared what breath he could to shout to Master Stonecutter. "Take their heads!"

He had no time to laugh at the loud reply. "I be take'n what I can!" The pile of writhing bodies that formed around the great ax wielder gave truth to his words as he lifted the angle of its travel to take them at their necks. Moments later the mountain man disappeared behind a grey swirling cloud of disintegrated foes. It was not long before the uncoordinated attackers were undone, and the two men met at the center of the camp.

"We done good, I be thinkin'." Fasurel moved around the area, quickly beheading the demon bloods that still lived. The man's height had made it easier to carve away their legs at the start of the melee, and he was amazed to see the wicked creatures still clawing after him with only their arms to carry them.

"Too good." The knight stared at the ground where he crouched near the tree line. "Too many tracks leading out to account for the small number of them we faced. It was a trap." Without another word, Silverwing drew an arrow from his quiver and shot it skyward. "We have to hurry!" The path of the arrow ignited and burst into a brilliant shower of light as it began to fall toward the earth, turning the moonless night into day. "God of Light save them, God save them all." The two warriors ran back toward where the other rangers had remained.

The bright glow rapidly diminished from the sky, but Lord Silverwing could see all he needed from the remaining light of the rangers' campfires. Easily three times the number of demon bloods Silverwing and Fasurel had slain formed loose patrolling groups, moving inside the clearing near the now ransacked camp. There was a rough circle of the creatures formed near the center of the encampment the pair of leaders had so recently left as well. The inner circle of creatures, growling and shouting in a language Lord Silverwing could not decipher, surrounded a handful of rangers and druids, some lying prone while others did what they could to heal the most wounded of their number. Some of the demon bloods waved what appeared to be makeshift clubs at their captives. The true nature of the weapons became apparent as several orcs within the central group bit deeply into the clubs, rending flesh from the bones of the limbs they carried. An unknowable number of his brethren had been torn apart, taken by surprise as the waves of demon blooded orcs had swept into the ranger's camp. A loose outer ring had formed around the inner ring that was taunting the captives. Each of the creatures forming that group faced outward, searching the darkness, tossing a large oddly shaped stone between each of their clawed hands.

"Their 'eads." the mountain man's solemn words confirmed with Lord Silverwing had also suspected. "Their 'eads!" Fasurel's bellow took Silverwing by surprise. The heads that had been torn from the slain rangers and druids became projectiles, striking Fasurel as he charged toward the demon bloods. Fasurel's fury awakened Silverwing's own. A flurry of arrows tore through the creatures nearest the trapped rangers just before the knight dropped his bow and rushed into the crowd of demon bloods. The pair of warriors hewed away the demon blood orcs that were directly in their path and made their way toward the wounded, intent on protecting those that remained. Silverwing tossed one of his swords at the feet of one of the less wounded rangers and turned to begin his harvest. He shouted over his shoulder at the young female as she took up the weapon. "Take their damned heads!" Instruction proved unnecessary, as she had already begun swinging the long blade out to the farthest reach of her toned arms. It was only moments before she disappeared into a deep cloud of disintegrating orcs, with only the occasional flash of firelight glimmering off the extended blade indicating she still moved. Lord Silverwing's arms began to grow weary despite the economy of his killing. The demon bloods would overwhelm them with sheer numbers if the battle lasted much longer.

Fasurel's initial fury diminished as he focused on the task at hand. There were too many of them to take with only the three remaining warriors. He had to do something and now was as good as a time as any. The mountain man drew a great breath and let out an inhuman bellow that dropped the ax from his hands even as the change took his form. Claws suited to digging in solid rock replaced the ranger's hands as a third pair of legs sprouted from his waist, ripping through his thick leathers. Thick scales sprouted from his skin to cover his form, as torn bits of cloth and studded leather plates fell away from his body. An elongated snout emerged to replace his mouth, filled with jagged teeth made for tearing. He wore his animal form as well as he wore his own, and set his claws and jaws to ripping the demon bloods apart with much more efficiency than his ax could have accomplished.

Master Stonecutter's call did not go unanswered. Several large lizards poured into the clearing. The ranger wielding Lord Silverwing's sword mimicked Fasurel's example in part and raised her voice to the woodland creatures. Her night piercing howl was answered in kind and a pack of wolves ran into the clearing, joining the swelling number of lizards, to kill the despoilers that had come into their homes. Before retrieving his bow, Lord Silverwing marveled for a moment at the giant lizard Master Stonecutter had become. The master archer delivered his arrows with vengeance. Once more the demon bloods felt his sting, and the encampment lit brightly with those slain by the rapidly flying arrows. The ferociousness of the animals within the area was matched by their summoners. The demon bloods fell like wheat before the scythe. It soon became clear that there would be no quarter given from either side. Withdrawal was not in the creatures plans, and the demon blooded orcs that remained would not escape, of that he was certain. Lord Silverwing turned to survey the landscape after he had exhausted the silver tipped arrows in his quiver, leaving the animals and the remaining ranger to destroy those that were left. The knight sensed that there was other prey in need of his attention. Somewhere in the darkness, a servant of these creatures' creator was present, and he intended to find it.

A leathery flapping of broad wings drew his eyes away from the violence. The prey had been spotted, and Lord Silverwing fired two arrows into the night, catching the strange creature unaware. The missiles pinned the imp to the tree where only moments before it had hopped from one foot to the other, taking in the chaos that littered the ground with bodies and blood. The creature tore its sickly wings, trying to free itself, but it was too late. Another arrow from its tormentor's bow lodged in its chest, leaving it drawing ragged breaths as the last of the demon blooded orcs were slain. Lord Silverwing moved to collect his prize almost casually as the thing renewed its struggle to flee. Its purpose here was complete. Its master knew the demon bloods had failed, but the knight had one last message to share with the creature's keeper before he killed it.

The ranger's grace was apparent to all who witnessed his ascent into the limbs of the tree. Lord Silverwing's usual knightly bearing and restraint, always evident to even casual observers among his new companions, disappeared, as he violently ripped the wriggling form from the tree. The ranger looked deep into the bulbous eyes of the imp as he pressed one hand against its body. He seemed unaffected by the clawing members of the creature as he spoke in a voice little more than a whisper. "Remember this face, Keeper. It will be the last thing you know of this world or any other." There was no warning as Silverwing formed his free hand into a fist and slammed it into the center of the staring imp's eyes, crushing its skull. The imp's body flinched reflexively with the force of the blow and moved no more.

"Good shot," Fasurel's rough voice carried up from just below Silverwing at the base of the tree, causing the knight to turn his head to look at him. "Nothin' like a good bone crushin' ta vent ya angers. If'n ya thinkin' ya able, we got folks needin' tendin' Jus' need a moment meself to get clothed an' I be joinin' ya wit' those remainin'."

Lord Silverwing noted the naked mountain man's makeshift loin cloth with appreciation for his modesty. "I guess that change is a terror on your armor."

"It is but I keep spare bits in me pack. Jus' never know when you might need a extra pair a' claws." Fasurel shrugged, turning toward his supplies.

The sight that met Silverwing's eyes as the mountain man walked toward his replacement armor brought a wave of laughter surging through him, almost causing the knight to lose his footing on the branch where he was perched. A plump, shining beacon reflected the dancing light from one of the nearby fires. Fasurel responded to the laughter without turning as his exposed flesh adopted a healthy red glow that Silverwing was certain matched the mountain man's face. "Wot? Ya act like ya never seen a bare rear afore. Getcha out that tree an' tend to the others." Silverwing did fall out of the tree then, landing with a solid thump that drew a laugh in return from Fasurel.

The healers among them, including Lord Silverwing, brought divine grace to bear, healing the most grievously wounded. The remaining two mountain men and Fasurel put their picks to work, digging a grave large enough to hold the rest of their fallen friends. Lord Silverwing spoke brief prayers over the remains, imploring the God of Light to recognize the sacrifice of each soul whose body was committed to the earth, and guide them safely home. Stones were then placed around the grave mound once the bodies were interred, in each representing a different divine power to honor the beliefs of the dead. Time was taken to offer prayers individually and to let those who lived recover from the terrible battle.

Later the rangers and druids gathered in a loose circle near one of the central fires of their encampment as Lord Silverwing took account of the ones who remained. Master Stonecutter stood at the knight's side, once more wearing his sturdy studded leather armor. "I am a stranger among you, though I have patrolled woodlands of my own as many of you have for years. We were not prepared for such tactics from these creatures. The weight of death that this failure allowed weighs on my soul alone. There were signs that I chose to ignore and I moved, with a lack of faith in the abilities of you all assembled here, to engage the creatures on my own. The mound where the dead now rest is testament to my lack of faith and wisdom. I will carry on alone into the desolate peaks. No more of you will be sacrificed for my folly. Collect your things and go home. Defend your lands and know that the evil that took place here will be avenged."

The assembled rose as one, quietly forming a line with a space left in the middle, and faced Lord Silverwing. Master Stonecutter moved to the space at the center that had been left open for him. The rangers and druids bowed before each dropped to one knee, except Fasurel, who rose from his bow to speak for the group facing the knight. "Ya not be rid of us tha' simple. We knew what we were in fer when we came an' we will be seein' it 'til the end. Ya can blame yaself if it ease ya mind, but we don' see it tha' way. We saved who we could an' those we couldn' are at peace now. More trouble comin' so we bes take our rest an' get ready to move fast in the mornin'" Fasurel waved away the others and moved to face Silverwing, the boots of the two men nearly touching. The mountain man's tone penetrated the knight's heart with his next words. "Ya cannot be blamin' yerself for what happened as we shoulda all been more alert, and we coundn' done no more good wit' us dying all together here than we could losin' the ones that fell with us apart. The dead would not have us shamin' them by not carryin' on wit' ya. Go on and gather your arrows, as I think ya will need every one before it is over."

As Fasurel finished speaking, Silverwing moved to the outer encampment where he had loosed his first arrows, noting as he went that the wolves still patrolled the forest. He could not help but wonder what his God intended for him, as he filled his quiver with the blessed arrows once more.

***

The passage opened abruptly into a vast cavern. Natural stone formations protruded at random throughout the demon's sanctuary. A throne that stretched toward the roof of the cavern dominated the vast area, flanked on either side by a bubbling crater nearly filled with lava. The boiling contents of the craters provided the only light in the cavern. The rear portion of the throne was capped with a ram's head carved from a black shimmering stone. The eyes were shaped with cut rubies and the fangs protruding from the ram's jaw had been cut from ivory. The beauty of the workmanship was lost in the evil images that dominated the throne's arms and base. The arms were cut in images of carnal violation. A Tharnorsa pinned a human female form to the arm of the throne on the right. The demon's fiery wings were drawn close to its sides and wrapped around the form of his victim so that only her head was visible. The left arm was a mirror image of the right with a succubus taking the Tharnorsa's position. The creature's leathery wings engulfed the human male below her, once more leaving only the head exposed. The demonic heads each stared down toward their respective victims with matching expressions that appeared to reflect cruel ecstasy. The human countenances were arched backward as though their abused forms sought to escape the gaze of their tormentors. The faces of the fervor possessed humans were the worst parts. They were locked in frozen looks of complete terror that had given way to numbness as their minds shattered.

Father Tur'morival knelt before the giant throne where the Tharnorsa sat, never taking his eyes away from the blackened hilt that lay at the demon's right hand. The hilt was decorated with intertwined dragons twisting around the handle, with their long necks curving outward to form the branches of the guard. The dragon's bodies were woven around nearly identical intricately cut crystals forming the center of the grip. Claws appeared to suspend each crystal at the top and bottom of the hilt. The crystals seemed to absorb the low light around them, as if offended by the illumination. "Must you keep that artifact exposed?" The demon's answer was immediate and the same as every time the two communicated directly. Heat surged into the priest's mind with the demon's ancient language, dark words blended into terrible images that would have driven most mortals mad with the slightest exposure. Father Tur'morival twisted his mouth in a rictus, enjoying the demon's mental touch.

It pleases me to see fear in your eyes on these rare visits. So much power in a mortal, and yet a broken sword's handle gives you pause. Yes, your fear tastes rich and is so much more delicious than the meager offerings of the orcs. As the demon touched deeply into his mind, searching for anything to twist the will of the man, Father Tur'morival pushed back.

The priest took only a moment to enjoy the shudder that traveled through the Tharnorsa's body before he spoke. "Do not toy with me, demon. I've no time to trifle with you. There is much to be done before our guest arrives. Where is Lord Silverwing now?"

The demon answered, though his displeasure at being pushed by the priest was evident as he leaned deeply forward. Father Tur'morival rose to his feet, taking a rapid step back as the demon's head came level with his own. That the Tharnorsa had taken the blackened hilt into his hand did not escape his attention. The implied threat needed no words. *I do not know where they are now but he is coming as we planned. That is enough to know. He will be surprised to see his old friend again, though I doubt he will be as pleased as I. You have news as well?*

"Yes, the child comes to us following in his mentor's footsteps. The assassins have failed to take him once more. It seems the reach of the Black Hand may be great but their fingers are cut away far too easily. I will have to deal with their master sooner than I would have liked. Once the two knights are captured, we will have little use for the killers."

You will move your followers against him. Mortals have such short sight. He would have been such a great ally, this Overseer, if you had allowed him free rein.

Tur'morival contemplated his answer before he spoke. "One who hungers so openly for power is never to be trusted. Have your dealings with me taught you so little, demon? I would think in your service to me you would have learned this much. Age has brought little wisdom to the Overseer, and that will be his undoing. Do not allow your own arrogance to be yours, Tharnorsa, as it was in the past. Faith is a powerful weapon in the hands of these knights, and I would have preferred to remove their weapons before bringing them here, but the failure of the assassins was anticipated and I have prepared. You will do what you have promised, and together we will destroy this world." Father Tur'morival turned from the demon to meet with his chosen of the Crimson Order. Lord Silverwing would arrive soon, and this time there would be no mistakes.

The Tharnorsa drew back into his throne, replacing the tainted hilt on the arm to the right. As Father Tur'morival withdrew from the cavern, the demon took time to reflect. He remembered the last time he and Lord Silverwing had met all too well. The knight had dismissed him from the world despite the careful plans of Father Tur'morival, a fledgling priest at the time, yet full of cunning even then. The surge of divine power had left its marks on the demon from that encounter, even as the Tharnorsa had reincorporated into the Abyss. The Unnamed One had seen fit to allow the twin scars in the demon's great chest to remain.

The fall of the Knights of the Golden Dragon would have been complete except for the faith of Lord Silverwing. The Tharnorsa recalled his and Lord Silverwing's last meeting with no pleasure. The other keepers of the light had fallen, leaving only the archer to face him and the tainted knights that had served the demon so many decades ago. The black servants had sacrificed themselves to the holy warrior despite the demon's influence. What drove the fallen knights to do so still troubled the demon, though in the end it made little difference. The Tharnorsa understood nothing of honor and devotion, but he remembered pain well. Lord Silverwing had drawn the strength of his God directly into his blades, then driven both the illuminated blades into the demon's chest, taking the demon completely unaware and placing it into throes of agony that persisted even as his corporeal form in this mortal world disintegrated. The demon remembered the last thought he had sent into the Knight's mind brain as the tumbling blades of the holy warrior had flown toward him, ignited with golden light. *Mere mortal, your God knows nothing of this place and you will not be given the choice to serve me, as were your petty brethren. I will find much pleasure in your torture before I feed slowly on your flesss...* and still the Tharnorsa felt the bite of the twin blades buried deep into his chest. Yes, the Tharnorsa would take great pleasure in fulfilling his promise when once more Lord Silverwing appeared before him, returning the pain he had been caused tenfold.

Father Tur'morival was cunning for a mortal and possessed an evil soul that nearly matched that of the demon before him. The priest had used the fall of the Tharnorsa to his advantage. The demon's arrogance was outdone only by his desire for revenge against the knight that had defeated him, leaving him marred for eternity. Father Tur'morival had learned much from the Tharnorsa in the time they had communicated before the demon chose to aid him. The Unnamed One all the creatures of the Abyss served was remarkable in his cruelty and desire for chaos, and the suffering the Tharnorsa had endured in the Abyss at his Master's hands had been without match. Father Tur'morival had found the demon all too willing to return to this world when the priest had reached into the swirling chaos, seeking the Master's scarred servant. Still the bargaining between the

Tharnorsa and the priest had been long, and the price of equality with the entity had been dear for Father Tur'morival.

In the end, the Tharnorsa had committed itself into the service of the Master of the Order of the Crimson Night for the promise of revenge and the priest's aid in bringing the Crimson Night itself to fruition. Father Tur'morival's use of the demons against the Knights of Bella Grey had proven only a partial failure, and had given the priest the last piece to controlling the greater demon completely. He had summoned the demon, placing him directly into the Knight's stronghold with instruction to destroy the only weapon that could stand against him, but the demon had had other plans for his summoner at the time. The demon had become aware of the depth of Father Tur'morival's connection to him too late, and had been forced once more into the Abyss with only half his prize. Father Tur'morival had withdrawn his power, and the Tharnorsa was once more left to the tortures of its Master. The Unnamed One had given the demon reason to give Father Tur'morival the last thing the priest needed. The Tharnorsa had projected its true name into the priest with the hope it would destroy him, but father Tur'morival's studies were not in vain and he was prepared. Taking possession of the Tharnorsa's soul had nearly killed the priest, channeling the demon's full powers into the soul stone, but the sacrifice had been worth it.

Loss of one's mortal flesh was a small price to pay for immortality when one's body began to wither. Father Tur'morival had found his body diminishing despite the strength of his increasing powers. Once he had taken control of the demon's soul and the power of the pure evil it possessed, the priest had remade his physical form. The thick scales that encased his weak true form gave him physical protection well beyond those of any pure mortal. There would be little challenge in undoing the young knight, despite what his visions had told him. The priest was certain his destiny was his own to make, as he had done so many times before.

Twelve priests of the Crimson Night Order awaited their high priest's arrival and knelt before his throne as Father Tur'morival took his seat. The seat of power for the order was unremarkable except for the two giant statues of Tharnorsa that flanked each side of the throne. Each obsidian figure held burning braziers with outstretched arms, lighting the humble throne of the Master in a wash of flickering light. Glimmering rubies that served as the eyes of the creatures shimmered in the darkness at a height just outside the light of the braziers' flames. The priests had learned quickly to remain at the farthest edge of the circles of light the braziers cast. Their master was not known for his patience with those that drew too near his seat of power. Marks burnt into the floor near the throne were all that remained of any brought before the Master after failing him. The inner circle had numbered many more priests in the past; some that had thought there was folly in the Master's plans or had felt another leader would better serve the Order. All these individuals, and those foolish enough to support these misguided followers vying for power, had been drawn from the Order and dealt with by the Father himself. No traitor left this sanctuary.

Father Tur'morival swiveled his hooded head to take in all the assembled priests. "The time has come, brothers and sister of the faith. Our old friend comes to pay his respects to our ally, and we want to make certain he makes it to the one that dwells beneath without hindrance. Those of you that are coordinating the welcome of Lord Silverwing will assemble your forces and take up the positions outside the keep as planned." Father Tur'morival centered his hooded visage on the priests in front of him before continuing. "Lord Silverwing had a measure of luck and evaded capture at the hands of our returning forces. His forces have sustained a significant loss at the hands of the demon bloods and, though the remaining protectors are stronger in spirit for their loss, we should have little trouble dealing with the few that remain. Those of you not forming the reception party will remain at the walls of the keep. Prepare the missile troops at the walls to take Lord Silverwing at range, and alive. All his companions are to be slain. If Lord Silverwing is killed, I will take great pleasure in torturing the one responsible for the failure through several lifetimes. His soul is beyond my ability to recall into this world, all of yours, however, are not. You would do well to remember that and take the necessary precautions to assure he is taken alive. Go to your appointed positions now." *ensure*

The priests rose as one, each in turn giving praise to their Master before leaving. Father Tur'morival extended a single finger of shimmering scaled flesh from beneath his robes, the deadly sharp claw at its tip reflecting the firelight from above him. "Father Ragone, remain here with me. I would discuss a matter of some importance with you before you go."

Father Ragone turned to face his Master once more, pulling back his crimson hood as he did so. For twenty years, the priest had served Father Tur'morival. Father Ragone was instrumental in the construction of the keep that served as sanctuary for the Master, and he knew every inch of the stone that formed it. His personal troops of demon bloods had created the throne room that served as the Tharnorsa's quarters, and he had appeared before the demon many times in Father Tur'morival's place. He had no reason to fear his Master, until the other priests left the room.

Once the two were alone in Tur'morival's chamber, the Master spoke. Father Ragone was amazed at how Father Tur'morival could sentence someone to death without even a minor change in tone or inflection. He had witnessed many such sentences in his time with the Master, but only now could he understand the paralyzing terror of being the victim of such a proclamation. "You serve two Masters, Father Ragone, and though I have known this for quite some time, I no longer have any use for your duplicity. Rest assured your years of faithful service are to be rewarded, and I will lengthen your agony no more than necessary. If you wish, feel free to charge this throne and perhaps I will kill you immediately. The Overseer did well in his choice of spies, and I would be interested in seeing just how strong one of the Black Hand really is. Do not dismay. Your brothers and sisters will be destroyed soon. Rogue assassins are trouble enough without a strong, organized band nipping at one's heels." Father Tur'morival seemed distracted as he brought his clawed hand from beneath his sleeve and pressed it into the folds of his robes. Father Ragone wasted no breath or movement as he closed the distance between himself and Father Tur'morival. The Master rose so quickly he seemed to stand without actually moving, as both his staff-wielding arm and the arm that had disappeared beneath his robes came out in front of him. Father Tur'morival held his staff in his right hand and a smooth dark-red orb roughly the size of a fist in his outstretched left hand. The two items, staff and crimson orb, glowed brightly in the light of the flames, though the orb seemed to magnify the intensity of the light it reflected. Father Ragone came to an abrupt stop, staring at the orb, as blood began to trickle from his eyes and ears. The doomed priest tried to speak, but no words escaped him.

Father Tur'morival smiled appreciatively. "Well done. You at least make an attempt at self-preservation, unlike the one who gave you over to me so long ago. Do you know that I placed your Master in his current position before your mother had given life to you? He has grown bold, but not wise. You would think one hundred years in service to me would make him smarter. You have the benefit of my personal touch on the way to oblivion; he will die in his sleep at the hand of his finest blade. I hope that brings your some measure of peace. Unfortunately, the entertainment I arranged for this evening has been delayed, so your suffering will have to suffice." Father Tur'morival found his victim's screams very satisfying for the time it took the burning to burst from within him and ignite his body.

15

Preparations

Tana's hunting party was gathered in the druid grove near Zanthfar. Gregor spoke with Mithrina nearby, gathering what news he could of Lord Silverwing and the group he had led into the mountains. "He would have made it deep into the lower mountains by now, Lord Lightsword, and should easily make his way to the source of the taint soon. Master Stonecutter knows the mountains as well as I know these lands, and the rangers and druids in Lord Silverwing's party were the best of those that gathered here."

"He is headed into a trap, Mistress Mithrina, and we must find a way to stop him before he reaches the Forsaken Mountains." Gregor made no effort to hide his concern for his mentor. "Lord Silverwing does not know the full power of the threat he rushes to face."

"Do not underestimate the strength of your mentor, young knight. He is knowledgeable and wise in years of training and study. There is little that he could encounter and be unprepared to face. He will do what he is called to do, as will the others with him, with little concern for the sacrifices that are demanded." Mithrina's words demonstrated her faith in the warrior knight even as Lord Silverwing drew closer to his fate.

"Mistress Mithrina, you do not understand. He is being drawn toward an enemy that is beyond his abilities. The blade I bear is the key to the defeat of Father Tur'morival, and without it Lord Silverwing will be slain. We must get word to him before it is too late!" Gregor's voice rose with each word he uttered until he was nearly shouting.

Mistress Mithrina seemed unaffected by the outburst, and maintained her calm bearing. "Accept his fate as he has, Lord Lightsword. We all commit our souls to the higher powers we serve. This is our calling. If he is to join the God of Light, Lord Silverwing will do so, and gladly, in service to his God. Do not belittle his role in a misplaced effort to save him. You will do what you are called to do, and so will he. "

Gregor lowered his voice, bowing his head in reverence to the druid before him as if to the God of Light he served. "Yes, Mistress Mithrina, God's will be done. How best am I to serve?"

"You will lead the remaining forces assembled in the near lands into the mountains, following the path taken by Lord Silverwing. Tana should be able to track him readily enough. If his enemy is drawing Lord Silverwing to him as you assume, you should have little difficulty in finding the evil that taints our world. The rangers and druids still patrolling the wild lands can be quickly recalled to join you. In a matter of a few days, you should be ready to go." Mistress Mithrina cast her eyes over Gregor's shoulder as movement at the young knight's back caught her attention. "Yes?"

Boremac appeared at Gregor's side, his face full of concern as he addressed the druid. "Begging your pardon, mistress, but I do not see the wisdom of sending in all the remaining protectors of the wood. The time we would lose in assembling the group would just give the advantage to the one we seek, by my way of thinking, and it seems he has advantage enough as it is. A small group of us would gain the element of surprise, and have a much better chance of getting in to Father Tur'morival's stronghold than an army of wood-keepers, no offense intended. They would see us coming from days away and the loss of good men and women could not justify the risk."

Mistress Mithrina cocked an eyebrow at the bold rogue's words. "What exactly do you propose, rogue?"

Boremac grinned at the measure she had taken of him. The druid did not mince words. "Well, Father Tur'morival has gone to great efforts to assure that Master Gregor is brought before him, so we do not want to disappoint him. The priest obviously needs the young knight alive for some purpose, or the assassins from whom we rescued him would have killed him. My dealings with the killers of the Black Hand, though minimal, have demonstrated their skills in the arts of death and shadow. They are rarely called upon to capture anyone they can kill."

Mistress Mithrina considered the rogue's words for a few moments before replying. "I see some wisdom in your words. Who do you choose to accompany the young knight into the Forsaken Mountains?"

"I think the path should be clear since Lord Silverwing passed through the lands just a few days before us. The priest that has set the path before Lord Silverwing, this Father Tur'morival, would have placed only enough obstacles in his way to make him unaware of the trap that was laid. The huntress, Tana, would come as a tracker, and Mistress Sephia should accompany us as well to scout the lands ahead of us. This would assure we do not alarm out target before we make his stronghold. The mountain man, Dramor, would be invaluable once we travel deep into the Forsaken Mountains, though I fear he would have trouble sneaking up on a blind, deaf man that was asleep." Boremac's last words brought an angry grunt from Dramor, but the mountain man could not deny the truth of it, and quietly grumbled to himself. "Still, his knowledge of the mountains would make him worth the risk. I will complete the group and educate the unwieldy in the art of moving unseen."

The leader of the druids nodded her approval. "If Lord Lightsword has no complaint, we will go ahead with your plan. I will obtain horses for the chosen, and you may leave at nightfall. The horses can speed you as far as the lower mountains, and perhaps you can overtake Lord Silverwing. Does this please you, Lord Lightsword?"

"I can find no error with the rogue's reasoning, and a smaller force should move more quickly." Gregor held little hope that they would catch Lord Silverwing before he faced Father Tur'morival. "You may know, Mistress Mithrina, that if Lord Silverwing's spirit departs his body, we cannot bring him back into this world without violating the code of the Knights of the Golden Dragon."

"Yes, Lord Lightsword, I am aware of the code you are bound by honor to keep. There is nothing I can do except pray that he is not sacrificed." She lowered her head as if entering into prayer at that moment. "Have faith in the powers we serve, Gregor, and know they have not forsaken us."

Gregor spent the remainder of the day making sure everyone carried enough supplies to take them to the Forsaken Mountains with a minimal amount of unnecessary weight. As the sun began to lower behind the trees, the small group he would lead gathered to discuss the journey. Tana was engaged in a heated exchange with Fang, and though Gregor could only understand the words Tana spoke, it was easy to interpret the growling that served as Fang's reply.

"You will remain here and I will hear no more of it!" Fang's snarl indicated her displeasure at leaving her companion's side.

"Don't use that language with me. I will not have you eaten, or worse, because of misplaced concern for me. You know that I can take care of myself." Fang raised her hackles as she barked out a rapid reply. "Don't bring that up again. Ancient history, pup, and I could have taken them without your help. There were only four, and they only stunned me momentarily." Fang lowered her tail and turned away from Tana, obviously done with the discussion. "Turn away from me? Get yourself to the woods and guide the wolves here. I need you to protect those who remain." Tana crossed her arms across her breast, watching as Fang lowered her head and slunk out of the glade. "Damn animal!"

"Yeah, the wolf's head is as thick as her mistress', it would appear." Boremac's snide grin disappeared as Tana turned on him with burning eyes.

Tana pointed her blade at the rogue before speaking. "Watch your tongue, thief, or lose it."

Gregor shouted at the pair a little louder than he intended. "Enough! We serve the same purpose and it's time you all start acting like it! No one has been pressed into this company, and the paths that have brought us together were not of our own making. If anyone doubts the cause that brings us together, leave now before you jeopardize the others later. Faith will only carry us so far. Unity must take us the rest of the way."

"Well spoken, Lord Lightsword." Mistress Mithrina's words turned Gregor away from the arguing pair. He bowed slightly in welcome to the leader of the grove. The druid nodded in reply and held out a small vial filled with cloudy liquid. "Take this draught. I pray you have no use for it. The liquid is a potent restorative that should only be used in the most desperate circumstances. It will heal even the direst wounds, though the imbiber will sleep deeply for some time. Should your own powers of healing fail, this will not." She turned to face the horses that were waiting for the group. "These animals will take you as far as they can and will return to me once you have released them. Go with haste and know the Goddess and God travel with you."

"Thank you, Mistress Mithrina, for everything. I have faith we will overcome the evil in the Forsaken Mountains, but I do not know what will become of the demon bloods and tainted creatures once the deed is done. There are many priests in service to Father Tur'morival scattered throughout the lands, and they wield terrible power in their own right."

"The others will be dealt with." The finality of Mistress Mithrina's words left no doubt in Gregor's mind that they would.

16

Fire and Fury

Lord Silverwing stood near one of the stone homes at a mining village, quietly talking to the miners. It had been three days since the remainder of his group had buried their fallen kinsmen and women. The rangers and druids that followed him had moved rapidly toward the Forsaken Mountains, intent on their purpose. Food and water grew scarcer as they traveled into the higher elevations, and the kindness of the miners had been essential as the group moved forward. Lord Silverwing thanked the mountain men for their information and supplies, and went to join Fasurel. Master Stonecutter was gathering news concerning the mines in the hands of the orcs.

Fasurel was scratching his head, clearly perplexed by what he heard from the scouts. "I don' get it an' I cannot say I much care fer it. Lookin' like the orcs done abandoned the mines all at one time."

Lord Silverwing paused to consider Fasurel's words. "That is strange after all the efforts they made to secure them. "

"They still guardin' one a\l/ the way up. Not many even there, though. Shouldn' take much ta make the entrance wit' even the few o' us we 'ave." Fasurel tightened his grip at his double-bladed axe, ready to destroy more orcs and demon bloods.

"How long will it take to reach the mine, Fasurel?"

Fasurel scratched at his beard, forsaking his puzzled head for a moment. "No more 'an a day the way we been goin'. Could match arms wit' the bastards by nightfall if'n we push."

"Better we push forward, then. We can camp in the mines, if we need to, and move through to the far side by nightfall tomorrow with some luck. The sooner we find out where all the ore and orcs have been going, the better I will feel. Finish gathering our supplies and I will gather the others. Night comes quickly." Fasurel shouted to some of the mountain men milling around the village as Lord Silverwing began to gather the last of their party.

Round up

***

The archers stood on a ledge overlooking the mine's entrance several hours later, arrows nocked and easily tracking the movements of the scattered orcs in the camp. The large bonfire at the center of the camp had served as a beacon in the night, allowing the rangers and Lord Silverwing to find the best position from which to attack them at range. Fasurel positioned the remaining warriors that preferred melee to a place opposite the archer's location, allowing for rapid engagement of any remaining enemies once the bowmen fired. Lord Silvering tracked the one demon blood that moved through the camp, as it snapped orders to its orc brethren. The small number of creatures assembled troubled the knight. He had not forgotten the lesson learned when the two leaders assaulted the demon blooded orcs' encampment, allowing half the number that followed him to be slain. "We need to fire as one. These orcs have shields and weapons. They will not go down without a fight, and we need to thin as many as possible before Master Stonecutter charges. If you cannot take your target in the head, take them in the chest. Do not leave this spot without my call. I need you pouring arrows into their numbers." The rangers nodded their understanding, their eyes never leaving their targets, and waited for their leader's call to fire.

"Now!" The knight's word was little more than a whisper, but it was enough, and angry shafts appeared in the orcs below, piercing many of the creature's skulls as the boar-faced humanoids brought their massive shields up to block the next volley. The single demon blood burst into flame where he stood as Lord Silverwing's arrow bore into the beast's eye socket. Lord Silverwing wasted no time, sliding down the rocky wall that sloped away from the ledge where he had stood moments before. He ignored the orcs that drew massive swords and turned to pursue him, as he ran to cut off the mine entrance. If reinforcements were to join the orcs around the fire, Lord Silverwing reasoned, they would emerge from the mine itself.

The sound of whistling arrows was everywhere at once as the archers at the ledge fired mercilessly at the backs of Lord Silverwing's pursuers. Fasurel's great bellow emerged from the far side of the encampment as he and his warriors engaged the remaining orcs. These orcs were not demon bloods, and were protected by their massive shields and thick plated armor, but the leader of the mountain men took their heads just the same. The great swords the orcs brought to bear against their attackers did them little good. Vengeance for the fallen fueled the strikes of all the masters of bow and blade, driving the rangers and druids alike into a fit of madness the orcs could not match or stand against.

Lord Silverwing was almost disappointed as the last of the enemies fell. Fasurel made short work of all that he met, and the killing efficiency of the archers was unmatched, assuring none of the orcs survived and only minimal wounds were sustained by the attackers. No reinforcements had presented themselves to face Lord Silverwing's blades. Fasurel's words drifted across the encampment.

"I know wha' ya' thinkin', Lord Silverwing, an' I agree. They weren' meant ta hold this mine."

"No, Fasurel, they were not. There were far too few of them to stand against us. Someone prepared this path. The question is, do we gain anything in finding another way?" Lord Silverwing sheathed his blades, awaiting his friend's reply.

"One way as good as t'other ta my reckonin'. Don' see findin' another way doin' much good. They know we comin'." Fasurel took up a torch from near the mine entrance, moving to the fire to light it.

Silverwing watched the mountain man light the torch and motioned a couple of the others to take up torches as well. "Yes, they know we are coming. I wish I were certain of who 'they' are. Might as well get moving. We don't want to disappoint whomever it is that has gone to such efforts to bring us to them. "

"Aye," was Fasurel's only answer.

***

Gregor found himself in darkness. The man before him was bathed in white light. The young warrior was dressed in armor similar to that worn by Gregor and bore the two blades of the holy warrior's mentor sheathed at his sides. "Master?" Gregor knelt before the man, certain the spirit of his mentor had left his body and was passing into the glory of the God of Light.

The vision of young Lord Silverwing smiled at the bowing warrior at his feet. "Rise, Lord Lightsword. You are equal in my eyes and should bow to no man or woman of the sword. Save your reverence for the priests of the Temple of Light and our God."

Gregor rose as he was told. "I pay respects to you as I see fit, Master. Have you left this world?"

"No, brother. It appears the God of Light has plans for me yet. I have come to guide you as I can, but time is short. You know the evil you must face, but you follow my path in error. Do not be misled as I have. You cannot fail. The huntress that follows my step will deliver you into the hands of the enemy, though this is not her intent. You must forsake my path and find your own way to the place where doom dwells. Follow the rogue. Boremac knows the ways of the shadows and possesses the tools to take you to the heart of danger. The daggers that led him to you in your time of need will guide you to the terrible danger you must face."

"I do not understand. How can I save you if I am to be delivered into the maw of the enemy?"

"I do not know, Gregor. I only know what has been shown to me. Have faith, young warrior, and the God of Light will save you when all others have fallen. We are warriors of the Light, sent into battle. Leave it to the priests to interpret the legacy of our actions." Already Lord Silverwing was beginning to fade as the light around him diminished. "You, Lord Lightsword, are to be the stuff of legends for centuries to come."

***

Tana knelt at Gregor's side, shaking him from sleep. There had been little need for the rattling at her hands. His eyes sprung open, startling Tana as she released him, and Gregor found he was sitting bolt upright with his hand at the hilt of his sword. "We have to follow Boremac." The words tripped over each other in their haste to make it past his lips.

Tana was shocked into silence and Dramor was the first to give answer, disturbed by the mere thought of following the rogue anywhere. The mountain man and the rogue butted heads often over Dramor's apparent lack of desire to move with anything resembling stealth. "Wot? Ya gots ta be yankin' at us now, Lord Lightsword. I mean ya no direspec' but wha' bring this on?"

Boremac snored loudly, indicating he was completely oblivious to the new development. Tana held her tongue for the moment, though her expression was pained. She had felt they had been well served with her tracking of Lord Silverwing. She had guided them easily to the place where Lord Silverwing's companions were buried and was able to surmise that the knight's remaining force had broken camp there only two days before this group had arrived.

"Lord Silverwing has come to me as I slept. He warned against following in his step and said the rogue can bring us to the place we need to find." Gregor related the dream to Dramor and Tana, rapidly covering the details of his mentor's appearance.

Tana could restrain her voice no longer as Gregor finished speaking. "Deliver you into the hands of the enemy? Why I would do such a thing, or even how I could, is beyond me. By all means, let's follow whomever you see fit, Master Gregor. As long as most of us are awake, we should rouse our new tracker. By your leave?" Tana did not wait for a reply to her request as she slipped toward the sleeping rogue with catlike grace. Two quick slaps across Boremac's face had the desired effect.

"I told you no one else could take your place, love. I don't know who that lass is." Boremac sat up, rubbing his eyes with his hands to clear the vestiges of sleep. "What? Why is it still dark? What the hell did I miss? I had the strangest dream. Tana, what are you doing right there and why are you looking at me like that?"

238

Gregor brought Boremac up to the present while Tana set out into the night to find Sephia. The rogue was less than happy with the new position he held. "So, what you are saying is, that Silverwing, whom you trust with your life, wants me to take you wherever these blades of mine lead, knowing full well that the reason these daggers glow at all is because you are in trouble? Is that about right? Let's not forget the urging to keep the faith once the rest of us have fallen around you. Tell you what, why don't you take the blades and I will have Tana just cut my throat right here. At the very least, I can save myself the walk."

Gregor smiled at the rogue. "Can't let you go that easy, my friend. You didn't expect this quest to be without its challenges, did you? We all have our roles to play, and immortality is nothing to fear. At the very least, the weight of sins on your soul should be cleansed with your sacrifice in service to the God of Light."

"That particular path to glory is generally reserved for knights, and I have no desire to die anytime soon. For what possible reason would I continue on this journey toward almost certain death? Think carefully before you answer, knight, and I will give you time to turn it over while I pack." Boremac, true to his word in this instance if no other, began gathering his meager items.

"You faced certain death to protect me from assassins, and now you would choose to turn your back on me when I need you the most? Have you learned nothing in the time that was spent in the Temple at Nactium? Do you have NO honor, rogue?" The young knight regretted his words, but the rogue had left him little choice. "I can ask no more of you than you are willing to give freely, Boremac. If I felt my trust in you was misplaced, you would not be here now, and Lord Silverwing has made every effort to see that you continue with us, no matter what fate holds at the end of the journey. Go if you must. God speed you and keep you."

Boremac dropped his gear and turned angrily to face Gregor. The holy warrior's words had cut him deeply, but it was the memory of Silverwing that forced the answer he gave to Gregor. "You know nothing of me, Lord Lightsword. You are the master of your own fate while those of us around you are made to bring you to face evil you cannot begin to comprehend. Blind faith is a wondrous thing. I will take you into the pits of the Abyss if that is what is required, just to see what happens when that golden light is stripped from your eyes. I will not die for a God that chooses to abandon his followers at his whim. I will take you to your doom to prove the strength of the word I gave your mentor. Be glad for that, and ask me for no more, for you will receive no more."

The soft clapping of a pair of hands nearby turned the two men away from each other to seek its source. Tana stood at the edge of the camp, taking in the exchange with Sephia standing at her side. Boremac's reaction was immediate as he narrowed his eyes at the huntress. "Shut up, Tana."

Gregor had to smile in spite of the path that was laid before this group. Some things would never change.

17

Into the Maw of Darkness

Lord Silverwing grew more anxious with each step up the sharply rising mineshaft. While the group he led had rested in the depths of the mountain, he had focused his will to contact Master Gregor. The holy knight had been as surprised by the form his God gave him as his student had. Many of the memories of the foolish youth he once was brought a smile to Lord Silverwing's face after the contact with Gregor was broken. Lord Lightsword, the older knight reminded himself. The youth that had come into Master Silverwing's care so long ago was no longer his student. The boy now was his equal, battle-tested and blessed with the touch of the God of Light. Lord Silverwing prayed he would live to see the knight Master Gregor had become in the time since the two parted.

"There be light, Silverwing. We comin' out the mine." Fasurel's call from the front of the party drew Silverwing back to the present; back to the task at hand. The knight knew the remaining rangers and druids were going to face a terrible enemy once they left the dark safety of the mine. Every member of the group was ready to face death, and Silverwing steeled himself to lead them into the unknown.

"Stand ready, Fasurel. I will take the first steps. Take the rear and be certain no one comes at our backs." Fasurel growled something unintelligible, clearly unhappy with taking the rear position, but moved past Silverwing to the back of those assembled.

Silverwing passed orders to the remaining hunters and healers as he took the point, attempting to marginalize the group's vulnerability once they emerged. The knight understood the arts of the battlefield, and lessons learned long ago served him well now, but all the planning in the world could not have prepared him for what was to come.

No creature moved near the exit from the mineshaft, and Lord Silverwing sharpened his ears, seeking any hint of an ambush lying in wait. If there were any creatures on the surrounding ledges at his back, they were far more disciplined than the forces Silverwing had encountered in their journey so far. The object of their mission was readily visible from the high perch, as Lord Silverwing focused his eyes on the small keep across the gorge in front of him. He knew with certainty borne of instinct that the cause of the evil plaguing this world dwelt within the unremarkable black stone walls of the stronghold. As if to confirm his suspicions, large humanoid figures moved across the buttresses of the keep. Even at this distance, Silverwing was able to see the glimmer of armor glinting red on the patrolling demon blooded orcs. Light from the lava flows winding around the building tinted the dark clouds overhead. The sky was blanketed in ash from some unknown source that kept the bowl of rocky cliffs in a near constant night. The swirling sheets of cloud snuffed out any sunlight bold enough to penetrate the gloom. Despite Lord Silverwing's purpose, he felt a tug of despair as he watched the humanoid guardians moving at the top of the keep and through the landscape at its base. He could find little hope that any of his forces would survive a direct assault on the stronghold, even with much greater numbers. The defenders he could see numbered in the hundreds. They would have to find another way into the keep.

"We cannot take the defenders at the front. There has to be another way into the stronghold that I cannot see from here. I will not throw the rest of you away for nothing." Lord Silverwing withdrew his bow from the sling at his back, nocking a silver arrow. "Looks like there is a makeshift road that leads to the keep from here. Ready your weapons and follow me down the mining path. Be alert. We will no doubt be challenged before we make the grounds near the keep." Silverwing was correct in his assumption, but his caution would prove fruitless.

The first of the archers in the group to fall had his chest penetrated by a bolt the size of a small spear. The only sound as the bolt was launched was the twang of the crossbow's lathe snapping forward to launch the deadly projectile. Those that were killed instantly were the lucky ones. The fist-sized tip of the bolt protruding from the ranger's chest extended metal prongs, lodging them deep within him. The demon blood that fired the missile dropped its crossbow to tug at a line made of thick rope, dragging its screaming victim into the air and up to the ledge where it stood. Lord Silverwing's arrow took the creature in the face, and the humanoid form burst into flame with the bite of the blessed arrow, but the damage had been done. The demon blood's victim plummeted to the rocky earth, his horrible screams silenced by the impact.

"Find cover! Get down!" Silverwing shouted out the warning in vain as he nocked another arrow and turned to find the next attacker. The surrounding ledges above the road filled with demon bloods, and more of their number boiled over the ledge at the hunters' feet; inhuman howls drowned out any further orders the knight could have given. The air filled with the giant bolts from the high precipice, towlines flying everywhere at once. Lord Silverwing fired arrows in rapid succession, destroying many of the crossbow wielders as they reloaded their weapons or attempted to drag their victims up the rocky slopes. His arrows were exhausted long before the numbers of the attackers were thinned; another of its kind replaced every creature he killed. The swelling number of demon bloods climbing to the road from below them were heavily armed and armored. All these enemies carried great swords and iron shields that dwarfed the weapons of their mountain orc brethren that Silverwing had encountered guarding the mine. The only possible path for escape would be blocked in moments if he didn't move quickly.

Already the ground had grown slick with the blood of the fallen rangers and druids. Lord Silverwing ran through the whirl of blades blocking him, beheading as many of the demon bloods as he could, as he moved to Fasurel's side. The mountain man was swinging his double-bladed ax like a man possessed, dispatching the circle of enemies crowding in on him several at a time. Silverwing brutally hacked his way into the center where Fasurel was making his stand, narrowly ducking under the stout man's spinning swings. "Go now! The others are dead or dying, and there is no reason for us all to be lost!" Silverwing brought his own blades into the melee and ripped through the waves of demon bloods, attempting to clear a path of escape for Fasurel.

"I won' leave ya to the fiends! We die together if'n tha' be the way of it! I won' go!" Fasurel's axe never slowed as he hollered his reply. Silverwing almost began to think they would survive until a heavy bolt shot past his head and impaled one of his attackers.

A voice filled with fury, but human no less, rose above the noise of the demo bloods. "Don't kill the ranger, you fools! The Master wants that one alive! Slay the bearded one and take the knight!"

The creatures were distracted by the order and turned to look toward the distant ledge where the call had originated. Silverwing took advantage of the creatures' loss of concentration and shoved Fasurel through the cloud of disintegrated orcs he had cut down toward the direction from which the doomed party had come. "Flee or I will kill you myself, Fasurel! Warn Gregor!" The knight paused only long enough to be certain the mountain man had disappeared into the ash cloud. He turned to track the line of sight of the staring demon blooded orcs that partially encircled him. A man stood high on the ledge above, clothed in blowing crimson robes and holding a long metal staff. Silverwing thanked the God of Light for revealing his enemy, and cut through the demon bloods between him and the figure, noting the man's head was exposed. Even as the demon bloods turned their attention back to the knight, Silverwing drew his bow and loosed one of the iron-tipped arrows at the priest's head. Despite the range, the arrow flew true. Silverwing was momentarily frozen as the priest's metal staff glowed brightly, casting an unearthly light the color of fresh blood, and the arrow deflected harmlessly away from the figure mere inches from his face. Though the knight could not be sure, he thought the man was smiling at him.

The demon bloods at the ledge behind Lord Silverwing took advantage of his pause. Two heavy bolts pierced both the knight's shoulders, driving him to his knees like great hammer blows to his back, as metal prongs clawed into his chest and arms. The successful crossbowmen began tugging the knight into the air almost immediately. Excruciating pain coursed through Silverwing's body as his feet left the ground. One of the demon bloods on the ground struck him violently with the flat of the blade of its great sword, and the knight knew no more.

***

Gregor and his companions were a mere two days behind Lord Silverwing when his mentor was captured. The group broke bread with the same people of the village where Silverwing and Fasurel had learned of the mine guarded by the only remaining orcs in the area. The intense discussions within the group, focused largely between Tana and Boremac about their current path, turned into an outright argument once they talked to the mountain men of the village. Tana felt the rogue was taking them directly down Lord Silverwing's path. "You have no idea what you are doing, do you? If we continue as we have, then we will no doubt meet the same fate as Lord Silverwing, for good or ill. Why are we following you? If we wanted to follow Silverwing's trail, I could have taken us there already. If isn't like he is hiding his passage through these mountains!"

Boremac returned her angry gaze. "Look, huntress. I did not volunteer to lead this doomed mission to save the world. In fact, I have no desire to speed into what will certainly be a most uncomfortable death for us all. Judging from the way I could replace our torches with these dagger hilts, I think it is safe to say Gregor is in serious trouble. We haven't even made it into the Forsaken Mountains yet. By the time we do, I will have to cover these damned things with something, and hope I do not need them to defend myself!"

Gregor returned from the group of villagers where he was gathering as much information as he could about Lord Silverwing's party before they had left. There was precious little to learn except where the others had headed after leaving the village. He shook his head as he approached Tana and Boremac, sad to see there would be no peace between the pair. He wondered yet again how they would ever accomplish their task when at least two of the five members in the group seemed to want to kill each other. He mumbled a short prayer to the God of Light before stepping between them.

"There is nothing to be gained in continuing to follow in Lord Silverwing's footsteps. The mine that was his destination may be the most direct course to follow, but as we have already surmised, Lord Silverwing walked into a trap of some kind. The vision he sent to me makes me think he may have suspected as much and gives us all the more reason to find our own way. There is a rough road worn deeper into the volcanoes of the Forsaken Mountains that will take us around the mountain that the mine Silverwing entered cut through. We have the advantage of Sephia and her falcon to scout ahead of us. We should be able to approach the place Boremac's blades lead without being caught by any roaming war bands. It is essential we do not allow the enemies to discover our path until we are ready to take them." Gregor stepped back from Tana and Boremac, awaiting their reply. He noted Sephia had silently joined the group and stood at his side, her falcon companion, Keen, perched at her shoulder.

Boremac was the first to speak. "I have no problem extending our journey into the mountain heights, Gregor. If we can all work together, we can at least postpone joining Lord Silverwing in his fate."

Tana chose to ignore the rogue's jibe as she addressed Gregor in her turn. "We can make the rest of the journey easily enough. Sephia and Keen can guide us beyond the reach of any threats as long as it does not interfere with Boremac's leadership too much."

"I am certain we will all put aside our differences to accomplish what is expected of us. The two of you *will* stop this constant baiting of one another." Gregor's tone allowed for no reply, and he waited for none. "We will gather what supplies we need and leave as soon as everyone is ready."

Dramor's bellowing voice carried across the village as he emerged from a broad building. "Lord Lightsword, I need a bit o' ya time!"

Gregor briefly issued tasks for the others to prepare for their departure and walked to where Dramor stood waving him over almost frantically. Gregor smiled at his waving form, thinking Dramor must have assumed the knight had gone deaf to not hear his call. The knight raised a hand in acknowledgment and went to speak with him.

"What is wrong, Dramor?" Gregor's smile disappeared when he saw the look of concern that colored the mountain man's heavy features.

Dramor lowered his rough voice and stared intently into Gregor's eyes. "Thar been a callin', Lord Lightsword, an' one I canna let pass. Master Stonecutter, the leader o' me clan, he is fallen an' I gotta find 'im."

"A calling? What do you mean, Dramor?

Dramor thought a moment before answering. "Our shamans, like yer priests I guess, sometime jus' know when somethin' terrible happens. I went ta pay respec' afore we goin' ta face tha' foes, an' the shaman say sumthin' terrible happen to Master Stonecutter. He still livin' an' near somewhere, an' I got ta go find 'im. I feel terrible bad ta leave ya an' the others, but I gots ta try an' find 'im. Like you an' yer mentor, I be thinkin'. Master Stonecutter be like a father an' a brother ta me an' I gots ta try."

"I understand, Dramor. You go and do what you have to for your leader. Go with the God's blessing, and bring him home safe." Gregor found he understood the mountain man's words better than even the knight himself knew. The holy warrior prayed Dramor would bring his brother home. He called for the strength to save Lord Silverwing as well, and felt at peace for the first time in a very long time. Lord Silverwing had often said that faith would carry the young knight, and Gregor believed it.

***

Lord Silverwing became aware of oppressive heat before he opened his eyes. His shoulders pulsated where the spear-like quarrels had penetrated them, but there was no longer any pain and they had been removed. The knight could only assume he had been healed by his captors for reasons that were their own. The answer to that question would come soon enough.

The rocky floor under his body burned him even through the protection of his leathers. His head was full of tearing pain as he felt the familiar invasion into his mind of the foe he had never forgotten. He knew the Tharnorsa was in front of him without opening his eyes. *Rise, Lord Silverwing, and see the devourer of this world. This meeting has been too long delayed.* The knight was violently jerked to his feet by unseen clawed hands. Silverwing took little comfort in feeling the weight of his swords in their scabbards at his sides.

The knight shook away from the grip of the creatures that had brought him to his feet. He saw the creatures move to leave the vast cavern as the demon on the throne before him waved at them dismissively. The creatures proceeded up a narrow stairwell that appeared to lead deeper into the mountain. The light cast by two giant craters filled with lava was adequate to their purpose, illuminating the throne and its occupant.

The dead will bear witness to your failure. The Tharnorsa's glowing eyes diminished the shadows near its massive head as it waved a broad scaled hand across the floor before the knight. The remains of the rangers and druids that were slain in the rocky terrain on the road to the keep had been scattered haphazardly across the rough floor of the natural cavern. *Do not worry over the bodies. They will be disposed of once I have finished with you. I am certain the Gods and Goddesses have already blessed their spirits with peace in honor of their sacrifice at your hands. I will honor them further in*

249

that they will not be fed to the demon blooded orcs in my service. Immolation in the pits will cleanse their remains. This mountain should have its due for its service to us. The Tharnorsa bridged its clawed hands in front of its chest, obviously enjoying invading the knight's mind. *Have you some reply, some cursed words against me, to which you wish to give voice?*

Silverwing stared into the darkness where the demon's eyes glowed. "You will receive no such pleasure from me, demon. The dead are beyond my prayers, and I will not waste precious breath speaking to your kind. You will find the taste of my blades has not changed since our last meeting." Despite referring to the blades at his side, the knight kept them sheathed. He wanted to know what this demon was really doing in this world, and more importantly, who had summoned him.

The Tharnorsa had remained in his mind and chose to respond to his thoughts as well as Silverwing's words. *You see I still bear the marks of our last encounter.* The demon gestured to the twin scars in his vast chest as he continued. *I have anticipated having the opportunity to give you wounds in kind for some time. My failure in destroying you caused no small amount of suffering for me in the Abyss. The Unnamed One has little tolerance for those of my position who cannot deal with blessed warriors, especially when so great a prize is to be taken. I was blessed with the attentions of the Unnamed One himself, and I intend to share the gifts he bestowed upon me with you in kind. The suffering I endured would kill you far too quickly to serve my desire for revenge, so we will spend long days together, enjoying the sounds of your screams.*

"You found no such pleasure with Lord Clamine, and you will receive none from me." Silverwing's defiant tone, or the events to which the knight referred, seemed to give the demon a moment of reflection. Silverwing pressed forward, sensing the demon's reaction.

The knight nodded to the resting place of his fallen brother's sword hilt, feeling a wave of sadness when he saw its blackened form. "You bear the hilt of the sword from the fallen knight, but his spirit lives on in all of us that remain. Your destruction is only a matter of time."

The demon's massive form began to diminish as it rose, standing in front of its throne and taking the hilt Silverwing referred to into its clawed hand. In moments, the demon stood in the form of a vaguely humanoid creature tainted by its true self. The horns and fiery eyes remained, though the mouth and other features of the demon were now vaguely human. Fangs protruded from the corners of the creature's mouth, and a thick split tongue darted out as it measured Silverwing at a comparable eye level. Large clawed digits dug into the rocky floor as if it were soft dirt, leaving small ruts as the Tharnorsa moved closer to the knight. A serpentine tail had grown from the demons lower back, and darted around the creature, shiny reptilian skin forming fleshy flaps at either side of the jagged stinger on the end. Silverwing was surprised at the change in the demon's form, but he was more disturbed by the voice that issued from the Tharnorsa's twisted grimace.

"There will be no end to my reign in these lands, Lord Silverwing. You are no threat to me now, and your pitiful student is of little concern. He is a knight in title alone." The demon's vile mouth turned upward into a mocking smile, as Silverwing reacted to the words concerning Gregor. "You have put much faith in a simple boy who knows nothing of what he will face. I am going to keep you alive so that he can rush to his doom in a misplaced effort to save you. The Master of this stronghold has long planned the events that led to this day, and, to his credit, he has used even me to the best of his abilities to take and keep power in this world. The priest has made a valuable ally. I am almost saddened that our association is nearly at an end. Rest assured, Gregor will be dealt with once he has served my purpose."

Lord Silverwing brought his swords into his hands as he answered. Each of his weapons was enveloped in the glow of white light and the knight readied himself to face the demon. "Master Gregor will never serve you, demon. He is destined to bring peace to this world and is touched by the God of Light. You cannot sway him."

The Tharnorsa only grinned in reply as the tainted hilt he bore sprouted a wicked blade. The black blade built itself from the hilt, enclosed in a deep red glow of its own as if in answer to the emanations from Lord Silverwing's blades. The single weapon the demon held was no longer than a longsword much like one of the knight's blades, an evil mirror to Silverwing's own. "We will see, Lord Silverwing. Let us end this banter. I owe you wounds and I hunger for the marring of your flesh. You note that I possess only one blade against your two holy swords. I will even the fight with the use of my tail and you will see that the blade I bear is equal in either of my hands. In addition, you should know that if my tail bites your flesh, you will be favored with an agonizing death as the caustic poison within its stinger taints the blood in your veins and dissolves your body. You may prefer that to the plans I have for you after I defeat you." The Tharnorsa casually spun the blade in one hand, demonstrating its oneness with the tainted weapon, before passing it to the other and repeating the action to emphasize its words. A drop of greenish fluid dripped from the demon's tail as it darted toward Silverwing, nearly touching the knight's forehead. "Prepare for death."

Silverwing tempted the demon with an opening move meant to draw an attack, seeking a suitable place to strike. The knight held one blade in a defensive position in front of his chest as the other blade darted out to find purchase in the demon's hide. The Tharnorsa dropped into a crouch, causing the attack to pass harmlessly over his shoulder; its envenomed tail swept the blade away from the creature's body. The wisdom of Lord Silverwing's defensive posturing soon became evident. The demon's black blade jabbed violently forward, seeking to penetrate the knight's chest. Silverwing's blade glowed with his movement to parry the demon's blade, as if it found the contact with the black blade offensive, causing the thrust to strike the floor. The white blade swung in a brief reversing arc, taking advantage of the opening the knight created, biting deeply into the demon's shoulder.

The Tharnorsa brought the blade up in a defensive posture of its own, moved to speak by the successful attack. "Well placed, Lord Silverwing, but I think you will find more than that is required to undo me." The weeping wound in the demon's shoulder knitted itself as the creature spoke, and the demon swept his tail high, nearly striking Silverwing's own shoulder in reply. The demon had obviously pulled the killing sting, and the knight wondered at his tormentor's mercy. It seemed it was not the creature's intent to kill him after all.

Lord Silverwing stepped backward, bringing his swords parallel to his chest with the tips pointing to the heavens. "You have grown powerful since last we met, and more cunning, but you will find you are no match for a master of the blades in service to the God of Light." A more aggressive approach would be required to disable the demon. It was only a moment before the knight saw the opening he sought. The first glowing blade in Silverwing's hand struck at the demon's black blade, gliding powerfully toward the weapon's hilt as the knight angled his own sword to force the Tharnorsa's blade toward the ground at his side. Silverwing ignored the swift darting movements of the demon's tail, focusing on his target with his second blade. A short downward slice carved the demon's weaponless hand away, leaving the dismembered claws curling into a fist on the ground.

The demon withdrew his own sword, nearly catching Silverwing's shimmering blade in its jagged teeth, as the creature retreated several steps to recover. A coarse growl hissed from the demon's tight mouth as the severed arm sprouted small bits of scaly flesh, slowly regenerating the lost hand. "It is good to see you will provide some challenge to me after all, blade master. Do not revel in your success too long." The demon brought his wounded arm up and flexed the stumps that were already forming to replace those cut from him, pointed tips emerging like the extended claws of a wildcat. "There is no mark with which you can mar this body that I cannot readily heal." As the demon finished speaking, he shifted his sword from its present hand to the newly regenerated one. Despite the Tharnorsa's words, Silverwing suspected there was something the demon feared. The implication of the demon's tightened grip on the sword's hilt, the claws of the wielding hand digging deeply into the creature's palm, was not lost on the knight. In his many years of struggle against evil, he had learned one lesson better than any other. The movements of one's opponent gave you more knowledge in the best way to destroy them than any words they chose to share. What did the demon fear? That was a question Silverwing had to answer quickly.

"You assume too much, light bearer." The demon spat the words out as if they were poison on his forked tongue. "You have no power here, and when this fight is over, you will lie on the ground at my mercy. In time you will plead for release from pain; you will even beg for the tortures awaiting you in the Abyss. Your God has forsaken you, Lord Silverwing, and in time you will curse his holy name."

These words were too much for the knight to bear. Silverwing crossed the two blades of his blessed swords before his chest and stepped into the demon's reach, meaning to limit the movements of the demon. The creature's step backward betrayed his intention, but Silverwing missed his advantage momentarily, and its venomous tail snaked between the two combatants. The tip of the demon's tail came between the knight's blades, pressing into the place where the two hilts touched and forcing Silverwing to shift his feet to maintain his balance. The strong tail's interference prevented Silverwing from striking at the demon's throat as he had intended, and opened the knight's defenses as he cut away the tail just below its scaly flaps, taking a step backward to get out of the reach of the demon's sword. Silverwing had underestimated the demon's desire to wound him, and the creature's speed. The knight realized his error too late as he felt the bite of the Tharnorsa's cursed blade sliding through his thin leather armor, the jagged blade ripping into his chest with the force of the thrust. Silverwing's lung opened to the hot air in the cavern as the demon withdrew his blade slowly, with a wet sucking sound. "That would be one wound we now share, knight. Do try to protect yourself better now that you know my intention. It is a pity about the tail. That will take a few moments longer to regenerate since I do not normally possess the extension. That piece is drawn from the ether to create the flesh of the tail, and will take longer because of its nature. You should seize the advantage while you have it." The demon drew the wet blade in front of his eyes, admiring the blood of his victim running down its length. "It is good to see you bleed the same as any other mortal, Lord Silverwing. I half expected this God of Light you serve to heal you. So much for the profit of faith and duty."

Silverwing wanted to reply, but found he could not. His wounded lung sapped his strength even as he prepared to engage the demon once more. Silverwing brought his blades to defensive positions once more at his sides, inviting the demon to strike out at him. The knight was already weakening, and he took little solace in knowing the demon's intention.

The demon lowered his own blade to his side. The blade master could not help noticing the demon had shifted his blade to the clawed hand opposite Silverwing's pierced lung. He stared at the knight knowingly as blood stained Silverwing's leathers. "You had a solid plan of attack. Unfortunately, your execution of the tactic failed to take all the potential elements of my defense into account. I nod to your skills and give you another attempt at beheading me. You no longer possess the power to destroy me, even with your God's intervention. Pray for that power and strike." The demon's head tilted backward, exposing its neck, as it spread its arms wide in mock submission.

Silverwing's blades ignited with divine force as he crossed the blades at his chest once more. The creature's sinewy flesh at his scaly neck flexed taunt as the knight stepped forward to deliver the killing cut. Silverwing summoned all the strength he possessed, sweeping his swords to either side of the demon's pulsing throat and scissoring the blades against the exposed flesh. Laughter burst from the Tharnorsa as each blade met the creature's neck, bouncing away harmlessly. The demon brought his own blade up as the force of the knight's attempt pushed Silverwing back, betraying the blade bearer. Once more the demon's sword stabbed into the knight as the knight's arms shot out to his own sides, a second wound to match the first appearing in Silverwing's chest. Silverwing stumbled, attempting to keep his feet under him as pain suffused his body and his strength left him. Peace would come soon. The knight knew there was no way he could survive the wounds, and he had no intention of healing himself.

The demon had other plans, and spoke to the knight as if he had read his thoughts. "There is to be no peace for you, Lord Silverwing. You will bear the marks of this meeting until I tire of your existence in this world. Your suffering will find you praying for death until all faith in your God has been extinguished. Allow me to tend your wounds." The touch of the demon's clawed hands was only the beginning of Silverwing's pain. The demon reached into his chest, expertly sealing the wounds with the fires at his command, and left only two large scars on the knight's chest to indicate Silverwing had been stabbed. "Rest for now, and I will have the priests tend to you. I want you fully aware when I begin to torture you, Lord Silverwing."

18

Hell's Doorway

The last of the warriors of faith, one devoted to the God of Light, two following the Goddess of Nature, and the rogue trusting in luck, sat near the fire in the middle of a desolate road leading into the darkness of the Forsaken Mountains. Gregor prayed quietly. He had taken up the habit each night of offering thanks to the God of Light, and entreating his God to provide safety for Lord Silverwing. The holy warrior knew what news Sephia's companion brought before the falcon had landed on her shoulder. Gregor had felt a surge of pain course through his body, bringing his head to his bent knees in front of him, and knew his master was made to suffer, or worse. Boremac was the first to notice that his daggers no longer glowed. The rogue wondered what it could mean.

Tana had risen to comfort Gregor, only to be brought up short by his raised hand. The young knight raised his head from his bent knees and shared his pain with the others. "I have failed my master. Lord Silverwing can find no peace. The Tharnorsa has him and I only pray the demon will allow him to live until I can reach him. Only his faith can save him now."

Keen, the falcon at Sephia's shoulder, dipped its head briefly as if in reverence as Gregor spoke. The bird related what it had witnessed to its companion with the light clicking of its beak and subtle wing flourishes. Sephia stared at Keen intently before she turned to address the others at the fire. "Lord Silverwing has been taken, and all those who traveled with him were slain. Keen followed your mentor's captors and has found a way into the place where he was taken. Keen was unable to see what lies beyond the entrance to the cave where the demon bloods dragged him, but no one emerged after entering. We will find Lord Silverwing there."

Gregor turned his face to speak directly to the Ardataure, the only remaining representative of the Ancient Forest Sephia called home. "Sephia, you must go to Mistress Mithrina and inform her we have found the enemy. She will want to assemble whom she can to purge the lands of this plague. We can find our way to the cave with your guidance and have no need of your scouting any longer. You are the fastest of our number, and Keen can fly ahead of you as well to deliver the message, I assume."

Sephia nodded in assent. "Yes, Mistress Mithrina will understand the message he brings to the Grove. I will go and do as you wish. Goddess protect you all." The keeper of the Ancient Forest disappeared into the dark night, heading down the road back toward the Grove in Zanthfar, after making a detailed outline of the best route for the group to follow to find the tunnel they would need to enter.

Boremac coughed into his hand to draw Tana and Gregor's attention. Gregor was not sure if it was the firelight, or something else, but the rogue appeared concerned. He waited patiently for the rogue to speak. "Master Gregor, or Gregor if you please and take no offense, do you really think it is wise to challenge a foe that appears to have so easily taken Lord Silverwing? The knight's skills, and wisdom besides, were far beyond your own. Even if we give you the credit of possessing some advantage by knowing whom you face, the power of the Tharnorsa and this possessed priest together would be your undoing. I see little profit in you facing the two of them at so severe a disadvantage." Tana voiced her thoughts with a huff at hearing the rogues' words, but chose to allow the men to continue their dialogue without interruption.

Despite the lingering pain in Gregor's body, he smiled knowingly at Boremac before replying. "They underestimate my commitment, and I doubt you and Tana have been factored into their careful planning. They expect only a young holy warrior bent on vengeance, not a cunning rogue devoted to self-preservation and a huntress who has skills that are unmatched among her kind. I think you can appreciate the advantage of surprise on the side of our meager group."

Boremac cocked an eyebrow at the knight's words, ready with a sharp reply of his own as if he had anticipated just such a response from the young man. "You sound more like your mentor all the time, holy blade. That is disturbing, to put it mildly. I suppose now you will perform the last of your sermons before we rush into the maw of death. Skip the speeches in honor of the God of Light. We should get down the road while night still covers us."

Tana spoke at last, breaking her silence after she had watched the two discuss the group's fate. "Gregor, you know it pains me to do so, but I have to agree with the bandit this time. Whether we are fated to live or die, we may as well get to the end of it. Sephia's directions will put us at the gates of hell by tomorrow after nightfall if we stop to rest during the day when the sun rises. Let's let the walk warm us and see if we cannot set the world right tomorrow."

***

Fasurel lay just inside the mine entrance where he and Silverwing had entered to travel to the other side of the mountain. The mountain man had regretted leaving the knight, and held little hope that Silverwing still lived. Fasurel had taken wounds of his own once he had entered the mine at the far side, when the demon bloods had hunted him down, intent on his destruction. The ranger had chosen the lizard form of his long dead animal companion to flee deeper into the mine shaft, but even six legs had not made him fast enough to avoid his relentless pursuers. In the end, he had turned to face nearly twenty of the creatures and had the torn flesh to prove it. His enemies had failed to capture or kill him, and his claws had torn them to bits in the end, but four of Fasurel's six reptilian legs hung useless from his body. Some amount of luck allowed the ranger to rip the heads from the last two attackers he had killed. Soon the wounds he had sustained would claim him, so in the end it had made little difference.

Fasurel awakened to the first sound of hope, certain he was having a fever dream brought by the loss of blood. His lizard form had given him just speed enough to find a hiding place, but not strength enough to get to a village. The rough voice of one of his brothers carried into the mine from the entrance near where Fasurel lay. Light, little more than a flickering blur at the opening, gave the only indication that the mountain man had been found, and Fasurel was thinking it was an angel of death coming to take him home. "Master Fasurel? Master Fasurel! Are ya there?! Shaman sent me ta gather ya! Ya there? Damn ya, ya bes' no' be dead, I come as fas' as I could!"

Fasurel scraped the ground with his remaining strength to draw the ranger's attention into the mine where he lay. He had no voice left to speak, but the scrabbling noises were enough.

"I 'ear ya, Master Fasurel! I 'ear ya! Lay still, ya' old fool! Gonna wear yerself out!" Moments later the sound of rough boots slapping the rocks sounded near where Fasurel lay, a mutilated giant in a pool of his own blood. It was the sweetest sound the mountain ranger could recall in all his life. "Went an' made a mess o' yerself, I see!" Dramor knelt down by Fasurel's unmoving form, noting the shallow rise and fall of his chest and the odd angle one of his legs was bent. "Lemme get ya fixed up. Bes' take your normal form as I doubt I can carry ya like this." Fasurel morphed into his naked bipedal form, with Dramor wasting no time setting his brother's broken leg and tying up the wounds Fasurel had sustained, holding his own healing gifts to the last. He set his hands to Fasurel's heavier bleeding wounds and drew on his limited powers to heal what he could. "Fraid I ain't much fer the healing arts, but that'll hold ya til I can get ya to the shaman. Gotta pick you up, Master Fasurel, an' I be feared it's gonna hurt awful. Grit yer teeth an' with a bit a luck ya pass out." Fasurel nodded by way of reply and gritted his teeth as he was instructed. The stout mountain man slung Master Fasurel over his shoulder like a bag of rocks and started off toward the nearest village. Fasurel's luck held once more, and the wounded ranger slipped into a gentle darkness as Dramor took his brother home.

***

The road was easy to follow, and no creature roamed near the path Sephia had laid out for the group. They had taken a brief rest at Tana's insistence as the midday sun heated the rocky path. Even Boremac, so used to exercising his tongue, had said little as they finished eating their remaining foodstuffs and saved only enough water for the return journey. No one thought they would be leaving the Forsaken Mountains, and each prepared themselves for the end in their own way. Gregor had spoken quietly with Tana before they started down the road once more.

Gregor removed the curative potion that Mistress Mithrina had given him so long ago and held it out to Tana. "Take this and heal Lord Silverwing, if his heart still beats in his chest. The sword of the Knight of the Golden Dragon must be restored. If I am to be slain, Lord Silverwing will be the only hope for destroying Father

262

Tur'morival. The future of the world should not be trusted to one so young. That is something the rogue and I agree upon." Gregor's eyes were filled with so many more things he longed to say to her but could not, not now when he was at the edge of his destiny and saw only darkness ahead of him.

Tana read the thoughts that the holy warrior could not disguise and brought her hand up to touch his cheek while she accepted the potion with the other hand. "You cannot see what is so plain to all of the others who look into your eyes, Gregor. We will speak of many things once this is over, and there is no other with which I would choose to share such gifts." Tana leaned close to Gregor and gently touched her lips to his, drawing her head back with a knowing wink.

Boremac's voice carried over to where Tana and Gregor sat, the rogue making no attempt to hide his amusement. "If you two are done saying your goodbyes, I believe we have a bit of unfinished business at the end of this road. Hate to break up the party, but no point in postponing the inevitable any longer." The rogue rose, dusting himself off before helping the other two to their feet.

***

The broken terrain before them defied description. Vast craters topped ever-growing mountains that poured lava down their sides and spewed ash into the blackened sky. Bits of landscape not covered by molten rock were permanently scarred with deep crevasses from the irregular rivers of glowing rock that poured, with no discernible pattern, across the Forsaken Mountains. No stars shown in the darkness above, and the moon did not dare peek from behind the great swirling clouds high above them.

"So, this is hell. The better I should know where I am headed when I get killed out here, I guess. Makes the trip terribly short when you walk right in like this." Boremac studied the landscape, looking for the telltale cave entrance of which Sephia had spoken. "Ah, there it is. Conveniently located between two broad flows of molten rock. Looks like we are out of luck, kids. We did all we could. I guess we will just have to head home now." As the rogue turned to start back the way they had come, Tana and Gregor grabbed him by the arms and went to take a look for themselves.

"You claim to be a capable guide, and you fail to note the bridge of stone someone has constructed. Narrow though it may be, it will serve our purpose." Tana spun the rogue around until he faced the cave entrance once more.

Boremac was moved to answer, "That, dear huntress, would depend entirely upon your purpose."

Gregor quoted the rogue's chiding remark from the campfire just a few days before. "I will take you to your doom to prove the strength of the word I gave your mentor.' Would you turn away from the chance to prove your word to the very man to whom you swore that oath? There is no hazard here, if the daggers you possess are to be trusted. In all likelihood, the danger to us all has passed, and Lord Silverwing only lies wounded, awaiting us to take him home." Gregor tried to sound hopeful but his own sad eyes betrayed his feelings as he voiced the thought. "Remain here if you must, Boremac. You are not bound to me, and you will prove to be of little worth if you are constantly checking your rear."

Boremac was never really sure if it was Gregor's words, or Tana's laughter after the words were spoken, that pushed him to continue. In the end, he factored it was each in equal measure. Later, as he reflected on where that choice had taken him, he realized that it

264

mattered very little what the cause had been. The effect ended up being much the same as it always was; Boremac up to his neck in the proverbial cow dung once more.

***

The imp messenger danced convulsively on Father Tur'morival's extended palm as it gibbered in the dark language of the Abyss. The priest rose from his throne and brought the stone into his free hand with one smooth motion, though the words he spoke to the imp conveyed no sign of pleasure at the information the creature brought. "The blade bearer is here? Why would the demon not share this with me? He will pay dearly for this deception. The Tharnorsa tests the limits of my patience. Lord Silverwing should have been destroyed when he was taken to the demon, and now this? What possible profit can the demon hope to find in keeping the young knight from me?" Even as the words passed Father Tur'morival's curled lips, the priest felt he knew exactly what the demon's intention was. The creature would find this summoner was not so easily undone.

The priest lifted the crimson soul stone even with his hooded gaze and spoke directly into it as the mists within ignited. Father Tur'morival directed his words into the demon's mind, making certain the cunning Tharnorsa could not twist the communication and its intent. Obviously the demon needed a reminder of the power the priest held over the creature. Father Tur'morival found it curious that he could not see through the eyes of his unwilling servant, but it did not matter. "You have disobeyed my commands for the last time, demon. Kill the knights and bring them before me now, or suffer at the hands of the Unnamed One for all eternity. This I command, and I invoke your name to assure your compliance, Siniamadrau!"

So you will comply

265

Father Tur'morival felt the surge of anger and pain that penetrated the demon's mind as its true name was spoken. The priest wished he could sacrifice the powers of the soul stone, dismissing the demon immediately, but there would be time for that once the two holy warriors were dead. Both Father Tur'morival and Siniamadrau shared a link that could not be severed, not yet.

19

Reunion

Several horrors battled to overcome Gregor as he entered the vast cavern. The boiling contents of lava-filled craters positioned at each side of a gigantic throne provided the only light. The grotesque throne itself dominated the center of the room. Its rear portion, capped with a ram's head formed of black shimmering stone and possessing glimmering eyes the color of blood, was nearly lost in the darkness overhead. The body of the throne itself depicted images too terrible for Gregor to contemplate. Two other forms drew Gregor's attention as the remaining three companions moved into the vast open area, walking slowly toward the base of the demon's throne.

The first was a vaguely humanoid creature with two horns curving out of its scaled skull, and eyes that flickered with flames. The creature's mouth bore ugly fangs at each corner, pointing at its razor-clawed feet. A thick, split tongue darted out of the creature's mouth at random intervals, as if the demon were anticipating its next meal. The serpentine tail darting around the creature's back, with shiny reptilian skin forming flaps at either side of a jagged stinger, seemed to have a mind of its own. The wicked appendage darted around its host, intermittently flaring its fleshy wings threateningly, and in the next moment resting at the demon's shoulder like a trusted pet.

The demon before Gregor did not disturb him nearly as much as the body lying on the seat of the massive throne. Even at this distance, the young knight could make out the shimmering pool of blood surrounding the figure. The swords at the unmoving form's sides confirmed Gregor's worst fears, though what remained of Lord Silverwing was little more than a mass of flayed flesh and tattered armor. Only the irregular rise and fall of his chest gave Gregor any hope at all.

The demon began to speak in a tone that was conversational, almost reverent, distracting Gregor from Silverwing's tortured form. "Lord Lightsword, I am honored to finally meet you. You have grown since our last encounter. Hopefully your wisdom and skill has grown to match your title. Forgive me. I assume you recognize me in my chosen form, so different from our last meeting. Allow me to refresh your memory." The Tharnorsa grew to its normal full height, shedding the skin of the humanoid form it possessed only moments before. The great demon stared down at the three humans before it with a broad grin dominating its features. It took a single step backward, scooping some unseen object from the arm of its throne, and brought its horned head down to meet Gregor's gaze. "I am certain you remember me now, young knight. The years have not erased that night from your memory." Not waiting for a reply, the demon re-assumed his humanoid form and closed the distance between the knight and himself.

Hatred burned in Gregor as he watched the demon approach once more. The knight stayed his hand, resisting with every bit of will he had the urge to draw his blade and cut the demon to pieces. The creature had not caused Boremac's blades to shine with their warning white glow, and there had to be some reason for it. The demon spoke once more, as if reading Gregor's thoughts. "Your God shares no warning because I am no threat to you, Lord Lightsword. We seek the same thing, you and I. Freedom from the evil that threatens the peace of this world. You know who your true enemy is. I am only a servant to that Master."

Gregor replied with disgust tainting every word he spoke. "Farther Tur'morival keeps you as his thrall? I find that interesting, but fail to see how we could possibly seek the same end to this conflict. I am here to avenge the souls you cast into the spirit world when you destroyed the Knights of Bella Grey. Your destruction will no doubt lead to Father Tur'morival's death as well."

"There is only one thing the Master fears, Lord Lightsword." The demon extended his clawed hand as the creature's tail danced around it, appearing to examine the hilt the he held before retreating behind his back. Gregor recognized the blackened hilt immediately, but made no move to take it. The knight sensed the dancing tail's movements had been a warning against attempting to seize the offered hilt. "You are correct, Lord Lightsword. It would be unwise to take the hilt from me. There is no power you can bring against me that would not end in your death, and we have a mutual enemy to deal with before you bear your sword against me."

Gregor felt he was walking into a trap directly in front of him, but saw no way to avoid it if what the demon said was true. "Why should I trust you at all? It would be better to send you back into the Abyss and take the hilt than to bargain with a demon."

The demon stared into the young knight's eyes, keeping his hand extended as he spoke. "Take the lesson offered by your mentor, Lord Lightsword. I have little doubt that he is the superior weapon handler of the two of you, yet here I remain while he lies in a pool of his own blood. Would you suffer the same fate in a foolish attempt to destroy me? You should forget the past, holy warrior, and look to preserving the future. Your death at my hands compromises all the people of this world, do not doubt that even if you doubt me."

Gregor was about to respond when the demon's eyes shut and the Tharnorsa took several rapid steps backward, clutching the hilt to its chest. The creature's body trembled as some unseen force shook it. Only the grip of its clawed feet, digging deeply into the rocky ground under it, held the demon upright. The violent fit persisted for several seconds, and the Tharnorsa spoke as if all breath had been forced from it when the shaking stopped, pushing words through lips bent by pain. "As you wish, Master."

The demon moved with blurring speed as it sprang to the seat of its throne where Lord Silverwing lay. Without warning, the Tharnorsa drove its stinger into the center of the failing knight's chest. Before Gregor had time to react, the demon swept Tana from his side and buried the venomous tip of its tail into Gregor's exposed neck. Boremac took only a moment to move between Gregor and the demon, but it was enough. The wicked tail snaked its way around the rogue's neck, cutting off the flow of air through his throat as the flaps of skin near the tail's stinger covered Boremac's eyes. "Father Tur'morival knows you have come. The poison I have injected should give you just enough time to find him. I will amuse myself with your companions until you return, if you return."

Gregor found his voice as the venom began to work its way into his body. "In the name of the God of Light, I command you not harm them!" The Elenondo metal of Onmea, the weapon forged by Master Firebeard in what now seemed another time and another life, ignited with white flame.

"Your God has no power over me, but I will honor your faith on one condition." The Tharnorsa tightened his tail's hold on Boremac's throat, lifting the rogue from the ground as he did. "Father Tur'morival possesses a stone which binds me to him and gives him some amount of my true powers. Do not destroy the stone, and your companions will live."

"You will be destroyed, demon, that I promise you, I will return with the stone when your Master has tasted my blade." Gregor began to turn from the demon as the Tharnorsa tossed the blackened hilt toward the knight, dropping Boremac to the floor.

"Your blade will fail, Lord Lightsword. Wield the sword of your long dead master, boy, and carve out the priest's heart."

Gregor grabbed the hilt from the air and brought the transforming piece to meet the blade he had carried for so long. A brilliant golden light infused the hilt, returning it to its former glory, as the sword was once again made whole. The young knight wasted no motion as he slid the holy sword of the Knights of the Golden Dragon into the scabbard at this back. Somehow he knew now was not the time to expose that blade, and he took Onmea into his gauntleted hands for now. Gregor turned, moving toward the stairs leading into the keep and the destiny set before him so long ago. Despite the poison coursing through is body, Gregor felt the reassuring weight of the weapon in the scabbard at his back and knew he would see the demon once more.

Father Tur'morival was surprised to see the young knight enter his chamber. He rose to greet Gregor, his priest's staff in one hand and the soul stone in the other. The priest looked at the knight with interest, noting the presence of the black blade Gregor carried and the odd halo of light that encircled the holy warrior's head. The priest was glad the knight had prayed for divine protection before facing him. It would make killing the fool all the more satisfying. "So, the demon has failed. I suppose it is only fitting that the pleasure of killing you will be mine. Come closer, knight. Bring your faith and your weapon against your executioner."

Gregor slowly closed the distance between himself and Father Tur'morival, both his hands flexing on the grip of Onmea. "This is the last day you will draw breath, Father Tur'morival. Your pet still lives but will be destroyed soon enough, once I have dealt with you."

The priest's staff and the soul stone became enveloped in the same crimson mist that Gregor had seen so many times before. Father Tur'morival's condescending tone as he addressed the knight infuriated Gregor, but he restrained himself from drawing the holy sword from its scabbard at his back. He might disagree with his rogue companion's chosen profession, but he could not deny the wisdom of what he had learned in watching Boremac face the assassin that had almost killed him. One should take a full measure of an opponent before striking to kill. "It is good that you know the true name of the one that will send you to your God. I wonder if your studies gave you wisdom enough to know that there is no hope for you, or any of the people in this land."

"You speak of the Crimson Night that you have labored so long to bring, I assume. There is no honor in taking demons as allies. Even if you were to open the gateway into the Abyss, do you think the demons that would pour forth will reward a mortal with anything more than an eternity of suffering?" Gregor closed the distance between himself and the priest as he spoke. Father Tur'morival was almost within his reach.

"The powers of the Abyss are readily controlled once one understands what is required. The Tharnorsa you have somehow gotten past does not call me its Master out of respect, I assure you." Father Tur'morival stepped forward, bringing Gregor within the reach of his staff. "You do not think I fear that sword you bear, do you? Kill me, if that is your destiny. Let us match weapons and see who falls."

The time for words was at an end, and Gregor drew from all his companions' fighting styles to choose the best way of striking the priest. Father Tur'morival showed no sign of recognizing the weapon resting in the scabbard on Gregor's back, and the young knight intended to take advantage of his ignorance. Gregor swept Onmea in a tight looping formation before him, attempting to draw a strike from Father Tur'morival's staff. The staff in the priest's hands spun end over end in a tight circle at a blurring speed, forming a shield of red mist before him. Gregor sighted a flaw in the defense immediately. If the arc of the staff could be halted as the tip faced the ground, the knight could possibly dislodge the metal pole in the priest's grasp. The problem was, if Gregor could not sweep the staff properly, his own weapon would be cast away and he would be disarmed. No one ever said the slaying of Father Tur'morival would be without peril.

Gregor thrust his black blade into Father Tur'morival's spinning staff and felt a wave of pain travel up his arms as the staff and sword made contact. The priest's staff swept the blade to one side, almost causing Gregor to lose his grip as the sword vibrated in his hands. The force of the staff's motion carried the knight's blade high to Father Tur'morival's left, telling the knight which direction the weapon was traveling at least. If the priest kept the staff spinning in the same direction, Gregor could take him with his next strike.

The young knight drew his sword back to a ready position as Father Tur'morival resumed turning the staff rapidly in his hands. The priest seemed to be unimpressed by Gregor's attack, allowing the knight a moment to retreat and regain his balance. Gregor nearly betrayed his intentions with a smile. Father Tur'morival's pause would prove to be his last mistake. The priest had resumed turning the staff at a much slower pace, building the speed as if he were demonstrating his lack of concern for the challenge Gregor presented. Now the knight knew for certain how to strike him.

Gregor moved toward Father Tur'morival and once more thrust his blade into the spinning staff, releasing the grip of his stronger hand from the hilt and twisting the sword's blade with the other to counter the force of the impact. Even as the staff was propelled into the air at the priest's side, Father Tur'morival countered the motion, moving to strike Gregor violently in the side of his head. As his blow slammed Gregor's head to one side, Father Tur'morival caught sight of the hilt of the true sword of the Knights of the Golden Dragon, and the priest stepped back. The holy blade had haunted the priest throughout his existence, ever since he had learned to use the true powers of the Abyss to preserve his mortal form. The blade, broken for so long and now whole once more, was the only holy artifact that could be wielded against him. The demon had betrayed him. Father Tur'morival drew his staff to his side, confused by his failure to prevent the restoration of the weapon that cast a halo around this petty warrior's head.

It was the only opening Gregor needed. The holy warrior's favored hand pulled the true blade from the scabbard at his back. Drawing on the lessons of Lord Silverwing so long ago, Gregor knocked the staff to one side with Onmea, delivering a staggering blow into Father Tur'morival's chest with the blazing sword of the Knights of the Golden Dragon. The priest crumpled to the floor, flesh withered by two hundred years of unnatural life replacing the thick shimmering scales that had covered him, and Gregor moved to kneel at the priest's side. Father Tur'morival stared up at the kneeling warrior, focusing his remaining strength to speak. "As it was foretold, so it has come to pass. Destroy the stone and destroy Siniamadrau, it is the only way. Destroy Siniamadrau." The priest's body rotted away until all that remained were bits of bone and a pile of dried flesh to show he had ever lived at all.

Gregor felt his strength lessening as he bent to pick up the glowing stone near the empty robes Father Tur'morival had worn. He rose slowly, returning the blessed sword of the Knights of the Golden Dragon to the sheath at his back and sliding Onmea into the scabbard at this side. The young knight doubted he would have the power to wield the weapons against Siniamadrau, but he raised his voice in entreaty to the God of Light to carry him back down the stairs to the demon's lair. "Blessed God of Light, I will do what you will of me and ask nothing for myself. Give me the wisdom to destroy the creature that has violated the Keepers of the Light who sacrificed themselves in service to you. Allow me to draw my final breath after the demon is no more and bow before your divinity once I have served your purpose." His heavy boots slowly dragged him to the stairs as he balanced himself carefully, running his gauntleted hand along the wall of the stairwell that led to the demon's throne room. Somehow he retained a grip on the stone in his other hand as each step weakened his body. Gregor swore he would do what must be done before his spirit left this world.

***

Tana had taken only a moment to stare at Gregor's retreating back as he headed to the stairs at the far side of the cavern. Boremac wasted no time picking himself up from the ground, and while coughing in an effort to clear his throat, launched into a verbal assault directed at the Tharnorsa that would have made the most callous sailor blush. Tana found a smile forcing its way to her lips as she watched the foolish rogue deftly dodge the demon's envenomed tail. Boremac quickly danced to one side, then the other, stabbing at the offending tail of the creature before him, the whole time holding out his shimmering daggers that were lit once more as the poison from the demon had been injected into Gregor. The huntress had to admit the rogue was brave. Insane, but no less brave for his lack of wisdom. "You will find me a more difficult opponent than the nearby dead

Silverwing and Master Gregor. Bring me your stinger so I can carry a proper treasure home! Come on, can you do no better than that? My mind is too slippery for one grown used to dealing with honorable warriors." Tana understood the rogue's warning, and cleared her own mind as she slipped behind the demon while Boremac bought her the time she would need. She focused on summoning her healing powers as she ran quietly to the demon's giant throne, praying the rogue could keep the demon from knowing her intent. She would not be able to heal Lord Silverwing or purge the poison with her limited powers, but she had to do what she could. Tana trusted it would be enough until she could use the curative Gregor had given her.

***

Boremac dusted himself off as the demon glared at him with hate-filled eyes. Even before the rogue had risen from the floor of the cavern, he had attacked the demon with a vitriolic series of curses, calling the creature's abilities and the demon's commitment to chaos and evil, into question. "Pity you can't kill me. I am pretty certain I can take you, demon. Do you honor the words you gave Master Gregor? Come, take me if you can!" Boremac focused his mind on the events of the past as he gave his body over to the reflexes he had honed in a lifetime of self-preservation. As he grinned at the furious demon before him, knocking the vicious stinger of its tail away from him with the flat of his dagger, he remembered events that had brought him here; when Silverwing shot him from the tree after slaying the assassins, waking up next to the goat, rescuing Master Gregor only to be captured himself. The demon would find nothing in the rogue's mind to give him an advantage. Just a little more time, that was all the huntress needed, and Boremac would do his damnedest to give it to her. "I know you can move faster than that, demon. Don't hold back on my account. You don't fear the simple daggers of a master thief, do you?" Boremac thrust both the daggers out at once, each still glowing dimly, toward the scars Silverwing had

276

given the creature long ago. The rogue noticed that the blades he held out, brightly shining when Gregor had first felt the bite of the demon's stinger, had diminished in intensity when the knight had moved deeper into the keep to face Father Tur'morival. Curiously, the enveloping golden glow was intensifying once more very slowly as the rogue withdrew the feint. "Looks like a nasty pair of scars you have there, demon. That must have hurt. The God of Light appears to be favoring me in our little dance. Why don't we make this easy for you? Drop that tail and I will stab you in the throat. Judging from the other victims of my blades, it will only hurt you for a moment. I never was much for extending death throes." Boremac slapped at the tail as it swept low around the demon's waist, seeking purchase in the rogue's leathers. "Come on, demon. This is just silly. Bow to a superior foe and go back to the Abyss." The demon drew back the tail, trembling with fury, and brought it high, preparing to pierce the rogue's neck in reply to his taunting. Boremac grinned with the knowledge that his little gamble had worked. He buried the two brightly glowing daggers into the scars of the demon's chest, dropping into a crouch and springing away from the Tharnorsa to land on his back several steps from where the demon stood.

Boremac wondered for years to come why he was not killed at that moment. Everything happened so fast the rogue could not make sense of what had taken place. The demon howled in fury as it leapt into the air toward where Boremac lay. The rogue saw that the hilts protruding from the descending demon were glowing more brightly that he had ever seen before, two small suns in the Tharnorsa's chest. The creature landed, digging its clawed feet into the rocky floor at Boremac's sides, and brought one of his clawed scaly hands to the rogue's chest. As the Tharnorsa pinned Boremac to the floor, impossibly long bloody claws emerged from the demon's other hand as he raised it over his head. The demon's intention was clear, and Boremac drew what he was certain would be his last breath.

"Release him, demon!" The command was little more than a whisper. "You are bound to the will of the keeper of the stone. Release him now."

Boremac released the breath his lungs had seemingly held for hours, still staring into the demon's eyes. The Tharnorsa's claws drew back into the hand over his head. The creature was not quite ready to release the rogue despite the command. "You will be dealt with in a moment, rogue." Boremac felt the truth in the demon's last words to him. Gregor was dying; there was no doubt in the rogue's mind. He was familiar enough with the last words of the dying to recognize them as Gregor spoke.

"Father Tur'morival is dead and the Crimson Night will not come to pass, not so long as there is breath in my body. You will submit, and you will be destroyed. Kneel, demon." Blood and greenish fluid trickled from Gregor's mouth as he spoke. The holy warrior fell to his own knees, the last of his strength leaving him as the demon's poison coursed through his body.

"You have returned with the stone as you promised, and I will allow your companions to live, though their lives will be an unending torture. I hope you will allow me to kill them when they beg for death, Master. You should speak on their behalf now. It will not be long until you succumb to the poison eating your flesh." The demon's condescending tone and the words concerning his companions gave Gregor the power to do one thing more. The demon had desired the stone whole for some reason, and if he were able to take it from Gregor's dead hands, his friends would suffer for all eternity. Still, Father Tur'morival had said that the stone must be destroyed to destroy the demon. What had ruled the priest's reasoning at the end? A desire for the destruction of his deceiver, or the bringing of the Crimson Night for which he had so long labored? Gregor had no choice. He brought the stone in his grasp even with his shoulder and focused all his remaining strength into shattering the orb against the cavern floor, whispering his last command to the demon. "Siniamadrau, I command you by your true name to exist no more. Your spirit will be diminished as your form in this world and the Abyss is extinguished. You will submit to the divine will of the God of Light as delivered by the Knight of the Golden Dragon, Keeper of the Light." A small crimson cloud rose from the remnants of the stone, slowly drifting to join with Siniamadrau as it shifted and flowed toward the demon.

White light enveloped Gregor's body as he fell forward with his head resting on the hot floor of the cavern. For the second time in his life, he lay before the towering form of the Tharnorsa that had slain the Knights of Bella Grey. Siniamadrau shifted into his true form, standing as high as the massive throne behind him. The demon's thoughts pierced Gregor's mind as the knight lay unmoving on the floor. *As you command, Master. I await the killing blow of your blessed weapon.*

As quickly as the pulsing heat of the demon had infused Gregor's body, it was replaced by the cool touch of divinity. *Rest, my young warrior. Your work here is done.*

Boremac sat up, staring at the immense form of the Tharnorsa whose shadow fell over the rogue and Lord Lightsword. He moved to Gregor's prone form, gently turning the warrior over and taking the knight into his lap as he knelt beside him. A tear trickled down his face as he examined the young sword master's withering body. Green tainted fluid replaced the blood in Gregor's pulsing veins as small pustules emerged from the knight's exposed flesh, breaking open and burning the surrounding skin. Boremac brought his hand to his mouth, wetting two of his fingers to check the knight's breathing, sensing only a shallow flow of air. He moved his hand over Gregor's open, staring eyes, and drew the warrior's lids closed. There was no reason for him to see any more death in this world. The rogue doubted Gregor could feel anything at all. A tiny shimmering point of light rose from the knight's chest, hovering over Gregor's body as if it were waiting for something.

The rolling thunder of a voice filled with rage flooded the cavern in the next moment and drew Boremac's attention away from the knight he held and the light hovering above Gregor's chest. "He who swears fealty to the God of Light as a Keeper of the Light remains a Knight of the Golden Dragon until the last breath passes from him in this world! Taste the blades that struck true so long ago, Siniamadrau, once again blessed with the divine power of the faith of a servant of the God of Light!" The Tharnorsa raged even as its body turned to stone, blackened by the holy force delivered into it by Lord Silverwing. The demon's body was rapidly enveloped with a surge of white light, turning to cracking stone as the energy traveled up and down its entire form. The demonic head shattered and the burnt stone it had become scattered across the ground at its feet. Silverwing appeared on the statue's shoulder and rode to the ground, jumping from one spot to the other as the pile of broken stone grew below him. All was silent for a moment, as the last of the demon's remains settled into a pile of small shiny rocks.

"NO!" Tana's voice broke as she watched the tiny light hovering over Gregor's chest plate glide through the air into the crimson cloud that now hovered over the pile of stones that had been the Tharnorsa, brightening momentarily as it absorbed the crimson mist. Once the mist was gone, the tiny light moved slowly in the direction of the young dying knight's body. "No!" the huntress repeated, running to kneel at Gregor's side.

Lord Silverwing came up behind Tana, offering what words of comfort he could. "Let him go, Tana. The God of Light has seen fit to release his spirit and destroy the demon for all time. Gregor feels no more pain and he will pass into the glory of the Light. His spirit will join the God of Light soon." Silverwing gestured toward the light hovering over Gregor's still form and made a sign of blessing to honor his student. "There is nothing we can do to prevent it. Let him go."

She did not turn to acknowledge the knight as she answered him. "No!" Her eyes met Boremac's as she issued orders to the rogue. "Strip him! Hurry, damn you!"

Boremac ran his hands across Gregor's armor, releasing the bindings and pulling away the plates that covered his body. The burning pustules were everywhere, eating through the cloth between the metal covering and Gregor's skin. Tana tore away the remaining bits of silken cloth as she tossed the armor plating and securing leather ties to one side, leaving Gregor's naked body exposed. Despite the weeping sores covering his form, the holy warrior's chest still rose and fell irregularly, as his lungs struggled to draw in air. Tana took a moment to look at Gregor, swept by a wave of despair, before she spoke in a whisper to the only one that could save him. "Goddess, I entreat you. In the years of my life protecting the wilds over which you reign, I have never asked for anything. The gifts I possess have always been used in service to you and for the glory of the natural realm." Tana reached out to take the tiny glowing light into her hand, staring into it as she prayed. "You are the mistress of the natural passage of all things. You have power over life and death of animals and plants, including the natural passing of men. Please, I beg you to remove the devourer from this servant of the God of Light. I have no power you do not give, and I cannot remove the scourge within him." Her prayer did not go unanswered.

The cavern filled with the bright colors of the wood in spring; the browns of tree bark, the deep green of the grasses and leaves, the clear blues of the flowing streams and still, deep lakes. The translucent female form that materialized near Tana wore a long gown composed of all the beauty of nature and the scents of thousands of flowers tingled in the nostrils of all those in the cavern. Long golden hair fell down the avatar's back to the floor, shimmering as if sunshine coursed through every strand. "Tana, my beautiful daughter and devoted huntress, I could never deny you. He will be whole once more. Give me the spirit of the warrior."

As Tana extended her hand, the tiny light that had emerged from Gregor drifted to settle at the center of the Goddess's forehead. The translucent form merged with Gregor's body, gently lowering itself into him. Gregor's eyes sprang open immediately, as the acidic fluid covering his skin turned into water and pooled around him, healing his wounds wherever it touched. The initial pain that Gregor experienced forced him to fill his lungs with air, crying out as his internal organs were made whole again. The young knight's features softened in moments as his body was restored. Soft, deep breaths began to flow steadily from his lips as Gregor fell into a deep sleep. Tana lowered her forehead to touch the knight's, wanting to be close to him, and was rewarded with the most beautiful smile she had ever seen, as Gregor's cheeks flushed with a healthy pink glow.

Boremac was first to break the silence, shifting uncomfortably under the holy warrior's weight. "Well....."

Tana looked up at the rogue and smiled, bringing a finger to her lips. "We should take him home."

Boremac only replied with a nod.

Epilogue

The nightmares had ended and Gregor was glad. He had made it back to his village in time for the planting season, and welcomed the simple smells of his father's farm and the feel of earth in his rough hands again. Tana had grumbled only a bit when she joined him in the fields, planting the seeds that would bring new life to the lands that had been troubled for so long. The huntress was of the feeling that the Goddess would provide, and she saw little need to dirty her hands when the plants did fine on their own. Their union was only a few days away and already the village's normally small population had swollen to the point of encroaching on the surrounding woods. Traders and woodsmen from across the lands had joined the many common people that had come to witness the joining of Tana and Gregor, and pay their respects to all those who had sacrificed their lives to restore the balance of this world.

Father Wallin insisted upon performing the ceremony that would link the rest of Tana and Gregor's lives together as they rebuilt the Order of the Knights of the Golden Dragon. Mistress Mithrina would join the priest of the Temple of Light, overseeing the rituals of devotion that were to be observed in honor of the Goddess of Nature. Gregor could not help but wonder what the future held for him and his bride. Peace reigned across the lands, and the bond between the Goddess of Nature and the God of Light their union represented was only one of the signs of the new strength of the protectors of the world. The new Knights of the Golden Dragon were being drawn from the servants of both deities; an occurrence unknown in all the history of the Order, and the new members would be trained in the service of both before being knighted. Already the number of the knights had grown by three: Dramor, the mountain ranger who had carried Fasurel to safety and struck a powerful blow against the blood orcs in the wild lands of Zanthfar, Tana the huntress, who had committed her life and ultimately her faith to Gregor, and Nadia, the healer and mistress of the staff who had almost been slain by the priests of the Order of the Crimson Night at Gregor's weapons trial. Gregor felt a bit of regret that Lord Silverwing would not be traveling through the lands with them, but the old knight that had been his first teacher had earned the rest. Lord Silverwing would join the priests in Nactium and oversee the final stages of training the knights that would fill the ranks of the Golden Dragon, and Gregor knew that his presence would be felt in the skills of each knight that the master of the blade and bow touched.

Master Fasurel Stonecutter had made a nearly complete recovery from the wounds and broken bones he had suffered, troubled only by a slight limp that hardly slowed the stocky ranger at all. He had remained in his mountain home, training new clan members to replace the terrible losses suffered by the guardians of the mountains. The rough mountain man had insisted on joining the rangers and druids in the woods with Mistress Mithrina after he was whole enough to take up an axe. He said simply that those who protected the wilds knew no boundaries when the lands were threatened. The threat of the barbarian orc tribes and roving goblin war parties was swept away soon after their demonic brethren had fallen along with their creator.

The day of the festivities Gregor was troubled. Master Firebeard, the blacksmith who had labored so hard at his forge for all the members of the group, was nowhere to be seen. The huge man would have been difficult to miss, even among all the milling strangers. Gregor had spent much of the day before, and the morning of this one, making inquiries and searching for the master weapon smith. Gregor reasoned that the man must have been delayed, and set to dressing himself in the armor the smith had fashioned for him in preparation for the binding ritual. Master Firebeard would not miss the union he predicted so long ago.

Gregor and Tana exchanged their vows of commitment, following the guidance of Father Wallin and Mistress Mithrina each in their turn. As the last blessings were offered, a path opened along the road to where the pair stood, and Master Firebeard struggled toward the bride and groom carrying an immense chest that was nearly as wide as the massive blacksmith was tall. The crowds grew quiet as the smith dropped his heavy burden to the ground, sending a tremor through the feet of all those near him. Master Firebeard raised his voice in exultation as he addressed Tana and Gregor. "Praise the Goddess and God alike! I feared I would miss the ceremony entirely. Looks like I have come at just the right time. Master Gregor, do not keep your lady waiting on my account. Kiss the bride!" Gregor embraced Tana, all too ready to intertwine his fate with hers. Only one person noted the solitary howl that rose from the woods nearby as Tana touched her lips to Gregor's. "Yes, I am truly happy at last," was all the huntress whispered as she noted the call.

Master Firebeard apologized for his delay, explaining he had found the great oaken chest outside the door of his shop two days past and surmised that the box was intended as a gift for the two, judging from the intertwined golden Dragons that served as the centerpiece of the lid. It was a struggle to find pack animals available to pull the wagon required for the delivery of it, delaying the smith's arrival even more. "There was no sign to indicate who sent the gift, or what it might contain, but the lock on the clasp is well beyond my abilities to decipher. There is not even a key hole that I could find, though I did not study it long."

Boremac appeared at the master weapon smith's side as if he had heard his name called, with each of his hands filled with a goblet spilling amber liquid. The rogue slid around to the front of the massive chest with grace that Filcher, Master Firebeard's pet weasel, would have envied. He handed the two drinks in his hands to Master Firebeard over the top of the chest, admiring the golden Dragons that adorned the lid. "Ah, excellent workmanship in the release. Let me see, there should be a pressure switch..." Boremac deftly probed at the shield in the center of the lock with the tips of his fingers. A small round portion near the middle retracted and set the tiny swords in motion, causing the two blades at either side of the decorative coat of arms to curve upward as if in salute. There was an audible click inside the mechanism, and Boremac smiled, appearing to be satisfied. "May want to stand back a bit." Without further warning, Boremac slid a heavy long sword out of the sheath of a nearby guardsman and wedged it between the lid and catch of the chest. The rogue gently levered the lid open and, with practiced caution, peered through the small crack he exposed. "Always best to check before you stick in your hand. Could be any number of nasty surprises inside."

Satisfied, the rogue stuck his fingers under the lid and flipped it open. The gold and gems within caused a great drawing of breath among all those who could see it. Among the wealth was a small envelope, bearing a small black seal of wax securing the top flap of parchment at the back. The front was marked with a simple inscription reading, "Lord Gregor Lightsword, Knight of the Golden Dragon". Gregor recognized the seal immediately as he received the letter from Boremac. There was no mistaking the mark of the Black Hand. The parchment read simply as follows:

Lord Lightsword,

It is with some pleasure that we inform you that with the death of Father Tur'morival, the contractual obligation binding

the Black Hand to assist in determining your fate is no longer valid. Our standard code of operation requires that the payment for said contract be returned to the living heirs of the original contractor. In this case, there is no such heir to receive the return of said payment, and thus we are obligated to dispense the contracted amount of collected funds as we see fit. We do not retain payment for contracts we are unable to complete to the satisfaction of the contracting party.

In light of your actions and the consequences of said actions, we have chosen to deliver said monies to you for dispersal, as you deem appropriate. On a more personal note, we thank you for your part in restoring balance to this world. Despite rumors to the contrary, the Order can find no profit in the destruction of the world we serve. Learn from the failure of your enemies and choose your allies carefully, Lord Lightsword. Remember that there is never light without darkness. We have chosen to accept no contracts that would bring us into direct conflict with you or those who will bear your name in honor of your sacrifice and noble deeds. The shadow of the Order of the Black Hand will not darken your back again.

There was no signature. Gregor folded the message carefully and waved Boremac over. "Master Boremac, you have shown grace and commitment far beyond your calling. Take the contents of this chest and do whatever you see fit with it. No one will remove the coin from this chest without your leave."

Lord Silverwing nodded his approval, as Gregor glanced over to where the fellow knight stood. The old Knight of the Golden Dragon, and soon to be mentor to those that would be honored to join the Keepers of the Light, seemed pleased with Gregor's faith in the rogue. Both reasoned Boremac was due some reward befitting his prowess, and what better gift than trust and coin could they offer?

For days after that eventful union, Boremac passed much of the coins and gems from the chest into the hands of the common people that had suffered so much in recent times, withholding only so much as the rogue could carry in his coin purses. The rumors that originated at the union of Gregor and Tana became stories and the stories became legends that grew and changed with each telling.

In time bards across the lands related the legend of the alliance of the God of Light and the Goddess of Nature who had joined to travel into the Abyss itself to destroy the Unnamed One, the Lord of the Abyss. The two divine forces had fallen in love, and their union had been blessed with a gift from the Dragon King, delivered by the great leader of the fire giants living in the Forsaken Mountains. Years later, Gregor smiled as he listened to the telling of the tale, he and Tana resting at an inn far from their home, and thought to himself....Some things will never change.